The Eye of the Storm

Kate Lace

Acknowledgements

A number of people helped me with this book. To them go my deepest and fondest thanks.

To Anita Burgh and Billy Jackson for having me to stay in 'la France profonde' so I could learn a little about French farming methods. They were endlessly helpful and hospitable, as were their many friends; in particular, their fabulous wine merchant, who found me a whole heap of information about Normandy in the war, and the residents of the local nursing home, many of whom had lived through it, and shared their memories with me.

To Ian, who had the idea for this book in the first place and who looked out dozens of books and pictures so I got some idea of the real events that happened at the end of June 1944.

To my friends, for their kind words and encouragement, and in particular Arlene King at Beaumont Hamel.

And lastly to the members of the RNA, who are the best support group any writer could hope to have, especially Jenny, Evelyn and Annie and the reprobates of the Oxford Chapter.

FACT

SS-Obersturmbannführer Jochen Peiper was a real person. After the war he achieved notoriety as a result of the Malmedy Massacre war crimes trial where the American Army tried to find those responsible for the murder of American POWs in the Ardennes offensive. He was sentenced to death but this was commuted to life imprisonment. He was released after twelve years. He tried to work in Germany but was persecuted by an anti-Nazi group. Eventually he went to live in the Haute-Saône in eastern France, hoping to achieve anonymity. On the night of 13th July 1976 he was murdered by a single shot from a British service revolver. The culprit was never found. Maybe this is why it happened …

One

An Hour Before Dawn, Saturday 24 June 1944

La Ferme de la Source – Normandy

'Take care, *Liebling*,' murmured Martine as she kissed her lover goodbye gently on the lips.

Otto held Martine by the shoulders and stared into her eyes. 'I'll try.' He shrugged to indicate his lack of power over the matter.

'And think about what I said.'

Otto nodded. He'd been thinking about little else since Martine had suggested the idea of desertion. It wasn't as if he wanted to go on fighting. He had never wanted to be part of Hitler's machine –even as a child he'd hated being in the Hitler Youth – but, like most Germans, he'd had precious little choice. However, the danger involved in deserting was immense – no less, of course, than the danger involved in continuing to fight; but which path would offer him the best chance of survival? He wished he knew. He'd only known Martine a matter of months and he didn't want to be cheated out of more time with her. He wanted a lifetime in her company; but what were the chances of that, given the current circumstances?

He pulled his uniform tunic on, buttoned it up; then, kissing Martine one last time, he picked up his boots and crept out of her bedroom and down the stairs. With the bedroom door open the sound of snoring reverberated from her father's room. The old soak had rolled in drunk again last night. They'd heard him crashing around the kitchen as they lay together in bed, both praying that he wouldn't barge into Martine's room. Not that he ever had, nor was it likely he would, but the sickening fear that he *might* was always there. Jean-Paul Bracque wasn't an aggressive man by nature, but, fuelled by calvados, the sight of the Boche in his house – in his only daughter's bed – might be enough to move him to violence. And they all knew where the shotgun was hidden. As usual, though, after a few minutes of bashing into the kitchen table and chairs as he stumbled about looking for food or drink, or both, he'd made his unsteady way up the stairs to his bed, where he had passed out almost instantly. Once the snoring started, Martine and Otto had allowed themselves to relax and had also swiftly fallen asleep clasped in each other's arms in the narrow little iron cot that had been Martine's bed since childhood.

Otto was certain, given the amount of booze Martine's father had probably shipped the previous night, that Jean-Paul wouldn't awaken now till late, giving him ample time to slip away, and the precaution with the footwear was more than likely unnecessary – but there was no point in tempting providence. Otto reached the kitchen, picked up an overturned kitchen chair and sat on it to put his boots on. When he'd finished lacing them up, he took his cap out of his pocket, set it on his head at the correct angle and let himself out of the farmhouse into the buffeting wind and lashing rain of a summer storm. The weather was marginally better than it had been for days – dear God! the storm earlier in the week had been terrible – but it was still bad.

Martine stood at her bedroom window and looked across the yard to the figure of her lover, just visible through the rain as he went through the gate and then strode down the lane that led to the road to the airfield. Had he been stationary, his field-grey uniform would have blended into the monochrome countryside, but his movement betrayed his position. In a few seconds he would turn the corner and be gone; so she watched until he did, not wanting, in these desperate and unsafe days, to lose a second more of his presence than absolutely necessary.

Otto disappeared from sight. She sighed, left the window and began to dress. As she pulled on her rough wool trousers and coarse cotton shirt, she heard the rumble of guns. *Are they closer than yesterday?* she wondered. Difficult to tell. She looked out of the window and saw the muzzle flashes off near the coast. A safe distance. A couple of days ago there had been a battle just down the road at Tilly. That had been terrifying. The shells had landed frighteningly near, the ground had shaken and the sudden, hideous explosions had made her want to curl up with her arms over her head. Then the barrage had stopped and the machine-guns had started up, but luckily it hadn't moved their way and since then it had been relatively quiet. Her father, cowering with her in the cellar, had muttered things about 'the Allies consolidating their positions' and 'engaging in flanking movements', but Martine didn't know whether this was old phrases from the Great War that he was regurgitating, blind speculation, or stuff he'd heard from his visits to the café in the village that might contain a shred of truth.

After the battle they'd seen refugees from Tilly fleeing, pushing handcarts, prams, bikes – anything they could lay their hands on – laden with basic possessions, frightened and not knowing when or if they would be able to return to their houses. She knew it was inevitable that the war would storm past their little corner of France like some terrible hurricane and Martine wondered if she should try to escape with her father, out of the line of fire. But she couldn't leave the animals and she was afraid that the thought of losing the farm completely might push her father right over the edge. Besides, they had nowhere to go and they were probably as safe, or in as much danger, as they would be anywhere in this region for the foreseeable future.

Martine pulled on her boots and slipped out of her room. Time to do the milking. The cows wouldn't wait just because there was a war on. Unlike Otto, she clumped down the wooden stairs. Now Otto was safely on his way, who cared if her father woke up? And just for once it would be nice if he did, then got out of his bed to help with the early-morning chores. But what chance of that? When her mother had been alive, and her father hadn't spent most of his time trying to find oblivion, there had been more than enough for the three of them to do. Now she seemed to be running the whole place almost single-handedly. She ran her work-roughened hands through her hair in despair. She woke up each day still feeling tired and by the time she got back to her bed tonight she knew she'd be completely exhausted. She sighed heavily. Feeling sorry for herself wasn't going to help anyone and surely the war couldn't drag on for more than a few months?

She entered the kitchen and went over to the range. She riddled the ashes and pushed some kindling into it. The embers still glowed from the previous day's carefully banked fire. In a matter of minutes the range was heating up nicely. She pushed a pan across on to the hotplate to boil up some water for coffee. Well, coffee was what she referred to it as still, but God alone knew what went into the grubby-looking grounds that she got from the grocery in the village. She cut a hunk off the end of yesterday's baguette, split it and shoved it in the oven to toast – as *tartine* it would still be edible when dunked in the coffee.

Ten minutes later, Martine was in the yard. It was almost light by this time. The glow on the eastern horizon was fading from orange to gold and the sky took on the colour of oyster shell. She picked up her hazel switch from where she had left it on the mounting block, opened the gate, gave it a shove to swing it wide and then set off to the meadow and the herd.

Gare Saint-Lazare – Paris

SS-Obersturmbannführer Jochen Peiper paced along the platform at the Gare Saint-Lazare, waiting impatiently for news that a driver had been found for the train loaded with around twenty Panzer tanks from his battalion, plus men, kit, ammunition, rations and service vehicles. His annoyance was manifested in the slapping of his blackleather gloves against the palm of his left hand and the frown that creased his high, broad forehead; he wasn't used to having his plans thwarted by inefficiency. Only a few days ago they had been in Belgium, resting and refitting, when the order came through that the battalion was to proceed with all haste to Normandy to provide reinforcements against the invasion. It was no small logistical feat to move an entire battalion of tanks such a distance and, until this hold-up, it had all happened with exemplary speed and competence.

But now, the first of the three trains that had been promised to take them from Paris to Caen was going nowhere for want of a driver. This was unacceptable. Peiper strode back down the platform again, anger welling up inside him. Some incompetent minion, no doubt, had failed to read the orders he had sent in advance and now precious hours were being lost. If he found out who was responsible he'd have them put against a wall and shot. This delay was tantamount to sabotage, he fumed. His battalion of Panzers might make all the difference to the battles in Normandy. If he was there, his tanks might stop and turn the tide of the enemy invasion. Peiper dwelt for a few seconds on what that might mean to him personally. He was already one of the most highly decorated soldiers in the SS. With another notable victory, his ascendancy would be unstoppable.

Winning wasn't going to happen, though, if he didn't get out of Saint-Lazare Station. He couldn't throw the enemy back into the sea from here in Paris. He turned on his heel again, his eyes searching for someone on whom he could vent his rage, but apart from his own men – and none of this was their fault – he could see no one. He sighed furiously and slapped his gloves against his hand again. *Where is that blasted driver?* he thought. He had remonstrated with the officer in charge of troop movements. He had issued more threats.

'But what am I supposed to do?' Major Kepplinger blustered.

'Find me a driver,' retorted Peiper coldly.

'I cannot produce what I do not have.'

'Then I suggest you find a solution.'

Kepplinger was tired, overworked and disinclined to be bullied. 'Or what?'

Peiper could barely contain his anger at this insolence. The last person who had spoken to him like that he'd shot. Admittedly it had been some nameless, insignificant Italian peasant who had refused to hand over food Peiper had requisitioned for his troops, not a German officer, but Peiper felt very tempted all the same.

'Just find one,' he snarled as he turned on his heel. He saw a French railwayman hurrying down the platform. Was this the driver? But no. The labourer jumped off the platform and wriggled into the space between it and the train and began greasing the axle bearings. Peiper, with nothing better to do, watched. The labourer glanced up as he moved from one flatbed to the next and met Peiper's gaze; then he dropped his eyes and moved quickly round the back of the truck and out of sight. There was something furtive and shifty about the man's actions. But surely no one would be foolhardy enough to tamper with the train under the eyes of a whole battalion of SS soldiers. Peiper narrowed his eyes as his instinct told him something was amiss; then he beckoned to his adjutant.

'That man – what's he doing?'

The adjutant looked in the direction Peiper was indicating, bent down to get a clear view under the bogeys and saw the labourer. He watched the man working for a few seconds and shrugged as he stood up again. 'Routine maintenance, I imagine, sir.'

Peiper scratched the cleft in his chin. 'Then why does he look guilty and nervous to me?'

'Does he, sir?' The adjutant bent to have another look just as Kepplinger hurried up. He abandoned his cursory investigation and straightened to hear what had to be said.

'I have a driver. He has just arrived. He was delayed …'

But Peiper held up his hand to stop the excuses. 'Just tell him to get the train ready to depart.'

'I have; he is.'

'Good. Lucky for you.' Peiper strode down the platform, forgetting his concerns about the workman now he could at last get his battalion away on the last leg of its journey, and making a final inspection of the loading, checking everything was in order before climbing into the carriage for the officers at the rear of the train: the men travelled with their tanks.

The labourer continued to grease the bearings of the front few flatbeds before quietly slipping away, taking his tin of carborundum-laced grease with him.

The English Channel, off Arromanches-les-Bains – Normandy

David Clarke was sitting on the deck of the landing craft, huddled in his greatcoat, with an empty pipe clamped between his teeth and his eyes shut. He used his pack as a pillow to cushion his head from the hard steel of the vessel, but there was no such protection for his backside beyond a few layers of uniform, and even in the fug of half-sleep he was aware of the damp cold striking upwards into his body. June it may have been, but the weather made it seem more like March. An appalling storm had lashed the Channel for days and their crossing had come close to being postponed; then the weather had abated just enough. From the start, the long journey from Portsmouth had been punctuated by the sound of seasick soldiers spewing over the side of the ship from the narrow deck that ran along the sides of the tank well. The noise of vomiting could be heard over the persistent pulsing of the ship's engines, the roar of the wind and the crash of the waves. David had almost succumbed too. He'd not suffered from seasickness himself before, but the sound of retching and the subsequent pervading sour smell was enough to turn the toughest of stomachs.

He was less apprehensive now than he had been for some days – this despite the fact that he and his men would be seeing battle within hours. In late May it had become apparent that his battalion was being held in reserve until after the main action of the invasion was over and he had been disappointed and angry. His men had been training for exactly this for months – years even – and why hadn't they been chosen? he'd wanted to know. Then the first radio reports and newspaper stories had come back and later the newsreel pictures, and despite the patriotic and optimistic nature of the reports, as an experienced military man, David had been able to read between the lines and conclude that many of the initial battles for the beaches had been bloody and desperate and the fight through Normandy was worse. While he was eager and ready to see active service again, he was not of a mind to see his men, many of whom he considered his friends, cut down by the enemy; he'd seen enough of that on the beaches of Dunkirk four years earlier, and the horror of it all still encroached on his dreams on occasion. Now, though, he dozed intermittently, rocked by the movement of the ship, and let his thoughts wander to his wife Gwen and their dog Jasper.

Off to the starboard a huge, rippling flash momentarily banished the dark from behind his eyelids. Instantly he was alert. The flash hurt his eyes and his ears were assaulted by a series of thunderous booms as the four-inch guns on the destroyer escorting them opened up. Then other ships followed suit. For a confused second David wondered if this was a barrage preparatory to landing before he realised that such an action would be shelling friendly forces. Adrenalin catapulted his brain into assessing what was really happening. The guns were pointing upwards and away from where the French coast would have been visible had it been daylight. Obviously some marauding enemy aircraft had been spotted and was being warned off. David hoped to God the pilot wasn't given to do-or-die heroics and took the hint.

Above Arromanches – Normandy

At 15,000 feet above David Clarke, Oberleutnant Gerhard Werner was piloting a Heinkel 177 bomber. It was tough, given the weather conditions. The gale tried to throw the aircraft around and he had to fight the control column to keep the thing on course.

A sudden gust made the plane buck and rear and Gerhard brought it back on course instinctively. He scanned his instrument panel. Flying blind like this was no easy task. It would be a simple matter to get disorientated in these conditions. His eyes flickered across the gauges. They were all reading as they should, and his instruments told him he was still flying straight and level. The cloud cleared again. Below them was the enemy's harbour at

Arromanches. His mission was to drop a huge mine in the approach to the entrance. If a ship entering or leaving set it off, it could hinder the enemy's resupply efforts for days, even weeks. He flew on a course to cross the target as steadily as he could. He willed his bomb-aimer to hurry up and get the job done. This was no place to be hanging around. Since the invasion this area was crawling with enemy night-fighters and as for the flak …

Just as he thought the word 'flak', a blinding orange burst of flame lit up the sky below him and to his left. He swore under his breath. The bastards had spotted him. Almost instantly the sky was peppered with deadly pom-poms of exploding shells. Gerhard could feel the plane bucking and lurching as the shock waves from the nearer shells buffeted his fragile craft. The jolts got progressively more violent as the gunners below began to get his range. He fought with the joystick, trying to maintain level flight when all his instincts were telling him to get the hell out of there.

'Bombs gone,' crackled the voice of the bomb-aimer in his headphones. Werner felt the plane leap upwards as the payload, a one-tonne magnetic mine, dropped clear of the bomb bay and down towards the sea off Arromanches. Instantly, Werner pushed the stick forwards and to the left, and the Heinkel responded by dropping her starboard wing and diving steeply. He hoped that the British navy's radar-directed guns would be slow enough in responding to his sudden change of course to give him a fighting chance of getting away.

His hopes were shattered when a salvo of six shells exploded just under his port wing. Several chunks of shrapnel tore through the flimsy fabric of the plane. Instantly a jet of flame burst out of the back of the wing. Werner knew the plane was doomed.

'Bail out,' he ordered his five-man crew. His bomb-aimer and his co-pilot grabbed their parachutes, kicking open the ventral crew hatch. As soon as their 'chutes were clipped in place they disappeared into the night. A few seconds later his dorsal gunner bade him farewell via the intercom. That just left his rear gunner.

'Get out, Dieter,' Werner yelled. There was no response. Dieter had fallen victim to another chunk of shrapnel. It had smashed through his Perspex cupola and then into his head, killing him outright.

Werner could feel that he was beginning to lose control. Without his co-pilot he didn't have enough power in his arms to hold the plane in level flight.

'Dieter!' called Werner more urgently. Fear was really beginning to grip him. He felt a loyalty to his crewman and it was his duty to try to save him, but his instinct was to save himself first. 'Go now.'

Still no response. Werner looked at the flames. Too bad for Dieter, but he'd given him as much chance as he could. Werner unclipped his harness and struggled out of his seat. As he did, the plane gave a violent lurch to starboard, throwing Werner off his feet. He grabbed instinctively at the back of the co-pilot's seat to try to keep his balance, but he missed and fell heavily. The plane began to spiral towards the sea and the centrifugal force, although not strong, was enough to keep Werner pinned in the awkward position in which he had fallen. The spinning became more intense and more extreme as the plane plunged downwards.

The magnetic mine hit the water just beyond the newly constructed Mulberry harbour at Arromanches. However, instead of falling directly into the main shipping lane it drifted off to the east as it sank, so it lay on the bed of the Channel several hundred yards from its intended target.

The bomber carrying the last two of its crew members hit the water a few seconds later about a quarter of a mile away. It disintegrated on impact and Werner was killed instantly.

David watched the flak bursting in the one clear patch amongst the heavy cloud cover above him, lighting up the sky like a thunderstorm. One of the fuzzy puffs of light didn't extinguish. Then, silhouetted against the orange glow of the flak and the fire, he saw three parachutes drift seawards. He looked back at the ball of flame that had been a German aircraft. Then suddenly the fireball was quenched as it hit the water.

One less Nazi plane to worry about, thought David without feeling.

There was no point in trying to get any more sleep. He pulled a letter from Gwen from his pocket. Dear Gwen, her letters were always so alive and yet so full of trivia, things light and gossipy and such as she thought would cheer him up. It was one of the reasons he loved her so much. He valued her letters and their normality more than he could say and he treasured each and every one of them. He gripped this one tightly so a sudden gust or squall wouldn't rip it from his grasp. He'd read it a dozen times already, but the familiarity of her words was comforting and he felt closer to her when he looked at the words she had written. He wondered if she was awake and thinking of him like he was of her.

Orchard Cottage

Gwen Clarke rolled over in the bed and looked at the clock. Instantly her state went from mildly dozy to wide awake.

'For God's sake, George.'

'Wha …?'

'Get up, George. You'll be late.' Gwen emphasised the urgency with a sharp jab to his ribs as she switched on the bedside lamp.

'Ow,' said George. He rubbed his side and glanced at his watch. 'Darn it,' he swore and, still massaging his ribs, he swung his feet out of bed and on to the bedside mat.

He quickly grabbed his vest and shirt. The chill morning air had already made his body come out in goosebumps. As he pulled his clothes on he flicked back the blackout curtain with one hand, just an inch, and had a look at the weather outside. It was terrible – pouring and blowing a gale – and he could hear the wind keening round the house. What an unbelievably filthy day. *What is wrong with this summer?* he wondered. No wonder the Limeys were always yakking on about the weather. Why couldn't they have a climate like they did back home? At least where he came from in America the summers were hot and the winters were cold. But here …Jeez!

Morosely he began to dress. Spending the night with Gwen was wonderful, but the ride on his motorcycle back to Thorney Island in the early hours was the penance he paid: doing it in a howling gale hardly made it worth the previous night's pleasures of the flesh. As he leaned back to pull on his trousers, Gwen pulled him off balance so that he flopped back on to the eiderdown. She leaned over him and kissed him.

'You will be careful today, won't you?' she murmured, looking down at him.

'Of course,' answered George glibly, not meeting her eyes. He didn't want a reminder of his own mortality. There were enough of those around the station each day. 'You're to come back safe to me tonight.'

'I'll do my best.' George pulled himself free of her grasp and stood up. He buttoned up his flies and then donned the rest of his kit. As he shoved his feet into his flying boots there was an impatient scratching at the bedroom door. With the laces still undone, George stumbled across the room and opened it, then sat down on the edge of the bed to finish doing up his boots properly. A large, elderly spaniel trotted in, the stump of its tail wagging, and licked George's hand.

'See,' said Gwen a touch petulantly, 'it's not just me who'll miss you if you do something stupid. Old Jasper will be inconsolable too.'

George looked over his shoulder at Gwen. 'Inconsolable' wasn't a word he would have associated with her. After all, when he'd first met her, her husband had been away months and she hadn't been inconsolable then – far from it, as he recalled.

George finished tying his laces. 'I'll let Jasper out into the yard, shall I?'

'Please.' She still sounded sulky. 'And give him some biscuits. Then he won't pester me.'

George knew perfectly well that, when he'd gone, Gwen would roll over again and go back to sleep. All right for some.

George dealt with Jasper and let him out into the garden as he left the house. Leaving him sniffing round the hedge, checking for traces of intruders in the night, George wheeled his motorbike from by the back door, through the gate and on to the lane at the front of the house. He tucked his RAF side hat under his epaulette and swung his leg over the saddle. A couple of quick kicks of the starter, then the motorbike engine puttered into life and he was away down the lane off the Downs towards Thorney Island.

It didn't seem like two months since he had first dropped in on Gwen – literally – by parachuting into her back garden after his plane had disintegrated on the way back from a raid. He knew he'd been hit by flak over Cherbourg but had thought he'd got away with it when the plane had suddenly started to judder violently as he approached the English coast. Something was obviously very wrong. He'd thought about throttling back to try to control the problem, but even as he thought about it there had been a violent bang and the plane had gone completely out of control. As he fought to get the canopy open he noticed that he had crossed the coast. Thank God, he thought: at least he wasn't going to get a ducking. He had a horror of the notion of parachuting into the sea, of being smothered by wet parachute silk and being pulled under despite the Mae West. No, give him dry land any day. If he'd wanted a close association with the briny he'd have joined the British navy.

With a desperate heave the Perspex shot back and locked. With a sob of relief that was whipped away by the freezing wind that now buffeted him, he unclipped his harness and pushed himself out of his seat. He was terrified of making the jump, but what choice was there? With a shove from his arms and legs he threw himself upwards and outwards and grabbed his ripcord ready to pull. Once clear of the plane he calmed down rapidly. Ripcord pulled, there was a fluttering and then a violent jerk. He'd done it. His heart slowed. *Piece of cake.* What had he worried about?

As he'd floated downwards he'd seen his Typhoon crash in empty fields, west of Chichester, out of harm's way. Then, suddenly, what he'd thought was empty countryside wasn't so empty after all. He'd been dangling under his 'chute watching the countryside drift around beneath his feet when a gust of wind caught him and swung him on to another track completely. Instead of heading for open fields he seemed to be heading rapidly for a cottage. He hauled on the lines and succeeded in steering away from the approaching building but – too late – realised that he was going to pile into the greenhouse on the lawn. He shut his eyes and braced himself for the crash. He felt a bruising thump on his left leg and heard the sound of smashing glass. A split second later came the jarring jolt of hitting the ground. He rolled on to his side and lay still. He could hear the tinkle of the last bits of glass dropping on to paving.

Slowly he opened his eyes. He hadn't, as he had feared, plunged directly into the greenhouse but had merely given it a glancing blow. Even so, a number of panes had been smashed. Behind him the parachute was slowly billowing to the ground, partly draping the wreckage, and partly the lawn, with a shroud of white silk. Gingerly George began to sit up and extricate himself from his harness. As he did so a volley of barking told him that his arrival hadn't gone unobserved. Looking up he'd seen a pretty blonde, accompanied by a black spaniel, making her way across the lawn towards him. It was about a second later he noticed the pretty blonde had a cigarette in her brightly rouged mouth. And it was a couple of seconds after that that he noticed she was carrying a double-barrelled shotgun tucked under her right arm.

'Hello,' he said.

The girl squinted her eyes against the sun to see him better. 'Oh God,' she said. 'You're not a burglar. Are you all right?' She lowered the gun.

George rolled his shoulders and moved each of his limbs gently. 'I think so,' he said, amused, rather than scared. 'Sorry about the glasshouse.' The dog stopped barking and trotted over to George, who squatted down and patted the animal.

'Good grief, you're a Yank. But you're ...' Gwen indicated his RAF uniform.

'British mother. Long story.'

'You'd better come into the house. You could be cut. Are you sure you feel OK?' said the woman. She took the cigarette out of her mouth with her free hand and blew smoke into the air.

George stood up gingerly and brushed a few shards of glass off his uniform, then reached into his flying jacket and took out his own packet of cigarettes. 'No, I think I was lucky. Nothing broken. Well, apart from ...' He inclined his head towards the damaged glasshouse. With his other hand he felt in his trouser pocket. No lighter. He tried in his other pocket. Nothing. It must have fallen out when he'd bailed out. 'I say, lady, you haven't got a light, have you?'

'Might have. But is it wise?' The woman regarded him steadily. 'You could be suffering from shock.'

George snorted. 'Hardly. I could really do with a smoke,' he said hopefully. Jeez, she was a pretty thing. Brave too, judging from the way she had been prepared to tackle a burglar. George was impressed.

'Come on.' She indicated the house. 'I'll find you a lighter. I'm Gwen Clarke, by the way,' she said.

'George Kelly.'

'Your mother named you George after the King?'

'My father named me George after George Washington.'

Gwen grinned, the smile transforming her face, making her look so pretty and approachable. Then she looked past him at the remains of her greenhouse. George turned round and gazed at the wreckage too.

'I'm sorry about the damage. How about I pay for it?'

'I should jolly well think so too. I was relying on those tomato plants. You can't get decent chutney for love nor money these days.' She switched her attention back to George. 'Follow me, and I might be able to find you a cup of tea too.' She swung the shotgun over her shoulder and strolled back towards the cottage. George took a few seconds to admire the curve of her hips under her tight skirt before he followed obediently in her wake, Jasper trotting beside them like an escort to a couple of cargo ships.

'So what are you doing in England?' was Gwen's first question when they reached the house and George had telephoned the air base to report his predicament.

'My father sent me over. He makes soda – you call it

'pop'. He wanted to open a factory here so he sent me and one of his directors over to look at places. That was in 1938. I sort of kept finding excuses not to go back and then it got too difficult. When all hell finally broke loose, I joined up.'

'What do your parents think?'

'They're as mad as hell, but there's not much they can do from four thousand miles away.'

'How very noble of you.'

George had never been called 'noble' before. He rather liked it. They then talked about inconsequential subjects: the weather, the dreariness of being rationed and the like. Gwen was easy company and George entertained her with some of the more outrageous stories of the chaps in the mess.

'Did you hear about Baghdad Smith – famous Great War airman?'

Gwen shook her head. 'Should I have done? And why on earth was he called Baghdad Smith?'

'Well, that was it. The chap went solo and was so proud he invited his family down to the airfield to watch him fly. After a bit he lands and offers his father the chance to accompany him on a few circuits and bumps. His dad jumps in the co-pilot's seat and off they go. Trouble is, Smith mucks up the take-off and rolls the plane. Terrible mess. And by the time they get things sorted out his dear old dad has popped his clogs and Smith has bagged his dad.'

Gwen roared with laughter. 'How cruel: Baghdad Smith! You're making it up.'

'Absolutely not.'

George noticed how the tip of Gwen's nose wrinkled when she laughed in a devilishly attractive way. He rather fancied seeing her again, but it wasn't an option if her old man was on the scene. He had spotted two photographs on the top of the piano. One was of Gwen in her WVS uniform looking a sight more stunning than most girls did in it. Beside it was a picture of an older man, in an army uniform. Was that her husband, or her father? Tricky to tell. And then there was the business of her wedding ring. And just as he was manoeuvring the conversation round to the subject of weddings and husbands and the like, the transport from Thorney Island turned up and that was that.

Of course, now, mused George, as he rode his bike down the deserted lanes towards the coast and RAF Thorney Island, he knew exactly what her marital situation was and he also realised that, had Gwen not been such an attractive woman, he might not have bothered to scrounge some panes of glass from his mate in the stores and might still have been none the wiser about her husband.

As it was, when he turned up one evening three days later and repaired her greenhouse, she repaid him with rather more than the mug of tea and a slice of bread and jam he'd expected, and he noticed that her wedding ring was no longer in evidence. He might have thought he'd imagined it if it hadn't been for the paler band of skin on her third finger. Obviously she didn't want any reminders of her husband, absent or dead, during their affair and so George didn't see why he should worry about him either. He was still curious, though; so, as they lay together in bed after he'd fixed the greenhouse, he asked about the photo on the piano.

'That's David,' she said matter-of-factly, taking a drag of a cigarette.

'And who is David?'

Gwen sighed, letting out a long stream of smoke. 'My husband. He's training "somewhere in England",' she added with heavy irony. 'Although for all I get to see of him he might as well be in Burma or Italy. They keep getting promised forty-eight-hour passes and they never materialise, or he bloody well turns the chance of some leave down.'

'Has he been gone long?'

'Months now. He was supposed to be coming home this weekend but he passed up the opportunity so his two i/c could go home instead. But what about me? What I want to know,' said Gwen, taking a final drag on her cigarette before stubbing it out with an angry frown, 'is why he didn't pull rank? Why didn't he insist on a chance to go home?'

'Maybe his two i/c had compassionate reasons.' George understood how the system worked. A good officer would always put his subordinates first.

'Huh. What about having some compassion for me? It's all right for David: he's got masses to keep him occupied. I'm lonely.'

'Just as well I'm here then.' George moved his hand so it slid down her curvaceous hip.

Gwen raised an eyebrow and rolled towards him. 'Well that's something at any rate.'

His visit on that occasion had established the pattern of all his other future visits: in return for a few minor odd jobs around the place Gwen repaid him in kind. George didn't complain and the arrangement suited him; after all Gwen was in it for the sex just as much as he was, and she certainly didn't seem to want any more of a commitment from him than to turn up when he said he would. If she had fallen out with her husband, that was nothing to do with him. It was his good luck he was around to comfort her when she seemed to need it. It was perfect, thought George: just what he wanted from a 'popsie', as his messmates were wont to call girls, until the war was over. The trouble was, it was starting to get more complicated than that. He was getting fond of her, even falling a bit in love. He knew he would have to back off. It was one thing to borrow her from her husband, but to take her away altogether – that was something else entirely. He'd been brought up to be a God-fearing, church-going, all-American boy; his parents would be horrified if they knew what he was doing. If he was honest, he was a bit ashamed of himself.

As George approached RAF Thorney Island, the sky in the east, despite the heavy cloud cover, was perceptibly brighter than the rest. George turned off the main road and steered his motorbike along the track that followed the side of the perimeter fencing to the east of the base. After about a quarter of a mile he came to a thicket of bushes. He stashed his bike in the undergrowth and then approached the fence. There was a narrow gap under the chain-link behind one of the hangars; George crawled through it, brushed the worst of the mud off the knees of his uniform trousers and then set off at a brisk trot towards the officers' mess. If anyone wanted to know what he was doing, he had the perfect excuse ready: he'd been unable to sleep and had gone out for an early-morning walk – which should be good enough to pass muster as long as no one considered what the weather had been doing. No one in their right mind would have ventured out before dawn unless they had to in this muck. He prayed he wouldn't get put on a fizzer for being off camp without a pass.

Near Carpiquet Airfield – Normandy

George Kelly wasn't the only person sneaking back on to base at that time. Across the Channel, Otto was also creeping back to his billet at the Luftwaffe airfield just to the west of Caen. As he walked down the Normandy lanes he saw to his right the sky was starting to lighten. He hoped he would get back without being spotted; he didn't want to risk being disciplined for being without a pass. But that was one good thing about the foul weather: any sentries round the camp would probably have their chins tucked in their collars and wouldn't be too keen to patrol. The others in his gun crew knew he was seeing a local girl and went absent from time to time, but they didn't know where the farm was. He'd kept as many details about her as he could private. Naturally he'd had to put up with the good-hearted but filthy banter about what he and she got up to when they met. It was no use explaining to the other soldiers that Martine wasn't that sort of girl. As far as most soldiers were concerned, *all* girls were 'that sort of girl', and as far as his comrades were concerned, French girls were only good for one thing. Some of the guys in his unit, especially the couple who had been on the Eastern Front, made it quite clear that what the local girls did, or more often *didn't*, want was of no consequence.

Otto glanced north towards the coast. Somewhere, not far away, was the enemy. He wondered how long it would be before they broke through and reached Carpiquet Airfield. In the distance he heard the rumble of guns firing. Away on the horizon there was a succession of flashes in the sky. Anti-aircraft fire. Otto paused and watched the shell bursts. Then he noticed a flash that didn't flicker and die. This one grew stronger and brighter and then began to fall earthwards. He knew that some poor bastard airman had been hit. He guessed it had to be a German. That anti-aircraft fire had been too far north and west to have been anything but the Allied defences. Otto grimaced and sighed: another German mother would be grieving.

On the brighter side, he thought, it wasn't his mother that would be getting a telegram. When the war was over he could look forward to life with Martine – and, judging by the way things were going, it wasn't going to be long. As far as Otto was concerned, the war couldn't end soon enough. He knew in his heart that if he got the chance he would surrender rather than fight. All he wanted was for life to get back to normal, and normal for Otto meant farming. Farming here or in Bavaria, he didn't care, but farming was all he wanted to do.

He passed a field of Friesian cows waiting by the gate for the herdsman to come and take them for milking. It didn't matter to the cows what was going on at the coast; they didn't care about the war; they needed milking and that was all that interested them – that and chewing the cud. Otto liked that about farming. What mattered in farming were the seasons and the weather, not politics.

Trouble is, thought Otto, *life isn't that simple. Not now, anyway.* It had been till the war had started. Until then his life had been mapped out: he'd work on his parents' small Alpine farm, he'd marry a girl from one of the nearby villages, and when his father was too old to carry on they'd take over. It was what had happened to his parents and his grandparents and had done for generations, and there was no reason to see why things should be different for him. It was a good life and he was lucky to have the possibility of such a stable future.

Then the war came and everything changed – changed for the worse. From the moment he'd been conscripted he'd been miserable. He was sent away to be trained at a huge barracks on the outskirts of Munich. He hated being crammed into a dormitory with twenty other men. He hated the orders, the shouting, the drills. He hated the drabness of the barracks, the scratchy fabric of his uniform. He hated being in a city, the lack of fresh air and most of all he hated the fact that he was no longer his own man. But he couldn't hate the enemy. It was not in his nature to hate *en masse*, to hate people he didn't even know. How could you?

After basic training, when he'd been sent to Dortmund to man an anti-aircraft gun, to begin with he had still found it hard to hate the enemy. But then the bombing started in earnest. Night after night the enemy bombers had droned overhead and the ground erupted and shook, buildings burned and people, whole families, died violent, dreadful deaths. He'd seen sights he knew would stay with him for the rest of his life: a limb, too small to be adult, naked and torso-less hanging from the one remaining branch of a shattered tree; disembowelled bodies lying beside the road; blackened corpses with grotesque smiles of startlingly white teeth showing through the remains of charred lips.

These sights inspired him to try his hardest to shoot down the enemy Lancasters and Halifaxes. It wasn't that he wanted to destroy the pilots but to prevent them from destroying everything around him. He didn't think he hated them – he hated what they did, certainly. But how, he'd asked himself could you hate someone you didn't even know? He'd known that Britain was getting the same treatment from the Luftwaffe; the papers were full of the heroic triumphs of the air force and you didn't need to be a scholar to understand that German bombs would be having the same effect on women and children over there too. It wasn't hatred that was the predominant feeling in Otto's heart; it was a sense of futility.

It was almost a relief when he'd been badly wounded by a nearby explosion; the bomb had landed only a matter of a dozen metres or so away and but for luck and a low wall Otto should, by rights, have died. It had taken a couple of months for the scars from the shrapnel to heal and then a further few weeks of recuperation for him to regain mobility in his legs. He was able to walk again but with a pronounced limp and he'd been considered unfit for the front line so had been shipped off to a soft posting in Normandy. After all, everyone knew the invasion, when it came, would happen round Calais, not further west – the logistics would be impossible.

Once he'd got to Carpiquet he'd been able to stop lying in his letters home, pretending he was doing well, sleeping properly and making friends. Now that he was back in the countryside and could feel grass under his feet, smell fresh air and admire the livestock in the fields, his letters were full of details about everything he saw around him. It was through cows that Otto had first met Martine. He'd been walking out in the country, enjoying a bright day, the winter sun low on the horizon, the air crisp and clear when he'd spotted a small herd of half a dozen cows of a type he was not familiar with. Mottled in dark brown and white with mainly white faces they were quite unlike the small, dainty Alpine cows he had grown up with, but they were healthy-looking beasts. He was admiring them when a sturdy young woman with curly dark hair, an attractive open face and large, beautiful brown eyes appeared at the gate of the field. In her hand she held a small switch and as she opened the gate the cows ambled over to her and walked through. Leaving the gate wide, the girl followed the last of the cows up the lane to the farm buildings. Otto waited until they had turned into the yard, then he followed too, but stopped at the gate. Seeing this sight had reminded him how much he missed the farm routine of home: the predictability and order of milking; the patience of the cows; the satisfaction of turning cream into butter and milk into cheese. Through the open door of the dairy he could see the first few cows waiting in their stalls until the girl got to them. Otto forgot the time as he watched her move her stool and pail along the line of animals, washing the udders and then swiftly and rhythmically stripping the teats of their rich milk. Otto itched to join in. It had been nearly two years since he had milked a cow and he found his fingers clenching and unclenching in the same rhythm as the squirts of milk streaming into the bucket. The girl became aware that she was being watched, lifted her head from where it was resting against the cow's flank and glanced round suddenly. Otto wished her a good evening in bad French. The girl ignored him and turned back to her task. Otto shrugged and left, remembering that he was the invader and not welcome. It was a shame because he thought she was a real looker. He would have liked to get friendly, but it didn't look as though there was any chance of that.

It was a couple of weeks later – late February – that Otto had next caught sight of the French milkmaid, as he thought of her. He was scratching one of the dairy cows on its flank with a stick he had poked through the fence as she came swinging down the lane with her switch. Otto smiled and got a stony stare back for his troubles.

'*Vache*,' he said pointing at the cow to eliminate any doubt about what he meant. '*Belle.*' He grinned broadly at her, trying to communicate how pleased he was to see her once more.

The girl looked away, but Otto could see it was to hide a smile of her own. An improvement on the blank indifference of their last encounter, although he was sure she was laughing at him and his execrable French, and the smile wasn't one of pleasure that they had met again. Otto was patient; he could wait. He wanted to make friends with her so as to have some contact with farm work again. It would be wonderful to get involved with the land and animals. He was sure he could gain her trust. And if he didn't? Well, there'd be his own farm waiting for him when he finally got back home.

Otto's breakthrough had happened in early March just after the cows had started to calve. The animals had been taken up to the farm and were in the barn where they could be looked after more closely. Otto missed seeing them out in the field and had wandered up the lane towards the main huddle of farm buildings, hoping to catch a glimpse of them – and, if he was entirely honest with himself, the farm girl. As he'd neared his destination, he'd heard the bellow of a cow in distress. To a man who'd worked with cows since he could remember, the sound was unmistakable. Without a second thought he'd opened the gate to the farmyard and hurried across to the barn. In the dim dusty light inside he could see the girl trying to help one of the herd that was obviously having a difficult time giving birth. Without thinking, he asked in German what the problem was. It was only when the girl replied that the calf was breech, also in German, that they both looked at each other in some surprise.

Before Otto could recover she'd added, 'Now get lost, so I can get on.' Then: 'Unless the German way is to shoot the animal.'

'We don't shoot cows on my farm. We help them, just like you do.'

The girl looked at him. 'You're a farmer?'

'Yes, we have farms in Germany too.'

The girl stared at him. 'Do you know about cows?'

Otto nodded.

'I could do with a hand. See that rope over there?' She pointed to one hanging over the wall of one of the stalls. 'I'd like to get it round the calf and see if we can't haul it out. Trouble is I'm not sure I'm strong enough.'

As she was speaking, Otto was stripping off his field-grey tunic and shirt. He grabbed the rope and tossed it to the girl, then washed his hands in the bucket of soapy water. 'Do you want me to get the rope on or will you do it?' he asked.

'I'll do it. Smaller hands.'

Otto watched her working. 'So how come you speak German?'

'My mother was from Alsace. She spoke both. She moved to Normandy to work. Then she met my father.' The girl spoke in short sentences punctuated with grunts from her exertions with the cow. 'There,' she said, after a couple of minutes work. 'It's on. Your turn.'

Otto took the rope and waited for the next contraction; then he took up the tension and pulled steadily. The girl patted the cow and murmured to it in French. The cow writhed and bellowed and Otto felt the calf slip suddenly.

He stepped backwards to regain the tension on the rope and, as he did so, the calf slithered free from its mother. Instantly, Otto grabbed a handful of straw and began to rub the dappled little creature.

The cow turned round to view her new offspring.

'Look,' said Otto, 'a heifer.'

'She doesn't speak German,' said the girl with a laugh.

'I forgot. Well you'll have to tell her she's produced a daughter.'

An awkward silence fell and the laughter died as if both of them suddenly remembered that they were conqueror and vanquished. Otto washed his hands in the bucket again for something to do.

'Right, I'd better get going.' He picked up his tunic and began to put it on.

The girl stuck her hand out. 'I had better thank you …' She paused, not knowing what to call him.

'Otto.'

'And I'm Martine.'

'Thanks are not necessary,' said Otto with a stiff little bow as he took her hand and then let it drop almost immediately. He was worried that she might not wish to be touched by a '*sale Boche*', as he knew the locals called them.

'I would offer you a cup of coffee but my father …' Martine shrugged. 'It would be difficult.'

'I understand.' And he did. The older generation had a deep hatred of Germany dating back a couple of decades. Not that his father's contemporaries didn't feel the same way about the French. Frankly, Otto was surprised Martine was being as welcoming as she was, given how long France had been occupied. Quite long enough for anyone, even those who couldn't remember the Great War, to hate the Boche just as a matter of principle. Perhaps Martine was more forgiving because of her mother's ancestry. 'Anyway, I must go or I'll late for duty.' Otto finished buttoning his tunic and, giving the cow a pat on its flank, he turned on his heel and left the barn. He knew he'd be welcome there another time as far as Martine was concerned. He should just keep out of the way of her father.

In the days and weeks that followed he saw Monsieur Bracque several times, but on each occasion it had been plain that Bracque was blind drunk. It was obvious that the 'difficulty' Martine had referred to seemed to be more to do with his dependency on the rough cider he brewed than with his feelings about the Germans.

'First my mother died, then the war started,' explained Martine. 'My mother said that he was never the same after Verdun. When he came back from the Great War he was always morose, never smiling, not the man she'd married. Then it all started again and it was just too much for him. I think he drinks to try to forget.'

'So do you have any help on the farm?'

'I manage,' said Martine shortly.

'But surely there's someone else?'

'Who? All you have left here are women, children and old men. You took the young men for *le travaille obligatoire*.' She sounded angry and Otto understood. His parents were struggling too. At a time when they should have been able to rely on their son and casual labour to do the heavy work, they were having to cope alone; all the young men were in uniform like him – that was if they hadn't died at Stalingrad.

As Otto walked between the thick hedgerows towards the airfield, his head bent against another heavy squall of rain, he knew he should be thankful for the fact that he had survived this far into the war. Which brought him back to the problem of Martine's suggestion.

Two

Dawn, Saturday 24 June 1944

Arromanches – Normandy

David stood up on the deck and eased his aching limbs. He was cold and stiff and longed to get off this foul-smelling bucket and on to dry land. He walked to the squat bow, or rather tried to, as the movement of the steel plating under his feet made him almost lose his balance with nearly every step he took. He leaned on the side of the ship and peered forward, towards France, the light good enough now for him to be able to pick out features on the land – what looked like a church on a cliff top, a fold in the hills that led down to a small harbour, the promontories and the beaches.

The *beaches*. Since 6 June the word had assumed a whole new and momentous meaning. Not long now and he and his men would be part of the invasion. It was a sobering thought.

A member of the ship's crew came forward.

'Captain's compliments, Colonel.' The young man's voice was raised to be heard over the thud of the engines and the racket of the wind and waves. 'He says would you care to join him on the bridge?'

David stared at this young sub-lieutenant, who looked barely old enough to be in long trousers, let alone in uniform. As he considered the offer, spray from a large wave slapped over the gunwale and splattered him with cold water. The idea of shelter was rather appealing.

'Thank you. I'd like that very much indeed.'

'If you would like to follow me, Colonel.' The junior officer led the way along the companionway and up a ladder, more nimbly and steadily than David could emulate, and then held the door to the bridge open for David to pass through.

David saluted as he did so and noticed, instantly, the smell of cocoa. God, what he would give for a hot drink. Perhaps something in his face gave away his thoughts.

'Get the Colonel a mug of cocoa, would you, number two. He looks like he could do with one.'

'Sir.' The sub-lieutenant left the bridge to comply with the order.

David stuck out his hand and introduced himself.

The Captain took it. 'Cyril Donnelly. Good to meet you, David. Filthy night. I'm sorry we couldn't offer your men better conditions for their crossing. Not built for comfort, these things.'

'Not to worry. My lot are a tough bunch. I expect they coped. Is it long before we arrive?'

'Not now. There's a bit of a problem though.'

David raised an eyebrow. 'Oh?'

The explanation was interrupted by the arrival of a pint mug filled with steaming cocoa. David accepted it gratefully. 'This problem …?'

'Ah yes. The problem is with the Mulberry.'

'I saw a report on the newsreel last week. What a wonderful idea.'

'Yes, it was.'

'Was?'

'Well, still is – mostly.'

David shook his head. 'I'm not following.'

'I've had a signal. This bloody storm has severely damaged it. Only certain ships are allowed to dock in the Mulberry. The rest – and that's ships that can get in close to the shore – are dropping their cargoes on the beach. I'm afraid LCTs definitely come into this category. You and your men will be getting your feet wet.'

'We'll manage.'

The Captain passed him a pair of binoculars. 'You'll see what happened if you have a look through these.'

David put the glasses to his eyes and adjusted the focus. The Mulberry was no longer the organised prefabricated construction he'd seen on the newsreel at the cinema the previous week. Now there were twisted and jumbled lumps of metal tangled together, some lying on the caissons, some hanging off. The straight lines of the outer wall had gone and instead it looked as if some giant sulky child had kicked it out of shape; but despite the disorder the harbour was still providing some shelter, and within the concrete basin the sea was almost calm.

'The tide is about right,' said Cyril. 'We'll land you actually on the beach just to the east of Arromanches. You shouldn't get more than your toes wet,' he added cheerfully.

All right for Cyril, thought David. It wasn't his toes that were about to go paddling.

David trained the binoculars away from the Mulberry and towards the beaches to the east. At first glance it seemed to be a scene of chaos. There were vehicles and men everywhere. Then, as he focused the field glasses he could see that the men were organised into chain gangs, manhandling cases of supplies into waiting trucks. However, interspersed among the lines of working men was the evidence of the struggle that had taken place there just over a fortnight earlier. There were burnt-out vehicles, shell holes, mounds of tangled metal that might have been shot-down aircraft, and in the other direction were a couple of monstrous bunkers – part of the Atlantic Wall that he'd heard so much about, no doubt – with their vast guns pointing randomly at weird angles and the concrete pocked with thousands of shell splashes. David lowered the binoculars and handed them back to the Captain, then took another sip of his cocoa. He wondered what other sights he was about to witness.

RAF Thorney Island – West Sussex

George opened the door to the briefing room and was hit by a wall of fug: cigarette smoke; stale air and the smell of imperfectly washed men and uniforms. It was warm and familiar, albeit not particularly pleasant. He squeezed himself through the press of bodies towards an empty chair at the side of the room. As he made his way to his target he was greeted by many of the other pilots. He responded to the welcomes with the same glib combination of banter and light-heartedness in which he'd received them and, having reached his chair, he pulled out a pack of Senior Service and lit up. He tried to look relaxed and confident though he felt anything but. His stomach was churning with nerves. When he'd first started to fly operations he'd felt invincible, but not anymore. He'd seen too many of his pals shot down and killed, wounded or maimed to have any remaining illusions about his own mortality. So when was it going to be his turn? George took a gloomy puff of his cigarette.

'Penny for them,' said Fred, a member of his section.

George forced a grin and blew out a long stream of smoke. 'Not worth that.'

There was a sudden flurry as the Wing Commander entered through a side door and everyone stood up. Silence fell, cigarettes were concealed.

'At ease, chaps,' he said. 'Those of you who have chairs may sit down. And you can smoke if you wish.'

The cigarettes reappeared and some chaotic and noisy seconds passed as the men settled down, took out notebooks, found pencils and prepared to pay attention. The Wing Commander pulled a blanket off a large map of

Europe set on an easel and picked up his pointer.

'This is the situation vis-à-vis our forces on the ground, as at eighteen hundred hours yesterday. As you can see, our troops occupy this section here.' The Wing Commander swept his pointer over an area of the map in a semicircle that encompassed a clearly marked area from the Cherbourg peninsula, around Bayeux and back up towards the coast at Ouistreham. He finished his flourish with a sharp tap with the point of the stick in the centre of the Allied area of occupation as if to underline his statement. 'Right – as the more observant of you will have noticed, the weather today is particularly tricky. However, it will be business as usual. A photo-reconnaissance Spit reports that there is a troop train carrying tanks just north of Paris ...' George listened as the Wingco rambled on about who the tanks probably belonged to and where they were going. He let his thoughts drift to worries about the danger of the mission. He came back to reality as the Wingco tapped once again on the map.

'... as such, attacking it should be a priority. Other than that, Red and Green Sections are to patrol this area,' – another sweep of the pointer – 'and to attack targets of opportunity. And with any luck there should be plenty of them. A murmur of laughter rippled round the room at the Wing Commander's attempt at humour. 'Finally, just to make sure we delay this train as much as possible, I want Yellow Section to bomb the sidings here.' He tapped the map with his pointer again. 'Caen.'

George breathed a sigh of relief and pitied the poor buggers in Yellow Section. Not an easy target. He'd been on a run there before. He didn't have to listen to the rest of the briefing to know about the flak and the other German defences. Not that he had to worry: 'targets of opportunity' were what he had to concentrate on. Great! – a morning of stooging around with his section and seeing what they could bag. Maybe he'd get through today unscathed.

As Martine walked along the same lane that Otto had trodden a little while earlier, she swung her switch at the banks of marguerites that grew along the verges. The sky was light enough now for colour to be returning to the scene, although Martine was in no mood to be lifted by the prospect of a new day. Besides which, being out at dawn, in the wind and rain, was neither welcome nor a novelty but a daily duty. She would have given anything to still be in bed, but that simply wasn't an option. As she made her way to the meadow to collect the cows,she gazed at the hedges. They were a disgrace: great wands of brambles and hazel waving about in the wind; the ditches underneath full of nettles and thistles; and the state of them was just a symptom of the neglect that vast areas of the farm and many neighbouring ones had fallen into.

Martine crested a slight rise and her attention was caught by a series of flashes on the horizon. She noticed one of the lights didn't disappear and then began to fall vertically. About thirty seconds later she heard the deep rumbling crash of the guns. More horror, she thought and turned away.

By the time she had milked the six cows and got the milk into the cooler the sun was well up in the sky, although it was hidden behind the thick pall of low stratus cloud. She took the cows back to the field before she got on with the next round of jobs to be done on the farm.

First she wanted to clear the entrance to the old root store under the barn, and at least that was a job she could do in the dry. They hadn't used this subterranean space for years and the entrance, in the corner of the barn, had long since been covered with some broken-down farm equipment, a disused mangle and an antiquated trap and harness. Martine would have used the trap again if their only horses hadn't already been taken by the German army for the war. She picked up the shafts and dragged the trap across the barn. Then she moved the old mangle. It was heavy and cumbersome and the legs left deep score marks across the beaten earth of the barn floor. Finally she heaved an old rusty plough out of the way, a scythe with a broken handle, two pails with no bottoms, the old horse harness, a pile of sacks, an old kitchen chair with no seat and a stack of timber. With the area cleared she swept the detritus of years away until she found the trapdoor. Martine kicked some loose earth away from the heavy iron ring that formed the handle and pulled on it. With a desperate creak from the ancient hinges the old wooden door opened. Martine let the door fall against the side wall of the barn and peered into the hole. At the bottom, some eight feet below her, was a small pile of shrivelled swedes. Other than that the space seemed empty. Not ideal, but it would do. She would stock it with some tins and a pail of fresh water and Otto could hide down there for several days. With all the farm machinery back on top no one would ever know there was a cellar below.

Martine gazed at the pile of junk she had moved aside and wondered about the wisdom of leaving it where it was. Who was likely to visit the barn over the next couple of days? Well, the obvious answer was her father and she didn't want him to know anything about what she had planned. God only knew what his reaction would be. Reluctantly Martine dragged everything back again.

Three

Early Morning, Saturday 24 June 1944

Orchard Cottage

Scrabbling paws at her bedroom door brought Gwen back to consciousness.

'Shut up, Jasper,' she muttered as she opened her eyes, but the dog either didn't hear or didn't care to pay attention, and the scrabbling continued. She glanced at her alarm clock, reset to a more civilised hour after George's departure, and saw that it was still much too early for it to go off. With an irritated sigh, Gwen flicked the lever to hold the little clapper in place, then pushed back the covers and sat up in her rumpled bed. *Damn dog.* She supposed she'd better get up and feed the mutt. Then she remembered that George had offered to let Jasper out into the garden. So how had he got back into the house? Gwen pushed her blonde shoulder-length hair back off her face with a cross little sigh and swung her feet out of bed on to the rug. With one hand she found her slippers and thrust her feet into them while with the other hand she reached for her dressing gown where it lay, draped over the end of the bed, and dragged it on. Really, it was too bad if George had left the back door open. Anyone could come wandering in.

Gwen pulled her dressing gown tightly round her to keep the worst of the morning chill off her, opened the bedroom door and, ignoring Jasper's ecstatic greeting of licks and tail wags, she made her way down to the kitchen.

She was met by the sight of an ample behind with a floral overall stretched across it pointing directly towards the door, the owner of which was kneeling on the hearth, stoking the range. Gwen recognised the figure instantly.

'Mrs Viney. What are you doing here so early?'

Mrs Viney straightened up her large figure a little, held on to the rail on the front of the range for balance and twisted round. 'Sorry if I disturbed you, Mrs Clarke, but I couldn't sleep. I got a letter yesterday, from my Bill, when I got home. Reading between the lines I think he's off to France today. Of course he couldn't say, not outright, but I'm that worried. I thought I was doing no good fretting at home I might just as well do something to take my mind off it. I hope you don't mind.'

'I see. Yes, I understand.' Gwen felt a little jolt of shock at the bad news. If Sergeant Viney was off to France then no doubt David was too; after all, they were in the same battalion. *Oh my God*, she thought. This was it. He was off on active service. A huge tide of worry whooshed through her stomach. Please God he'd be all right.

'Have you heard from the Colonel? He'll be off too.'

Gwen shook her head. 'I haven't had any letters for a couple of weeks now.' She bit her lip as she thought back. 'The last one I had didn't say anything about them joining the invasion.'

'Well, they may not have known then. And you know what the post is like. I expect you'll get a whole bunch of letters soon.'

'Maybe.' She felt a sudden rush of guilt and anxiety – guilt because of her affair with George, and anxiety ... well, anxiety for two reasons. On one level she was worried about David: he was going into active service and who knew if he was going to come back again? The thought of her husband facing terrible danger was a ghastly worry. She might be fooling around with George but underneath she really did love David. He might do things that annoyed her a bit, he might want a quieter life than she did, but despite that he was always so kind and thoughtful. And she knew he loved her. Having an affair when he was safe in some training camp was one thing, but now he was off to fight the war proper … well, he deserved better. Gwen was ashamed of herself. What had she been thinking of?

And over and above her anxiety for David and her worry for his safety she had another worry: what if Mrs Viney had seen George leaving because she'd arrived ages earlier than she ought to have done? This was what really concerned her: getting caught. Gwen felt her cheeks burning at the thought of it. She didn't want Mrs Viney to see her face in case she looked as guilty as she felt. She turned away to hide the evidence of her conscience. Once she was sure she had her colour and her expression under control she reached over the still-kneeling figure of Mrs Viney, picked up the kettle, then walked across to the sink to fill it. Casually Gwen glanced around to see if there was evidence that Mrs Viney had been there for more than a few minutes. No, there were still crumbs on the kitchen table and a couple of unwashed plates lying around. Mrs Viney was a creature of habit. Every morning she would come in, take off her coat, get the fire going to make the tea. Once she'd downed a good strong cuppa she'd tidy the kitchen before getting going on the rest of the house. If the kitchen was still untidy, Mrs Viney couldn't have been at Orchard Cottage for any more than five minutes. Gwen breathed out with relief and felt her heart rate slow slightly. George had been gone almost an hour; there was no way Mrs Viney would have seen him near the cottage. She turned off the tap and returned to the range.

'Did Sergeant Viney say anything about the Colonel in his letter?' she asked brightly.

'Sorry, Mrs Clarke, he didn't. He said they'd done a lot of training recently, and he told me their rations weren't much good – as if any of us are eating like kings. I imagine if that was all he had to write about, other than they were off on "a boat trip" today, that means the Colonel is fine and most things are going on just as they always have …'

'Apart from the fact,' interrupted Gwen, 'that they're probably now all in France.'

Mrs Viney nodded. 'Well, yes. Apart from that.' Silence descended as both considered the possible imminent danger that their menfolk were in.

Gwen returned to her room. As she sat at her dressing table, pinning up her hair, she considered the possibility of telling George not to come and see her any more. This incident had brought home to her what a foolish game she was playing – and how much she was jeopardising.

She'd never intended to start on an affair. She knew it was dreadfully wrong of her: David warranted her loyalty, especially now of all times. It was just that she'd been so fed up and lonely – and angry with David – when George had parachuted into her garden. Looking back she knew she shouldn't have lost her temper with him about giving up his leave. George was probably right: Tom Allen, David's two i/c, might well have been in greater need of a trip home than David himself, but that wasn't the point. She'd been so looking forward to seeing him again and she'd felt so let down, when he'd told her it wasn't possible, that her disappointment had bubbled over into rage and she'd seen red. Gwen had tried everything to persuade him and then she had accused him of not caring about her and he'd told her not to be so stupid and she'd slammed down the receiver. She'd then spent thirty minutes pacing around the drawing room waiting for David to ring back and apologise, but he hadn't. And she couldn't ring him because he'd rung her from a call box. She had gone to bed that night feeling wretched: angry with him for giving up his leave, angry with herself for losing her temper – and terribly lonely. The next morning the loneliness had receded somewhat and going to work had helped; but, on her return, the feeling had recurred as had her resentment at playing second fiddle to the battalion and Tom Allen. She'd still been simmering with annoyance and disappointment when a glamorous Yank had fallen out of the sky and into her life.

Not that any of that was any sort of an excuse. She was well aware of that. But, she reasoned, she had to face realities. There was no guarantee that David was going to come back from the war. Come to that, it wasn't guaranteed that she was going to survive it either. With life so desperately uncertain could she really be blamed for trying to grab some happiness, a little fun and a bit of excitement?

She sighed, stabbed a pin into her French pleat and took another puff on her cigarette. She knew she was weak. David deserved better than her. He ought to have married someone who wouldn't let him down so very badly, as she had. But then he'd been the one who had chased her. She hadn't made the running in their romance; he had. She made a little moue at her reflection. Not that she'd played hard to get, she admitted to herself. She'd been terribly flattered he paid any attention to her. He'd been quite a catch after all – a hero of Dunkirk, one of the youngest lieutenant colonels in the army, good-looking, reasonably wealthy, old family – what girl wouldn't have wanted to be wooed by him? Of course, she hadn't thought about the age difference then. She had been swept along by the moment, but the ten years between them had soon become apparent once they settled down into the routine of married life. When she'd wanted to go out, David wanted a quiet night in. When David had had leave, she'd wanted to go to London, while he wanted to go walking in Cumberland. If she'd wanted to spend an evening listening to gramophone records, he wanted to listen to the news on the Home

Service. Gwen tried to be interested in the same things. She thought that if she made the effort she'd get used to his way of things and she'd grow to like them, but the truth was – and it had taken her a while to admit it to herself – the things he did bored her to sobs. She was too young to be leading the life of a middle-aged woman. For heaven's sake, she was only twenty-two. She ought to be having fun, dancing, going to parties, wearing pretty clothes, not stuck out in the country with no company other than the dog. Being in the WVS helped. At least it got her out of the house every day and it gave her some human contact, but her work was pretty mundane and the women she worked with were mostly old enough to be her mother. What she did might be useful – essential, even – and it gave her the chance to meet and talk to people; but it wasn't fun and sometimes it was damned hard work.

It wasn't as if she'd ever been able to have much fun. She'd been sent off to that dreary boarding school at eight, her parents being stationed out in India. She had had to spend her holidays with a succession of elderly relatives or, just sometimes, a friend's family. Every couple of years or so her mother had come over to England for a holiday, but she and Gwen were virtual strangers when they met, and getting further apart with each successive visit. The one bright spot on the horizon had been her mother's promise to send her to finishing school and then give her a proper London season. Well the war had put paid to that. Her parents were stuck out in Delhi, she was stuck here and there was no chance of escaping to the promised fun of Switzerland. So she'd swapped school uniform for war work and the chance of learning how to dance and cook for rolling bandages and make sandwiches.

Gwen sighed heavily at the thought of all that she'd missed out on. She could hardly remember a time when clothes and food hadn't been rationed, and as for the dreariness of the blackout and the shortage of petrol ...

As she had these thoughts, she knew she was being unutterably selfish, but was it so wrong to be young and pretty, and just to want some enjoyment?And George was fun – no doubt about that – and different; and right from the start he'd made her laugh. She hadn't laughed for a long time before he arrived on the scene. At the thought of some of the good times she'd had with George she smiled as she slipped into her uniform. She finished buttoning her blouse, straightened her tie and took her jacket off its hanger. She did it up as she ran down the stairs. As she reached the bottom she glanced at her watch. Good grief, was that the time? All that daydreaming in her room had almost made her late.

'Mrs Viney,' she called as she grabbed her handbag from the hall table and took out her purse, 'I'm expecting the grocery boy to deliver some things this morning. Could you ask the boy to tell Mr Goodbody I'll go on my day off to settle my account. Oh and there are some clothes in the bathroom that need to go through the copper. Could you be a love and see to that?' Gwen took a loaf out of the bin and cut herself a slice, then spread it with a dab of marge.

'You should have a proper breakfast.'

'No time,' Gwen replied indistinctly with her mouth full as she slipped her arms into the sleeves of her waterproof.

Mrs Viney shook her head in disapproval as Gwen grabbed her hat and sped out of the back door.

After Gwen had cycled off, Mrs Viney bustled about the kitchen, wiping down the table, tidying away the clean crockery off the draining board, trying to keep her thoughts from straying to what might be happening to her Bill. She'd known that he'd get sent to France sooner or later and she was glad he hadn't gone across a fortnight earlier. Not that it was any less dangerous now. Jerry was still putting up a fight. Still, her Bill said he had a lot of faith in the Colonel and that he was a good sort, for an officer. Nan Viney hoped he was right. She wasn't sure about his wife. Bit of a flighty young thing. Then she smiled to herself. Flighty she might be, but Mrs Clarke had a heart of gold and Nan thought that she could do far worse than work for such a nice lady. All she needed was a baby to settle her down. But fat chance of that happening till after the war was over.

Nan Viney was brought out of her thoughts by a knock on the door. That'll be the grocery boy, she thought. She wiped her hands on her apron and went to answer it. The young man proffering a brown paper parcel tied up with string was patently not delivering the week's shopping.

'Oh, the laundry.'

'That's right, missus. I can't come Monday. I did tell Mrs Clarke last week. Has she forgotten?'

'She didn't mention it to me,' Mrs Viney grumbled. 'I don't know if she's got the laundry ready to go back.'

'I did tell her,' the youth insisted. 'Either way, it's one and six, please.'

'Hang on.' Mrs Viney took the parcel and put it on the kitchen table, then she found her purse and the right change before panting up the stairs to the back bedroom. The laundry was ready: Mrs Clarke hadn't forgotten – apart from leaving the money, that is. Not that that was a problem. Nan knew she had enough to pay in her own purse and Mrs Clarke could pay her back tomorrow. She picked up the dirty linen, wrapped up identically to the parcel she had just taken in, and the laundry book sitting on the top. By the time she'd returned to the front door with the dirty laundry and handed it and the money over she felt quite puffed.

'There you go.' She checked the book. 'Two sheets, two pillow cases, one tablecloth and three blouses.' The lad noted down the items listed in his book and, taking the money, went off whistling. Mrs Viney returned to the kitchen for a cup of tea before getting on with the rest of her duties for the day. And now there was the bed to change as well. She imagined Mrs Clarke would want her to do it. It would save her employer a job on her day off. Finishing her tea, Mrs Viney took the parcel of clean laundry upstairs and began stripping Gwen's bed.

En route from Paris to Caen

The troop train ground slowly along the tracks, the suburbs of Paris becoming more frequently interspersed with areas of farmland. Peiper leaned back in his seat and gazed sightlessly at the slowly passing view. He was not interested in anything except reaching Caen as soon as possible, but this unbelievably sluggish crawl was making him almost as frustrated and angry as he had been at the station. The other officers in the compartment eyed him warily; brilliant commander he might be, but his temper was terrifying. No one wanted to antagonise him with some seemingly innocuous comment that he might take the wrong way. They sat in silence, but they were all thinking much the same: they were all worried that this train would make a perfect target for any passing enemy bomber. And they all knew that they could expect no Luftwaffe air cover – there was none, although to say so was tantamount to treason.

The countryside slipped slowly past the window. They passed through a number of towns and villages and a couple of times they saw other trains waiting in sidings or on loop lines for them to pass. Peiper was pleased that they seemed to be getting priority over other railway traffic. However, their progress was never fast and from time to time they slowed down even more, as they passed gangs of malnourished slave labourers repairing sections of track that had been damaged by enemy bombing action. They were passing one such group when Peiper noticed the normally expressionless and sullen workers were displaying signs of animation and they were pointing and gesticulating at the train. Peiper's curiosity was aroused. He stood up, dropped open the window of the compartment and carefully leaned a little way out. The acrid smell of the smoke from the engine made his eyes water slightly; then he realised that the smoke wasn't coming from the engine but from the axle housing of one of the flatbeds. Peiper swore under his breath, then pulled his head in. He was about to reach up and grab the communication cord when there was a desperate squealingand juddering. The train braked suddenly and he was flung backwards into the lap of one of his subordinates. Peiper grabbed the edge of the lowered window to regain his balance and hauled himself to his feet. By now the train was almost at a standstill and flames were apparent. Soldiers carrying buckets had jumped down from the trucks, no doubt obeying orders from the NCOs, and were running along the track towards a nearby stream. The NCOs were organising other soldiers into a chain gang down to the water's edge, some thirty metres away. The slave workers were also co-opted but rather more brutally. Peiper could see that the situation was largely under control, but he decided he wanted to see for himself the extent of the damage to the truck and whether it was going to delay them for long. Being stuck in open country in broad daylight was a far from ideal situation.

He exited the compartment and strode down the corridor to the door. He jumped the metre or so on to the track without hesitation and headed towards the scene of activity ahead. The soldiers and slave workers were now formed up in a line between the train and the river and buckets full of water were being passed rapidly from hand to hand. Peiper reached the burning axle as the first of the full buckets did and he was close enough to hear the hiss of the water as it hit the red hot metal. Billows of steam were added to the black smoke of the burning grease and Peiper had to turn away to shield his eyes from the stinging combination. Through narrowed lids he thought he saw a trail of smoke wisp away from the other axle on the truck. He ran a couple of yards and bent down to examine it. Perhaps it was his imagination. He reached out and touched the wheel bearing and leapt back as the metal burnt his hand. One seized wheel bearing was unfortunate; two was sabotage.

'Get the men to douse all the wheels,' he yelled at the nearest NCO. The NCO looked bewildered. 'Just do it,' he roared. 'And organise some men to keep watch for enemy aircraft. We're like rats in a barrel waiting to be shot at here.'

Around him men with buckets ran in all directions to carry out his orders, while others climbed on to the tanks and grabbed machine-guns. The train had an anti-aircraft gun mounted near the engine and another at the rear, but it would not be much of a deterrent to the enemy – certainly not enough of one to prevent them trying to destroy such a prize as a stationary train loaded with Panzers. Peiper moved away from the smoke to better view that his instructions were being followed. By this time all the officers had disembarked from the train too and were either helping deploy the men or making sure that the axles were getting cooled sufficiently. He could see the train driver running towards him. Peiper beckoned to his adjutant.

'Sir,' said Captain Kowal, running over.

'I need you to translate.'

'Sir.'

The train driver stopped by the still smouldering wheel housing and scratched his head. Peiper strode over to him.

'Explain what has happened.'

Kowal translated. The driver shrugged his shoulders and said it must have seized.

'Tell him I can see that. But what made the other bearings seize, or nearly seize too?'

The train driver didn't meet Peiper's gaze and shrugged again. Peiper drew his pistol and cocked it. A look of terror crossed the driver's face.

'Sabotage,' he said.

The word needed no translation. It was the same in German as French.

'How?'

The driver knelt by the track and scraped some grease off the housing, his hands protected from the heat by thick leather gauntlets. He looked at it closely. He then removed the glove from his left hand and gingerly checked to see if it was cool enough to handle. He rubbed some of the grease between his forefinger and thumb.

'There's an abrasive in the grease. Carborundum, sand – he doesn't know,' translated Kowal.

Peiper swore, then said, 'Gare Saint-Lazare.'

His adjutant nodded. 'The workman.'

Peiper sighed heavily. 'So how do we sort this mess out?'

The driver looked at the grease on his fingers then said, 'You'll have to clean all this off the axles and then re-greasethem. Even then I can't guarantee it'll work. The bearings may be damaged.'

Peiper waited till the adjutant translated, although he guessed from the despondent tone of the driver that what he was saying was not good news. Angrily he ordered the adjutant to set the men to work as soon as all danger of further fires was over. 'And get them issued with rags soaked in petrol. I want the grease cleaned off properly. Understand?' Peiper returned his pistol to its holster now he no longer had need for it. It had served its purpose although he'd never had any intention of shooting the driver – that would have hardly improved the situation. Not that the driver knew his life had never been in danger.

David stood on the windswept sea wall of the small French village and surveyed the beach below him. The tide was low and the grey sea and the crashing waves were in the distance although the constant roar of the wind and waves still swept up the beach and drowned out most other sounds. Milling over the vast expanse of damp sand were men and vehicles. Where, ten years ago, families with children in bright summer clothes would have sat on the sand or rolled trousers up and hitched skirts to knee level to paddle in the sea, now there was frantic activity from khaki-clad adults, and dun-coloured lorries. In amongst the chaos were the men of his battalion.

He'd been told to find the Beach Master's HQ, which he had done, and, having received his immediate orders, he now knew where his battalion was to go next: a holding area where his men would get a meal and the opportunity for rest. Sadly for David, he had to report to Divisional Headquarters, so there would be no break for him.

He passed his orders to the RSM, who got the troops organised and into a convoy. About an hour later they crawled across the damp, pale sand to the slipway that led off the beach, then on to a metalled road. The road snaked down and up a couple of steep inclines where a river cut through the hill obeying its own imperative to reach the sea, then up they went to the top of a high piece of open ground, which afforded a spectacular view over the whole area of coast that the British had only recently taken. The scale of the Mulberry harbour, when seen from this vantage point, stunned David. He wondered who on earth had had the imagination to conceive such a project. Of course it was no longer quite as it should have been. The terrible storm had wrecked parts of it; but the majority of the breakwaters, jetties and moles still seemed to be functioning pretty well and, what with the huge expanse of beach that was exposed at low tide, David thought that the issue of keeping the troops supplied was going to be relatively straightforward. Or, at least, as straightforward as keeping nearly half a million men in food, fuel and ammunition was ever going to be.

Off to his left David could see a field hospital that had been erected, the khaki tents adorned with vast red crosses on white circles. He noticed with a slight sense of surprise that there were nurses moving amongst them. Then he reasoned that there was no reason why they shouldn't be there; after all, the fighting had moved on considerably and this area was almost as safe as being back in Blighty. To his right was the holding area. A military policeman in a glistening oilskin cape began directing their convoy through the gate and into the field. David's driver swung the wheel and took the jeep off the tarmac of the road and on to the metal trackway that the sappers had laid to stop vehicles getting bogged down on the waterlogged grass. They followed directions past rank upon rank of tents until another policeman indicated they should park up and showed them where to find the field kitchen and food.

David jumped out and stretched. He was still stiff from that awful sea crossing and furthermore his uniform remained damp. He was no worse off than any of his men, and he knew he had to remember that. Wouldn't do to complain about his own lot in front of them. He let most of his men go past before he joined the straggling column heading to the field kitchen. As he approached it, he could smell the delicious aroma of bread baking. No doubt they were likely to be served porridge or some other filling stodge. He'd have given his back teeth for bacon and eggs, but what were the chances of that these days? Fresh bread would be good, though, even if it would have to be margarine that topped it, not butter.

David was right. Breakfast was big hunks of bread and marge, porridge and a pint mug of tea, but even so it was hugely welcome to almost all of his men – even the ones who had still been looking pale – and David himself wolfed it down. Nothing like sea air, he thought, for giving you an appetite.

Once breakfast was over his men were formed up again and taken back to the tents allocated to them so they could rest before they were thrown into the thick of the fighting. David called for his driver and set off for Creully, where Divisional Headquarters was to be found.

It wasn't far to the Headquarters, but the journey was tricky. The roads were filled with troops and trucks either going back towards Arromanches for more supplies or going towards the front line to reinforce the offensive. Furthermore, the few villages they drove through were all severely war-damaged and they had to avoid lumps of rubble and potholes. The churches especially seemed to have taken a battering because the spires and towers were such perfect locations for lookouts or snipers. It was heartbreaking to see such wanton destruction all around. He wondered what had happened to the inhabitants. He hoped most of them had found shelter or had escaped. There were precious few locals around now, that was certain.

The road from Asnelles passed the château, as he had been promised. It was in a fold in the hills below the main body of the village of Creully. They turned off the road and through the gates. Ahead was the beautiful old building, looking mostly undamaged, and in front of it was a mass of vehicles, radio masts, and other military paraphernalia. A military policeman stopped them at a makeshift barrier, saluted and demanded to see some identification. David handed over his ID card.

'On your way then, sir,' said the MP as he snapped another salute.

They drove on slowly along the drive. David noticed that the estate hadn't escaped entirely unscathed. There were a number of raw, brown craters pitting the bright green grass. The battle for Creully might not have been lengthy or vicious but it had still left its mark. *Even here*, thought David, in deep countryside and away from the coast, the Allied invasion was harming the very people it had come to save.

His driver pulled up on the gravel sweep outside the front door to the château. 'Wait here,' said David stepping out of the jeep.

'Right oh, sir,' replied his driver.

As David strode to the entrance the driver parked up nearby, took his beret off and lit up a smoke.

Inside the door was a desk behind which sat a couple of military policemen, who wanted to check his pass.

'I'm here to see Colonel Cole,' he said.

One of the MPs scrutinised his ID card. 'Yes, sir.'

'Up the stairs and follow the corridor along to the right,' said the other.

'Is there a canteen around here? I'd like my driver to be able to get a cup of tea.'

The MP heaved himself out of his chair. 'I'll give him directions, sir. Best you get on.'

David took the shallow stairs two at a time. At the top a gloomy, unlit corridor led off to the left and the right, flanked by doors most of which were open. He could hear the clatter of a couple of typewriters and the sound of male voices involved in what appeared to be a very animated discussion. A couple of clerks were bustling about importantly, ferrying files and papers from one office to another. David turned to his right and headed towards the first room he could see.

He poked his head around the open door. Inside were half a dozen trestle tables covered in maps, signal pads, radios and paperwork. Around them officers examined the positions of Allied and enemy forces as represented by coloured pins, flags and map symbols. There was a low hubbub of voices as options for a variety of possible strategies and tactics were discussed.

A young captain looked up. 'Can I help you, sir?'

'Colonel David Clarke reporting. My battalion has just been landed on Gold Beach and is currently in the holding area above Asnelles.'

'Oh jolly good. We've been expecting you. Welcome to France.' The junior officer introduced himself. 'I've just been posted into the HQ so I didn't get the chance to meet you when you were training in England. Take a seat and I'll get someone to bring you some tea. We'll take you to the Colonel in a few minutes.' The captain gestured to a folding chair at the side of the room and David wandered over and sat down. He felt slightly disappointed that he hadn't yet come across any of his chums. The HQ had gone out to France a couple of weeks before his battalion had received its orders and he was anxious to catch up with the news of the staff and other units that they had come to know so well during the preparation for the invasion.

A couple of minutes later a clerk came over with a mug of tea and a bowl of sugar. The spoon in the sugar had obviously been used several times already, judging by the encrustation on it. He settled down to wait. War had ever been thus, he mused: frantic, sometimes terrifying activity, for short periods, followed by hours, or even days, of boredom. He sipped his tea and wondered how Gwen was getting along. Did she know he was in France? Was she worrying about him? And although he didn't want Gwen upset, he did rather hope that she was. He still wasn't entirely sure she'd forgiven him for not coming home for that weekend those several weeks back.

West Sussex

Gwen cycled along the same lane that George had ridden

along on his bike some three hours earlier. In the distance was the sea, though today it didn't sparkle like it ought to in the summer but rather gleamed dully. She thought about the French coast, hidden over the horizon, and wondered if David was there yet. She'd seen the newsreels and furthermore she'd seen the casualties coming back through Portsmouth. She was under no illusions about the battle in Normandy and what it was costing, and now her David was going to be a part of it. And she felt rotten that the last time they had had a telephone conversation it had been so acrimonious. If only she could go back a few weeks and tell him how much he meant to her, instead of snapping at him for giving up his chance of leave. She'd written him lots of letters since, trying to make things up to him, but it wasn't the same as actually speaking to him. The bottom line was – and she realised this with startling clarity now – that his fuddy-duddy ways might irritate her, his loyalty to his men and his way of putting them first had enraged her, but she loved him and she couldn't bear the idea of anything terrible befalling him. And she desperately wanted him to know it.

Too late, though. Now he was in danger – or was about to be – and all she could do was pray that it wasn't going to cost him too much. She tried not to think about what that personal cost might be, but she was no fool and knew the odds on his safe return were not outstanding. She half-wished she was still in ignorance regarding his whereabouts. If Mrs Viney hadn't told her about 'her Bill', she wouldn't have heard yet. She sighed disconsolately. Well, she knew now.

The hill steepened somewhat and Gwen applied the brakes. The rubber pads squealed unpleasantly against the metal of the tyre rim. She pressed the brake levers harder and the bike juddered to a crawl. For a few hundred yards Gwen concentrated on her riding rather than on any thoughts of David. She rounded the final bend in the lane before the junction with the main road and the gradient levelled out. A couple of minutes later she had hidden her bike behind the hedge at the bus stop and was straightening her hat and skirt. She took her handbag and gas mask from her bicycle basket and waited patiently for the bus to arrive. She wondered what she would be required to do that day. She prayed she wouldn't be asked to deal with cleaning up the walking wounded as they arrived back, though. It wasn't the injuries that she found so repellent, although often it took her all her courage to look at some of the more disfiguring wounds without flinching – it was the smell. She couldn't get used to the stench of clothes that hadn't been properly dried or changed for weeks, or the reek of soldiers who had been unable to wash for days on end. Sometimes it was so overwhelming she was afraid she was going to gag, and that wouldn't do. Even Gwen knew the soldiers had been through quite enough without being humiliated by some female who was oversensitive to a bit of a pong. She'd hoped she'd get used to it, but it was no good. In the years she had worked for the WVS, whether she'd been dealing with victims of bombing raids, refugees or troops, she had never been able to cope with the odour of unwashed bodies.

The sound of some vehicle grinding up the hill towards her brought her out of her thoughts. Good – the bus. She clambered on and paid her fare to the conductor standing on the platform, before making her way to the back of the single-decker. The windows were misted up and the air was fuggy with cigarette smoke. As usual there were only a few seats available and Gwen squashed herself next to a lady of ample proportions with a shopping basket on her knee. Gwen realised that she had made a mistake as soon as she sat down. She had only a few inches of seat on which to perch and every time the bus went round a left-hand bend the large lady oozed another inch or so towards the aisle. Gwen wanted to move but knew it would be obvious and hurtful if she did. She turned sideways slightly, so both her feet were in the aisle, and braced herself against the human landslide as best she could.

'Nasty again, isn't it?' said the fat lady.

'Hmm.' Gwen really didn't want to talk. Besides which, if she became engaged in a conversation, she could hardly conduct it with her back virtually completely turned to the woman. Yet if she sat square on the seat she was in every danger of being peremptorily shoved on to the floor.

'Can't be much fun for our boys in France,' her neighbour continued undeterred.

'Indeed no.'

'Still, it should all be over by Christmas.'

'So they say.' Gwen opened her handbag and took out a packet of Craven 'A'. She lit up and blew the smoke towards the roof of the bus. She hoped this would indicate she really wasn't interested in talking.

'Off to work then, are you?'

'Yes.' Good God, what would it take to make this woman shut up?

'Portsmouth docks?'

'Yes.' Gwen debated about getting off at the next stop and waiting for the later bus, but that probably wouldn't get her to work on time.

'My son-in-law works there. In the docks. He's a crane driver.'

'Really.'

'Been working ever so hard lately.'

'I can imagine.'

'Says without the canteens your lot provide he doesn't know how they'd have kept going. He can't say enough about the WVS. How wonderful you ladies are. Always cheerful, always happy to give anyone a hand. Wonders, he says. Blooming wonders.'

Gwen took another puff of her cigarette to hide her

embarrassment. She'd been so mean to this poor woman and she was only trying to be kind.

'Thanks. We're only doing our duty.'

'No, there's duty and doing things the way you ladies do. Credit to the country you are.'

Gwen shrugged. The bus pulled over at the side of the road.

'And here's my stop.' The ample lady hauled herself to her feet and Gwen stood up too to allow her to pass. 'My son-in-law's called Tom – Tom Greenaway. If you come across him, don't let him give you any flannel.'

'I won't,' said Gwen as the fat lady huffed and puffed her way down the narrow passage between the seats.

'If he does, you tell him you'll tell Bertha,' she said with a jaunty wave as she got to the door.

Gwen nodded and smiled. And what were her chances of coming across Tom Greenaway amongst the thousands of men who worked in Portsmouth docks?

The bus pulled away again and Gwen sank into the comparative luxury of a seat to herself. She shuffled over to the window and used the back of her glove to wipe away some of the condensation so that she could see out. Given that it was late June, the weather was startlingly unseasonal. Grey clouds scudded across a grey sky, a stiff wind blew and the pedestrians on their way to work were huddled in mackintoshes and coats. On either side of the road was evidence of war, though Gwen had long since stopped noticing the bombed-out buildings or craters. At the start of the war she'd recoiled in horror at each new manifestation of the war's random violence. She would gaze out of the windows and wonder about the casualties, the damage and the awfulness of having your house blown to bits and everything you possessed smashed and wrecked. But she didn't any more. She knew far too many people who had been bombed out and who were making the best of living with relatives or friends to be able to spare a thought for any stranger's personal tragedy now. She knew that if the worst happened to her little cottage, there would be precious little sympathy for her either. It wasn't that people didn't or wouldn't care; it was just there was too much awfulness around for anyone to have the time or the luxury of being able to focus on an individual.

The bus progressed through the suburbs of Portsmouth, then through the city centre itself. If it hadn't been for the piles of rubble and bricks, the boarded-up windows and the defiant notices announcing that business was 'as usual', it could have been an ordinary day in any big town. The bus finally stopped at the entrance to the dockyard and Gwen shuffled off the bus behind a dozen or so others all heading for the same destination. She queued patiently at the dockyard gates while the sailor on duty checked their passes.

'Morning, ma'am,' he greeted her as he scanned her ID card. He handed it back and let her pass.

Gwen passed through the gate and into the hurly-burly of the dockyard. Everywhere she looked there was frantic activity. Ships were being loaded and unloaded, troops were being mustered or marched and Wrens, matelots and officers were busting about with an air of importance. Gwen hitched her gas mask on to her shoulder and stepped out to the WVS office to find out what the day had in store for her.

Four

Mid-Morning, Saturday 24 June 1944

Carpiquet Airfield, Caen

Otto had managed to get back to camp undetected by dint of crawling under the perimeter wire and then sneaking to the latrine area. Once he was there, no one would comment about a soldier returning to his billet from an early-morning call of nature. However, he'd hardly crept into his camp bed when the alert had sounded and he'd had to race out and help man one of the airfield defensive positions – a single-barrelled twenty-millimetre cannon. He'd been sitting with his crew of four on the gun now for over four hours, aching with lack of sleep and the damp, bone-numbing chill of the overcast, wet, windy June morning. His tunic and trousers did not offer much protection against the elements. He wished he had a coat to wear.

For some time now they had heard the intermittent drone of enemy aircraft, but they had been flying above the lowering cloud and neither Otto nor any of his comrades had caught a glimpse of them through the occasional breaks. However, as long as air activity continued in their area they had to man the gun. As the sun had begun to climb in the sky behind the heavy cloud cover, the day had got marginally warmer; but Otto still felt frozen. He tried to tell himself that he would have thought this almost tropical if he'd suffered on the Eastern Front, but it didn't help. He tucked his hands deep into his armpits in an effort to warm them. He let his chin sink on to his chest. He'd just let his eyes shut for a few seconds …

The shouting of his comrades startled him. Instantly he was wide awake. He could hear the sound of an approaching aircraft. He swivelled so that he looked towards the direction of the noise and squinted to try to sharpen his vision.

One of the crew frantically turned the handle to traverse the gun into the right direction.

There it was! Just above the horizon, racing towards them. More turning of handles as the muzzle of the gun was depressed to the right trajectory. Then the gun opened up. The first twenty-round magazine, firing at three rounds a second, was used up just as the plane crossed the edge of the airfield. Otto handed the gunner another full mag. It was clipped on and the firing continued. The noise of the rounds and the Typhoon at full throttle zooming overhead was deafening. The aircraft was directly above them and then, with that distinctive change of engine note, it was going away from them. The gun was swung through one hundred and eighty degrees so they could continue firing. The mag emptied and the gunner stopped. In the near silence that followed they stared after the jinking, weaving enemy aircraft as it shot away from them towards the east. Perhaps they'd get it on the way back.

A few months ago, even as little as a few weeks ago, the Luftwaffe would have scrambled and taken that Typhoon on, but now all that was left on this airfield was a couple of burnt-out wrecks and the remains of two other aircraft that had been cannibalised for spares until there were no aircraft left that might ever fly again. However, Otto and his comrades had been told categorically that their job was now to deny the enemy this airfield. Strategically it was hugely important and that was why they were expecting the imminent arrival of a crack SS-Panzer Regiment.

Otto sighed. That arrival was the cause of a big problem for him. With SS-Panzer Regiment 1 sharing the airfield with them, things would be bound to change. Not that discipline was lax now, but the SS had a reputation for doing things differently – very differently. Otto knew that once they got to the airfield his chances in this war would alter considerably and not necessarily for the better. With the SS around and about it became less of an option to surrender to the enemy at the first opportunity, which was what Otto had planned. He was as patriotic as the next man and was more than prepared to defend Germany, but he drew the line at France. As far as he was concerned, if the French wanted it back, let them have it. He'd fight to the last to protect Martine, but he wasn't going to die fighting for this scruffy square kilometre of French grass that surrounded him now. He recalled the discussion he'd had with Martine.

'If the SS are coming you've got to get out before they arrive.'

'It's not as easy as that.'

'It'll be harder when they are here.'

Otto conceded that she was right.

'*Bien sûr j'ai raison*,' she'd said with an irritated shake of her head.

Otto looked at her uncomprehending.

'Of course I'm right,' she'd repeated in German. 'I've worked out the perfect place to hide you. All you have to do is walk off the airfield, come to the farm and I'll do the rest. If you can keep your head down for just a few days, a week at the most, until the Allies get to us, then all will be well.'

But Otto still had doubts. Slipping off for an illicit couple of hours with his girlfriend was one thing; deserting was something else entirely. On top of which he wasn't sure he fancied the idea of being trapped in some little hidey-hole while a battle raged around. His imagination flicked around a number of deeply unpleasant scenarios most of which involved him being trapped under rubble or in a burning building. He knew it might never come to that. He might get taken prisoner, which was what Martine had planned.

'Better that than being shot in battle,' she'd said pragmatically.

But the trouble was, supposing he got caught by his own side? He would end up being shot anyway. Realistically he knew he had just two options: fight or flight – and both of them carried risks. Otto sighed. He wished he could see into the future; then he would know which path to take.

La Ferme de la Source – Normandy

Martine was hot and bothered by the time she'd finished getting the root store covered with farmyard junk again. She wanted a wash and to cool down, but there was no point in doing that till she'd finished work for the morning. Sighing, she made her way across the yard to the hen house and opened the door. Inside, sheltered completely from the elements, the atmosphere was warm and dusty. In the corner one of the hens was broody and sitting on the nest clucking quietly. The sound she made was one of the farmyard noises that never failed to comfort Martine. Her spirits lifted despite her tiredness. She picked up the basket from its position by the door and began to collect the eggs. She worked swiftly, rummaging through the soft hay for the hard round shapes. She found a dozen. Good, she thought: enough to cover the quota plus a couple for the farm and a couple for the black market. She took the basket out with her to the yard and went over to the pump. Placing her valuable load carefully by the trough, she yanked the handle up and down. The water that gushed was icy cold, but Martine plunged her hands under the jet and then splashed her face and the back of her neck. Having done that, she filled the pail that was there, picked up the basket with the other hand and lugged it all into the kitchen.

Her father was sitting at the table staring into a bowl of coffee and chewing on a lump of stale bread.

'*Bonjour, Papa,*' said Martine as she deposited the pail on the drainer by the sink and put the basket on the table.

Her father grunted in reply.

'I'm going to the village in a minute. Do you want anything from the shop?'

'We need soap.'

Martine sighed. She knew that. But what were the chances of any of that being available? 'I'll see what I can do,' she replied. 'What have you got planned for today? If you feel up to it, the gate to Long Meadow needs seeing to. One of the hinges isn't right. And the pigsty needs new straw.'

'*Plus tard.*'

Martine sighed. It was always *later* with her father. Then he'd forget; then she'd have to remind him; then he got angry and called her a nag. But she couldn't do it all herself, though God only knew it felt as if she did. *Mon Dieu*, she thought, she was doing the work of two grown men most days.

'Please,' she said. It was worth a try.

Again her father grunted and hacked off more bread. Not knowing if her father's noises meant he was going to help out or if it was his way of ignoring her, Martine dropped the subject She went to the larder and brought out the big flour crock. She dug a hole deep into the flour, buried two of the eggs from the basket and returned the crock to the larder.

'The Boche will kill you if they catch you doing that.'

Martine shrugged. 'They won't. Besides, we have to live too. They get plenty from us.'

Her father said nothing and dipped the last of his bread into his coffee.

Martine then put eight of the eggs in a bowl, which she put on the dresser, and slipped the last two into the pocket of her trousers.

'And do that hinge,' she said as she flung a shawl over her shoulders and picked up the empty basket. She banged the door loudly as she left the kitchen. Not that she held out much hope that he would. Something else she'd have to find time to do no doubt. Angrily she stamped off to the dairy to load a small churn of milk and a kilo of butter on to the handcart before she walked down the lane to the village.

She clumped away from the house in her heavy work boots. She wouldn't be surprised if, once she had left, her father also made his way to the village to add to the profits of Bernard, the café owner. If he did, the hinge would be forgotten. Martine wondered if the next time Otto came to the farm perhaps he could fix it for her. It wouldn't hurt to ask.

As she walked down the lane a British plane passed over her head. A few seconds later she heard the guns at the airfield open up. The sudden volley of crashing thumps startled her and she jumped. To the north she could bear the intermittent rumble of distant guns. She'd heard the people describe the sound of distant guns in the Great War as being like thunder Now she had the chance to hear gunfire for herself she thought it was nothing like it. It wasn't a natural sound at all: sudden booming crashes that came out of the blue. Sometimes they heard the eerie whistling of unseen shells passing overhead to hit German positions near Caen. Martine could only hope the gunners had the range right when she heard that.

It was about ten minutes later that she reached the little village – a cluster of stone and brick houses with grey roofs built round the church, the café and the shop.

Outside the church was the memorial to the sons of France who had given their lives in the Great War. Most of the names were familiar to Martine. Their families still lived in the area – or those family members that the Germans hadn't taken away to the labour camps or for the *travaille obligatoire*.

Martine had chosen her time for her visit to the village carefully. The glistening street that ran through it was deserted – not a German in sight; there never was in the late morning, and it was even more unlikely given the lashing squalls that swept through every few minutes. As Martine came to the first of the houses of the little settlement she turned off the road and on to the path that led along the stream at the back of the houses. When she came to the fifth gate she opened it, pushed the handcart inside and shut it again. Then, with her basket on her arm, she retraced her steps and walked along the street, picking her way between the puddles, to the shop.

Martine nodded greetings to a couple coming out of the little store and exchanged a few worried words about the progress of the invasion. When were they going to be liberated? they asked each other *sotto voce*, careful to make sure no one else was within earshot. If things had been dangerous before, they were worse now. The Boche were twitchy, the Resistance were carrying out God only knew what raids, and putting everyone in danger from reprisals.

Martine didn't want to dwell on the bleakness of their outlook. '*Alors*, I must get on.' Martine bade the couple farewell and hurried into the shop.

'*Bonjour, madame, monsieur*,' she said as she entered the little store, manners dictating that she should greet both people present – the proprietor, Mme Boiselle, and the customer waiting for her to wrap some cheese and add the package to the small pile of other purchases.

'*Bonjour, mademoiselle*.' The shopkeeper's eyebrows

were raised just a fraction.

Behind the customer's back Martine nodded and Mme Boiselle smiled, but it was a smile of acknowledgement – not friendliness. Her lips might have moved but her eyes stayed cold and hard, like a pair of black olives. A message had been given and received, that was all. Martine knew some locals were only too aware of Mme Boiselle's black-market sideline, but obviously Monsieur Hervey wasn't one of them. One couldn't be too careful about who knew what – a word in the ear of the authorities was enough to have whole families deported to God only knew where. Though, if Martine had felt she could have got away with it and not been implicated herself, she would have quite liked to snitch on Mme Boiselle and see her carted off. Serve the old biddy right.

Mme Boiselle finished serving M. Hervey and dealing with the ration coupons and money. Martine waited patiently for him to leave the shop, her shawl dripping water on to the wooden planking and forming a pool round her feet, before she began her own business.

She didn't bother with any further pleasantries. 'I'd like some tins of ham and milk,' she said. 'As many as you can spare.' She didn't think that was likely to be very many.

'Stocking up?'

Martine shrugged. Why should she tell the old bat anything? But she had to say something. 'With things being as they are …' She left the sentence unfinished, and shrugged. Mme Boiselle reached under the counter and brought out four tins. One was ham, one was a tin of peas, one was soup and one was milk. 'That's all I can let you have. It's not just you wanting stuff, you know,' Mme Boiselle said curtly.

Martine knew full well that even if she had been the only one wanting stuff she still wouldn't have got any more. 'There's a churn of milk and a kilo of butter in your garden,' Martine said somewhat pointedly, pushing wet hair out of her eyes. She reached into her pocket and brought out the two eggs. Mme Boiselle had them spirited away under the counter in a trice.

'And here's the money for the last lot.' The old woman snapped open the drawer under the counter and pulled out some francs.

Martine let it lie on the counter. They both knew that Mme Boiselle was paying less than the market rate. But then she was also taking the bigger risk. Martine dropped her gaze first and with a shrug she swept the coins up in her hand and shoved them into a pocket. She knew Mme Boiselle didn't really like her. Martine suspected it might have been because her repellent husband was always giving her the glad eye. Not that she encouraged him; quite the contrary, but he didn't seem to get the hint.

'I don't suppose you have any soap?'

Mme Boiselle laughed. 'What do you think?'

Martine thought that she didn't have any soap because of who was asking. That was far more likely. It was obvious to Martine that if it wasn't for the black-market goods she supplied to the shop, Mme Boiselle would find that she had very little available for Martine to buy at all. But she wasn't going to let the old bitch know how much it riled her to be treated like this. She smiled sweetly. 'Oh well. *Tant pis*. I thought I'd ask. What I wouldn't give for a proper wash and clean clothes.'

A door at the back of the shop opened and M. Boiselle entered. He nodded at Martine and as soon as he saw his wife wasn't watching him he followed it up with a lecherous wink.

'*Bonjour, mademoiselle*. I trust your father is well.' He licked his wet, flabby lips. Martine suppressed a shudder.

'He is when he's sober,' said Martine shortly. 'The tins. How much?'

'The two eggs will cover it.'

'Right. I'd better go. Work to do.'

'I've emptied your cart,' said M. Boiselle. 'Come through the shop to get it.'

Absolutely not, thought Martine. She wasn't going to risk getting caught in a back room with the old goat. 'My boots are dirty. I'll go round by the lane.'

'No, that doesn't matter. Save yourself a journey,' M. Boiselle insisted.

Mme Boiselle gave her a hard stare. Martine returned it. If Mme Boiselle wanted to make something of her husband's offer, she had better take it out on him. Martine had nothing to do with him and wasn't going to, ever, under any circumstances. He was the last person she would encourage. Even if all the men in France died except him, Martine would still find him completely resistible.

She bade the couple farewell and left, aware that Mme Boiselle was still looking daggers at her. Stupid old cow.

'She's a sly one and no mistake,' said Sylvie Boiselle. 'It's too bad the way Jean-Paul carries on. If he was ever sober, he'd see her game.'

'She's not that bad. And she's a hard worker, like her mother.' Robert didn't add that Martine was also a looker, just like her mother.

'But her mother knew how to behave. She was a good woman. She made Jean-Paul a good wife. I can't see Martine being a good wife to anyone. Mark my words, that girl will come to a bad end.'

'She'll be all right with the right man. That's what she needs: a man.' Robert thought that he could probably solve a lot of Martine's problems, or the problems he perceived her to have, if only the little trollop would give him half a chance.

Sylvie Boiselle shot him a look. 'Hmmm. And with all the young men away, where's she going to find one of those?'

Robert didn't answer her. He was thinking about sorting out Martine's 'problems' and what it might be like.

Sylvie continued, 'And that farm isn't much of a prospect for anyone to take on. Jean-Paul has let it go to ruin. The old soak should be ashamed of himself.'

'But she'd be a catch. A little beauty like her.'

Sylvie sniffed. 'Little beauty, my eye. Little whore more like.'

Above Normandy

At just over 2,000 feet, when George took his eyes off his instruments or glanced at the ground instead of at the sky around him, he could see the countryside beneath him in fantastic detail. The clouds immediately above his cockpit may have been grey and dreary but the land below was startling in its green intensity, criss-crossed with hedges and lanes, splattered with random, darker-green splodges of woods and coppices and little settlements clustered by some useful feature – near a bridge over a river, at a crossroads or in the shelter of a valley floor. At this height he could see the type of stock in the fields, the size of the gardens behind houses in the villages, and ten or so miles away from the front line it was easy to imagine the war didn't exist at all. It all looked remarkably peaceful and normal and all very chocolate-boxy compared to the big open spaces he was used to back home. *It isn't going to last*, thought George dispassionately as he zoomed on towards Caen. The locals were going to get shaken up in the near future. The war was coming their way – no doubt about that – and probably before the end of the month, judging by the position of the troops he'd only just overflown. Around him were the three other planes in his section, keeping station with him, their leader, just to the side and behind him, providing extra eyes for each other and cover in case they got bounced by an enemy

Messerschmitt. Not that there was much of a chance of that.

At 2,000 feet they weren't out of range of light flak, which made George a little uncomfortable. By rights they should have been at around 10,000 feet, but this cloud cover meant that they had virtually no chance of spotting any targets. Nothing for it but to fly underneath – which wasn't ideal, thought George wryly. And it was tough flying straight and level. The wind buffeted them terribly and he had to constantly fight the stick and rudder to stop the plane getting bounced all over the sky.

In the distance he could see Caen: the ancient grey-stone castle on the grassy hill looming over the houses below it, the spires of its various churches and abbeys pointing skywards and the muddle of grey roofs of different heights and pitches that flanked the network of narrow streets.

Suddenly, bright flashes of exploding shell peppered the sky around him. *Damn*. Just as he'd feared. His heart rate shot up and he felt a clench of excitement knot his stomach as adrenalin kicked his senses up to full throttle. Instinctively George applied stick and rudder alternately so that his plane swung left and right, banking first to one side then the other through the sky, like some sort of drunken albatross, Out of the corner of his eye he saw his section scatter, the other planes veering off away from the source of danger. Below he could see the anti-aircraft gun emplacement that was firing at him from the side of a disused-looking airfield, and for a split second he caught a glimpse of ant-like figures of men manning it, trying to get a bead on him, and then he was directly above it and beyond, still swinging to port and starboard for safety's sake but rapidly heading out of danger at nearly 400 miles per hour.

A few seconds later it was all over. He was safe, his Typhoon seemed to be untouched, his heartbeat returned to normal. But he felt he'd had a lucky escape. Time was he'd have felt exhilarated and invincible, but once again he noticed he was drenched in a clammy sweat and his hands were still shaking.

He flicked the switch on his radio. 'OK, Red Section. Settle down; the action is all over now.' He said that as much to reassure himself as the others.

'Roger, Red Leader,' his section acknowledged in turn as they regrouped in their positions on his wing.

The section flew on, keeping tight with George as they headed towards Caen and their intended target. As they approached the city, George gently banked to starboard, his section keeping in formation so that his course would take him to the south and east – the railway line, where the troop train was supposed to be, was on the Paris side of Caen. On this bearing George knew he would cross the line and only had to follow the railway to find the prize – assuming the Int was correct. He could see the dull, gun-metal glint of the Orne as it flowed through the centre of the city and near it the sharper, brighter, straighter shine of the railway. *Bingo*.

George banked his plane again and flew parallel to the track, peering out of the cockpit in the hope of spotting his quarry. The ground slid rapidly beneath his wings – hills, woods, pasture, crops – but all the time he kept position with the line. Then he saw the train. There it was; a long line of trucks, laden with large grey shapes. No doubt about it, the shapes were tanks. But something wasn't right. George gave it a second look. Then realization dawned. The train was stationary. There should have been a stream of steam trailing back from the funnel, but what he could see was a rhythmic emission of steam, a puff about every second and the steam was being whipped away sideways by the breeze. A sitting duck. Yes, they couldn't fail! But equally, he realised with a sick feeling, it would be easier for the ack-ack gunners on the train to get a bead on them if they weren't moving. He took a deep breath to try to steady his nerve – and his hands.

'Target ahead, Red Section. Follow me.'

George pulled back gently on the stick and moved it fractionally to his right while his right foot applied just a squeeze of pressure to the rudder bar. His Typhoon responded by gracefully arcing upwards in the sky, away from the train, while just behind him the other three Typhoons followed him, keeping perfect station. At 2,000 feet George brought his plane back into straight and level flight and flew away from his target, just below the cloud base. When he judged his position to be perfect he brought his plane around through 180 degrees and lined up on the troop train.

'Attack, attack, attack,' he called into the radio as he pushed his stick forward and flicked open the button ready to fire the eight rockets housed in the wings of his plane.

He could feel the G shoving him back into his seat with brutal force as his plane plummeted towards his quarry, the engine screaming as his speed approached the maximum. Streaks of thin white flame shot past his cockpit as the gunners on the train opened up on him, but at this speed he knew he was a difficult target to hit and anyway almost every bit of his concentration was focused on his gun sight. As the Panzers on the flatbeds began to fill it, he pressed the firing button and saw the white streak of smoke whoosh into the distance as the first pair of rockets shot away. No recoil, no kick, just a pair of lines in the sky heading towards the target. Then he pressed the button again. The next two went, and again and again. As the last pair left, the first pair hit the target and exploded with a huge mushroom of flame and black smoke. George pulled the stick up hard and, with a sense of intense relief, felt the lurch as speed was converted to height and he soared away from the devastation. *Yes, another attack survived.*

He looked over his shoulder to observe the effect of his strike and was satisfied to see that several of his rockets must have achieved direct hits. Even if they hadn't destroyed the tanks, they would make it impossible for the train to move for the foreseeable future. Over the radio George could hear the next of his section going in for the attack as he gained height and prepared to circle out of ack-ack range until they had finished their work.

'Jolly good show,' he muttered under his breath as he reached his chosen vantage point and could look down at leisure at what was happening below. One thing was certain: the tanks weren't going to be causing a problem to the Allies for a while now.

South-east of Caen

Peiper strode along the edge of the ballast that held the sleepers in place to oversee the task he had set his men. Under every set of bogeys were several soldiers, all lying on their backs wielding petrol-soaked rags, trying to eradicate every trace of grease from the wheel bearings. Still smarting from the delay in Paris, his anger was now fuelled to a towering rage. Added to which was the worry that they had no cover. At least in Saint-Lazare they'd been hidden from enemy action by the station roof, but here ... *Gott im Himmel*, how much more exposed could they be? They needed to get the axles cleaned up and to be moving again as soon as possible. Six hours ago all he'd had to be furious about was the delay. Now the delay wasn't just costing them time: it might well be about to cost him his battalion.

Peiper strode along, weighing up possible courses of action. They could wait here and hope they weren't spotted. Given the weather it was possible the RAF might not be flying. Or he could order his men to unload the tanks from the train. At least if they were scattered it would be harder for the RAF to attack them. But if they weren't spotted by the enemy it would cause extra delay loading the tanks back on to the train again once it was ready to move. He shook his head as the possibilities whirled around. He cast about for someone to kick metaphorically.

He came across his adjutant, who was looking at the sky nervously. Obviously he too was worried about the RAF. He'd do, Peiper thought viciously.

'How long?' he snapped.

'The men are working very hard.'

'I can see that. How long?'

'Difficult to tell.'

Peiper took a deep breath. *Give me strength*, he thought. Which imbecile had thought fit to promote this idiot to Hauptman? 'Ten minutes?' he prompted sneeringly. 'An hour?'

'Probably about thirty minutes.'

Thirty minutes. God, thought Peiper, plenty of time for the whole of the RAF to gather and try to blow them off the face of the earth. 'Get this lot moving,' he yelled. 'Get them to put some effort into this. I want results and I want them soon. And get a detail to move the loading ramps to the back of the train. I want everything unloaded.'

'Sir ...'He swallowed nervously. 'Sir, what with the men detailed to provide air-defence cover and the rest cleaning the axles, I'm not sure ...'

He didn't get to finish his sentence. 'I don't care how you do it. Co-opt some locals. Get the labourers to help, but just do as you're told.'

The adjutant swallowed. '*Jawohl.*'

He was about to run down the track to expedite the order when Peiper gripped his arm, preventing him from leaving; but Peiper wasn't staring at his adjutant, he was looking skywards. Kowal followed Peiper's gaze. He was staring up at the black bulk of the engine, up to the top of the funnel. And beyond it, high in the sky, a flash of light, just a pinprick, had caught his eye. Then he saw it: a formation of four aircraft just visible as small black shapes against a slightly less dark cloud.

'Enemy aircraft!' Peiper yelled, his voice hardly loud enough to be heard above the wheezing of the engine. He ran back along the uneven and treacherous ballast, stumbling and almost falling as he passed the tender. 'Enemy aircraft!' he yelled again. But this time his warning was lost as the gunners on the first flatbed, also observant, opened up. Peiper looked skywards again. The plane was plummeting towards them at terrific speed. Then he saw streaks of white flash forward from the aircraft's wings. And again. Then more. Eight in all. Rockets!

The first two missiles struck the rear of the train. The explosion was deafening and a huge orange fireball billowed into the air. Moments later the blast wave struck. A wall of hot gas struck Peiper and that, coupled with his unsure footing on the ballast, was enough to make him miss a step. He found himself falling sideways into the undergrowth at the side of the track. He lay there for a second, disorientated and stunned, then the next salvo of rockets hit. This time they landed, so far as Peiper could judge from his position, on the other side of the train. He scrambled to his feet again, yelling for the men to get out from under the flatbeds. This was no time for them to be cowering like a load of schoolgirls. They were members of the SS, for heaven's sake. They should be out and fighting. As he threatened and screamed at his men, the third pair of rockets exploded. This time one hit one of the Panzers beside Peiper. He didn't see where the other one went. The tank disintegrated as a large charge of high explosives blew a section of armour plating to bits. Peiper felt another hurricane of hot gas rush past him, blowing him off his feet a second time, and the noise of the explosion left his ears ringing violently.

Peiper realised that the situation needed controlling. The soldiers were well trained and doing their best, but they needed more direction. He yelled at the NCOs and anyone else within earshot to get the men to drive the Panzers off the train.

'Get them moving, damn you,' he screamed, his eyes bulging with the effort of making himself heard over the bedlam of the attack and its aftermath.

Frantically he saw the NCOs trying to round up the soldiers who had scattered away from the train in an effort to distance themselves from the relentless and deadly aerial assault. A salvo of rockets landed twenty metres wide of the railway line, blowing a couple of craters in the field. Peiper mentally thanked God for this momentary breathing space.

'Get the tanks off the train!' he yelled again. Deciding to lead by example, he made his way to the rear of the train, ordering soldiers to accompany him as he passed them. By the time they reached the last of the wagons he had gathered a party of about forty men. The NCOs had rounded up some more. The main priority was to get the officers' carriage out of the way so that the tanks could be driven off the back of the train. 'Get it out of the way and get the loading ramp in place!' he yelled as he clambered up on to one of the flatbeds. He saw an NCO bring a couple of lengths of rope and tie them to the buffers. The men took up the strain.

Above him he could see a second aircraft starting its descent. Around him machine-gunners and the two anti-aircraft positions opened up with a hail of bullets. *Please God, let them bring the bastard down,* prayed Peiper. He forced himself to take his eyes off the Typhoon and concentrate on what he was about to do. He hauled himself around the front of the tracks and climbed on to the body of the tank; then he heaved up the hatch to the driver's compartment and slipped inside. A strong, deeply unpleasant smell of engine oil and stale body odour rose up from the space, but Peiper ignored it as he squeezed his body into the hard, functional seat. He pressed the button to start the engine. Even over the racket of events around him, the thunder of the machine-guns, the scream of the diving aircraft's engines and then the sudden, violent noise of a rocket exploding, Peiper could hear the engines fire and feel the throb as the whole vehicle began to shake. Having got the tank ready to move, he clambered out of the driver's hatch once more and over the main body of the Panzer. He could see the men had managed to drag away the officer's coach. A couple of soldiers were finishing securing the ramp in position. Ignoring the smoke and noise of the attack raging around him, Peiper climbed back into the tank and pulled the two levers that controlled the tracks. The tank began to move. With his head proud of the compartment Peiper concentrated on watching the progress of the tank, making sure it moved straight back. The last thing he wanted to do was drop it off the side of the wagon. The Panzer moved about four metres, then he felt gravity begin to take over as the rear of the tank tipped over the back of the wagon and on to the ramp. Peiper gunned the engine again and slowly allowed the tank to haul itself backwards a few more metres. Then he felt the angle of the tank change once more. The rear must be off the ramp. He revved the engine harder and the tank levelled out in just a second or two. As he pushed one lever and pulled the other, the tank swivelled and Peiper drove it into the adjoining field.

Once away from the mayhem he killed the engine, hauled himself out of the cramped compartment and looked back. He saw with relief that several other tanks were moving and one was about to clear the train. Further along the train he saw soldiers laying planks over the gaps between the flatbeds to get some of the service vehicles off too. However, at least half a dozen tanks and several trucks were burning wrecks. He scanned the sky. The Typhoons seemed to have gone, but their lightning attack had done more than enough damage. Besides which, with the railway engine destroyed, their only chance of reaching their objective was to drive across country.

'Damn,' muttered Peiper under his breath. Angrily he punched his balled fist into the palm of his other hand. If – if he found out who was responsible, he would have them shot. No, he thought, he'd shoot them himself.

Creully – Normandy

'Colonel,' said a young staff captain approaching David, holding out his hand. David stood up and shook it. He was pleased to see Jim Grant, whom he regarded as a very competent chap. 'Welcome to Normandy, sir. Nice to see you again. Pleasant crossing?' Jim Grant began to move towards the door. David gathered up his beret, gas mask and service revolver and followed him.

'Frankly no,' replied David with a wry smile. 'Hardly luxury class.'

'Rotten weather,' Jim observed. He glanced behind him at the window. 'Looks like it might rain again at any minute. Wouldn't think it was June, would you?'

David grinned and shook his head. My God, he thought, here we are in the thick of a war and the British are still discussing the weather.

'No, it's been a shocking summer.'

'It hasn't done our offensive much good.' Jim shook his head. 'Not good, not good.'

'No, I can see that.'

Jim set off again along the corridor. They arrived at a door at the end.

'Here you go, sir,' said Jim. 'You're expected.'

He opened the door without knocking and stood back to

let David pass. Feeling faintly apprehensive – what he heard next would determine what his battalion was going to encounter for the foreseeable future – David walked into the room, stood to attention and saluted. The room was massive, with high ceilings, ornate plasterwork, and at the far end he could see a trestle table with Colonel Cole sitting behind it. Between him and the table was a large armchair.

'Come in, come in,' said a slightly irascible and strangely familiar voice that emanated from the armchair.

David brought his hand smartly down by his side and took another couple of paces into the room. Where had he heard that voice before?

'Who are you?' The tone was more than slightly imperious. Obviously someone used to having subordinates jump to it.

'Colonel David Clarke.'

'So what's your regiment?' asked the voice. The speaker had a hint of a problem annunciating his 'r's. With a jolt David realised just who this was.

He gulped and said, 'The Third Battalion King's Yeomanry, sir.' God, was it OK to call Monty just 'sir'? He shook himself mentally. Of course it was, he told himself. Monty was an army officer, not God or the King.

'Jolly good. Arrived today?' Monty peered around the back of the chair and gave him a long stare.

David walked right into the room so that the great man didn't have to crane.

'Just landed, sir'

'Then you need briefing so you can join the fray. We want soldiers like yours up at the front just as soon as you can get there. I'll leave you to it.'

The Field Marshal stood to leave and David stiffened and saluted again. As he passed by, he noticed he was really quite short, almost weedy-looking, and then he berated himself for thinking any thought that belittled such a brilliant leader.

'Right,' said Colonel Cole. 'Let's get on now, shall we?'

David moved up to the trestle table. Now he was close up he could see just how exhausted this staff officer was. He'd heard Monty worked his staff hard. It now looked as if that rumour was an understatement.

'Sir,' said David.

'Come and have a seat where you can see this map properly. I take it you've had some food or a cup of tea at the very least since you landed?'

David sat in the folding chair that was opposite the Colonel's and thanked him for his enquiry. 'I'm fine. The holding area was looking after my men very efficiently when I left to come here.'

'Good. Glad to hear something is going smoothly and as intended.'

David assimilated these words and said nothing. This wasn't what he wanted to hear. The Colonel's demeanour and tone rattled him rather more than he cared for. He knew that the British and Canadian troops had had a relatively easy time of things on the beaches – well, relatively easy compared to the Americans – but it didn't sound as though things were going as planned right now.

'Right then, David, this is how things stand at the moment.' The Colonel pointed out the forward British positions and the various enemy units they faced. 'As you can see, there are heavy enemy troop concentrations here and here.' He pointed out a line of enemy positions that ran roughly between Caen and Saint-Lô. 'The main battles so far have taken place here and here, and the Americans are having a tough time pushing south and east.' Then the Colonel went on to outline, in general terms, how things had gone since the invasion and the immediate plans. 'Now, we particularly need more infantry just here.' He pointed at the map. David bent forward to look at exactly what was being indicated. It was a minute village – well, a hamlet really.

'Brouay?'

'Well, actually about half a mile east of there. Of course, when you get there you may find things have moved on a bit further. You'll get an exact location from Brigade HQ.' The Colonel stubbed a finger at the map again. 'There's BHQ – or that's where it was according to this morning's briefing. Anyway,' continued the Colonel, 'our objective is to capture Carpiquet Airfield as part of the push for Caen. As far as we know the airfield there is not heavily defended, though we have had intelligence that an SS Panzer regiment is heading our way, so the sooner we get this particular objective the better.'

'Right.' David tried to inject a note of positive confidence into his voice – confidence that he wasn't sure he felt.

'I suggest you report to BHQ right now, then return to the holding area and make arrangements to move your battalion up tonight. That is, of course, if that is in agreement with the Brigade Commander's plans. I'll send a signal to BHQ telling them to expect you in the next hour or so.' A thought crossed the Colonel's mind. 'You have got your own transport, haven't you?'

'Yes, Colonel,' said David. 'My driver's waiting with my vehicle.'

'Good, then I suggest you get going. The sooner you get your orders from BHQ the sooner you can get back to the holding area. If your luck's in, you'll have a few hours off duty before you are needed at the front line.'

David saluted and left, wondering when Colonel Cole had last had a few hours off duty. Not for weeks, by the look of him.

He returned to his vehicle.

'You'll never guess who I've just seen, sir,' said his driver excitedly as David climbed into the passenger seat.

'Montgomery?' hazarded David.

'Yeah.' There was obvious disappointment in his driver's voice at having his thunder stolen. 'So you saw him too.'

David didn't want to boast about his close encounter. 'I caught a glimpse.'

'Oh. Well he walked right past me, sir. And I saluted him.'

'That will be something to tell your grandchildren.'

His driver obviously wasn't looking to make long-term plans. 'It'll be something to tell my girl. She'll be dead impressed.'

Five

Afternoon, Saturday 24 June 1944

Portsmouth Dockyard

Gwen was pouring tea from a vast urn for dock workers. The weather had eased a little from the driving rain of the morning and it now consisted of the occasional squall, although the wind was still whipping around the corners of the buildings, making the naval officers walking past hang on to their caps. She was working in what was called a mobile canteen, although, if the truth be told, it hadn't moved from its position near the *Victory* for months now. As a rule Gwen liked working in the canteen. The workers invariably flirted with her and she enjoyed the banter from the men. However, today she felt out of sorts and didn't bother trying to josh with her customers – men who had been coaling up one of the ships in dock. They were all as black as miners with their white teeth showing in startling contrast to their grimy skin when they smiled and thanked her. They must have sensed that she was not in the mood for joking and teasing as they left her alone and moved off. Marjorie, Gwen's co-worker, glanced across at her from time to time. This wasn't the Gwen she knew and liked.

The tips of Gwen's fingers were also black from occasional and accidental contact with the stevedores' filthy hands. Every now and again she wiped them on a cloth under the counter, but that was now so grubby itself that it almost put more coal dust on her than it took off. After the dockers had collected a mug of tea from Gwen, they were given a potted-beef-and-tomato sandwich and a biscuit by Marjorie, and then they moved off to find somewhere to perch – a bollard or a step or the dockside – while they ate their snack.

'Goodness! There are a lot to serve today,' said Gwen conversationally. Without thinking she pushed a stray tendril of hair off her face and left a smudge of black on her forehead.

'Do you think so? Perhaps you're just tired.' Marjorie stopped serving and faced Gwen. 'Are you sleeping properly?'

'Fine,' lied Gwen. Obviously, with George staying at her house the night before, *sleeping* had been the last thing she'd done.

'Hmm,' said Marjorie, seeing straight through the fib. Apart from anything else, the circles under Gwen's eyes told a different story.

'I think you're being very brave, my dear.'

Gwen shrugged, not quite understanding. She didn't think doling out tea and sandwiches to dockers made her eligible for a medal. 'No more than anyone else.'

'It's not fair on you young ones. People like me have lived our lives. We've had our share of fun and good times. Not like you.' She smiled kindly at Gwen. 'Besides which, what have I got to worry about? I know where the ones I love are and that they're safe.'

Gwen knew that Marjorie's husband was a doctor and her children were away at boarding school in the country.

'Oh come off it,' said Gwen. 'Life's not easy for any of us. If we're not trying to make something out of nothing, we're having to queue for rations, or make do and mend, or dig for Britain.'

'Or keep mum,' said Marjorie with a laugh, joining in with the list of government slogans. 'It's not just things like that which are a worry though, is it? I imagine you're worried about that brave husband of yours.'

'Well …' She was now, of course. Now that she'd heard Mrs Viney's news. 'Actually I am a bit. I've heard he probably sailed to France today.' Last night, however, David could hardly have been further from her mind and she certainly hadn't worried about him one jot. Gwen felt another little jolt of guilt at having to own up, albeit only privately, to being so disloyal and unfaithful.

'Oh, my dear. No wonder you haven't been sleeping.'

Gwen was hit with another little whoosh of guilt. She smiled at Marjorie's well-meaning kindness.

The drone of aircraft overhead distracted her from the conversation. The air-raid siren hadn't gone, but even so Gwen looked up nervously to make sure they were friendly. The four craft were flying in formation and Gwen recognised them as Typhoons. She wondered if George was in one of them. At the height they were at, they were probably returning to Thorney Island.

'I wonder what they have been up to,' she speculated out loud.

'Giving Jerry a bloody nose, with any luck,' said Marjorie with vehemence.

'Goodness, Marjorie. You sound fierce.'

'I just want this war over and done with so we can all get back to normal.'

'Normal. Yes, that would be nice.' Though Gwen thought that she could hardly remember what 'normal' was like any more.

RAF Thorney Island

As soon as George had taxied to the dispersal area he shoved back the cockpit canopy and unbuckled his harness. Around him were the other three aircraft from his section, the props winding down and clunking to a stop, and across the grass from the perimeter track he could see a jeep bouncing over towards them ready to pick them up.

George clambered out, impeded by his parachute, and jumped off the trading edge of the wing. Back on the ground his nerves receded and it was easier to appear gung-ho.

'Any luck, sir?' asked his flight engineer as he kicked a chock under one of the wheels.

He made a point of inserting a note of confidence into his voice. 'I should say so. Took out a German troop train.' Just as he finished speaking another pilot ran across the grass towards him, whooping with delight.

'Did you see those soldiers scatter?' he shouted as he approached. 'I wonder if they've stopped running yet.'

George forced a smile and nodded. 'Good show,' he agreed, using the RAF vernacular.

'That'll teach Jerry to park up in daylight.'

The other two pilots from Red Section came over, shook George by the hand and clapped him on the back, delighted at what they had achieved.

'How many tanks do you think we destroyed?' one asked.

'Enough,' said George. 'The gun-camera film will give the details.'

'I got the engine,' another boasted. 'It'll take a while to sort out that mess. There won't be anything running on that line for a day or two.'

'Come on,' said George. 'Let's go and tell Int Section what we've been up to.'

'Yeah, and then find out what they've got planned for us next.'

George was rocked by a sick feeling in his stomach. Wasn't dicing with death once a day enough? But of course there was bound to be another sortie. There was plenty of time for the ground crew to refuel their crates and bomb them up again. However, quite apart from the fact that he felt that every time he took to the air he was shortening the odds of his own survival, he was shattered.

Too much bed and too little sleep, he thought. Which brought him back to the problem of Gwen. He was getting in too deep with her. A little harmless fun and some slap and tickle ... but it was going too far now. He had to see her and explain that it was over. He wondered how she would take it. Perhaps he could put it to her that he needed more rest than he was getting; flying while half-asleep wasn't the way to get through it unscathed. Gwen would understand that – surely. Besides which, he'd caught her staring rather sadly at the picture of her husband several times recently, when she'd thought he wasn't looking. George was no scholar, but even he could guess she was missing him more than she was letting on. It was time to call it a day. But gee, how was he going to do that?

George yawned. Sheesh, he was pooped. What with still feeling rattled over that encounter at Carpiquet, plus the fact that all he wanted to do was take a nap, he didn't think it was a good idea for him to fly again. If he'd been a learny-makey pilot, instructors would say he'd had enough for one day. But not now. Now he was a veteran he wouldn't get any choice.

The jeep arrived and the driver drove round George's Typhoon to park up facing the right way. George clambered into the front seat, the privilege of the section commander, and slumped down, lost in thoughts about Gwen and flying and mortality. The other three climbed into the small space at the back and grabbed hold of the sides. With a jolt they set off towards the Station HQ. Perched behind the driver Wilf noticed his leader's glum expression. He leaned forward and jabbed George's shoulder.

'Cheer up, George,' yelled Wilf over the noise of the engine. 'Tell you what: suppose I promise to buy you a drink in the mess tonight. Would that make you smile?'

'Blimey, that would make anyone smile,' said Fred.

'Except his bank manager,' said Dusty. There was a

burst of laughter from the others.

'He'll have to dust off his chequebook specially.'

'Shake the moths out of his wallet.'

George couldn't help smiling at the flak that poor Wilf was drawing. 'You're all right, Wilf. I'm out tonight.'

'Where are you off to?'

'Hot date, I reckon,' said Wilf. 'Who is it, then?'

George shrugged. 'None of your business.'

The three other fliers exchanged knowing looks.

'All right,' said Wilf. 'We won't ask any more questions on the condition you have one pint with us before you go.'

'We'll see.'

'We certainly shall,' said Wilf. He tapped his nose at the other two in the section to indicate that they weren't going to let George escape that easily when they returned from their next sortie. Dusty and Fred winked back at him.

'Anyway,' said George with enthusiasm he certainly didn't feel as they drew up outside Station HQ, 'we've got a debrief and another mission before then.'

He jumped out of the jeep and strode into the building hoping he looked keen and energetic. Wouldn't do the men any good if he let them see how he really felt.

They ambled in and up the stairs to the Int Section office.

'Any luck, lads?' asked the Flight Lieutenant on duty.

'We shot up that troop train you wanted dealing with near Caen,' said George.

The Flight Lieutenant cocked his head. 'Really? How much damage?' Fred, Wilf and Dusty gave animated details of their attacks. 'So out of the twenty or so Panzers you think you've disabled half a dozen.'

'And completely blocked the line. We got the engine too, don't forget. That'll take some shifting,' said Fred.

'Besides which, they were unloading the tanks as we left,' added Dusty.

'You mean they may be giving up on the troop train and going cross-country?'

'You're the Int wallah,' said Wilf indignantly. 'You tell us what they were planning on doing.' There was a burst of laughter from his comrades.

'That's right,' said Fred. 'We're paid to fly; you're paid to think.'

'George?' The Flight Lieutenant looked at the section commander.

'It looked that way to me. Or it could be they were unloading the train so as to make it a harder target for anyone else.' George shrugged. He didn't really care. He just wanted some sleep. If they got away from here soon, he might get the chance of forty winks in the mess before the next sortie.

Finally they escaped, having been briefed on their next mission, which was to attack a German position in the village of Fontenay.

'Piece of cake,' said Fred cheerfully as they left and headed for the mess for a cup of tea and a sandwich. 'How hard can it be to hit something big and stationary like a church?'

'But if it's an observation post, don't you think they might observe our arrival?' said Dusty with heavy emphasis.

George was trying not to think about the implications for this mission. Apart from the fact that it was on the German front line and in the midst of some of the heaviest troop concentrations, it was bound to be protected against air attack. What were their chances of coming out of this one unscathed?

He felt sick again and hurriedly lit up. A smoke might calm him down. George took a deep drag and felt the buzz of the nicotine. That was better. He looked at his watch.

'Right, we've got an hour before we're due to fly again. I'm off back to grab some tea, toast and forty winks.

Coming?'

The other members of his section agreed that was a good idea and together the four airmen strolled from Station HQ across the grass to the mess.

South-east of Caen

Peiper stood in the field beside the railway line surrounded by his officers. He had weighted down a map of the area on a makeshift table fashioned from some stacked-up ammunition boxes and a couple of planks. Behind him most of his soldiers were busy removing the last of the vehicles from the battered troop train while a small party of men retrieved the bodies and buried them in hastily dug shallow graves. The air around them stank of burning oil and God alone knew what else. Trails of smoke wafted around as the stiff breeze caught them and eddied them around the area. The field itself was pocked with massive brown splashes and craters where rockets had exploded, and around the train were several burnt-out vehicles. It was a depressing scene of chaos and devastation. He turned his concentration back to the map and his officers.

'As you can see, we are here.' He pointed to a position on the railway line about twenty-five kilometres south-east of Caen. 'Our troops are fighting the British along this line here' – he ran his finger along a minor road that ran west of Caen from Carpiquet to Caumont. 'To get there we have to cross the River Orne. I received a radio report from Divisional HQ at Fresney-le-Puceux,' – he stabbed his finger at a tiny village to the south of Caen – 'that the bridge near there is open. So, we will proceed due west from here to this point,' – he indicated the bridge he meant – 'and then once we have crossed we can swing north to Carpiquet and await further orders. Now, I want all the remaining vehicles that we have to move off into the cover of the wood over there,' – he swung round and indicated the one he meant. 'Once it's dark, we'll move out.'

His officers moved forward to study the map and to make notes on the route Peiper wanted them to take.

'Looks all right,' one muttered. 'But what happens if the bridge is blown?'

Peiper shrugged as if indifferent. 'We'll find a way over somewhere else.' He shook his head impatiently. 'We don't need to worry about problems before we come across them.'

His briefing over he ordered a couple of subordinates to clear away his improvised table and strode over to the train to see how his men were progressing.

He caught the arm of a passing senior NCO.

'How many dead and injured?'

'I think it's about seven dead and sixteen injured, sir.'

Peiper nodded. All things considered, they'd escaped quite lightly. Given the ferocity of the attack, it might have been much more serious.

'It was because most of the men were out of their vehicles attending to the axles it wasn't worse,' said the *Spiess*.

Peiper thought his sergeant major was correct. Given the suddenness of the attack, the men travelling in their tanks would have had little or no chance of escape.

'What is the state of the wounded?'

'A couple with superficial injuries, two with burns and the rest are pretty bad.'

Peiper swiftly weighed up his options. 'We'll leave them here to be collected later. And what is the damage to the vehicles?'

'Three Panzers destroyed, two too badly damaged to move. And we lost quite a few of the soft vehicles.'

Peiper nodded. Again, considering how exposed they'd been, it could have been much more devastating. A deep throbbing roar began to fill the air as his men started the engines of their tanks and moved them away from the train, up the hill towards the small wood that covered its crest. The cover the dense canopy would provide should be enough to shield them from the RAF for a few hours. Once darkness fell, they could get on their way. At least, this far south of Caen they were out of reach of the enemy artillery as well. It would be a different matter once they crossed the River Orne.

Near Arromanches

The RSM was watching out for the return of David and approached his vehicle as it rolled to a halt in the holding area. He saluted his commanding officer and opened the jeep door.

'Ah, Mr Brown. The very man,' said David as he stepped out of it. *Dashed uncomfortable way to travel*, he thought, as he stretched and eased his back. 'I need to brief the officers. Would you round them up for me and ask them to come to my tent, please.'

'Right away, sir.'

David turned to his driver as the RSM marched away. 'And can you get someone to rustle up something for me to eat? I seem to have missed out on lunch.' His driver nodded and dashed off. David pulled the flap back of the large tent that had been allocated to him. There were half a dozen camp beds against one wall and on the other was a trestle table and chairs. If the camp had been full to capacity, David had no doubts that he would have been sharing, but he was lucky that there was enough space for him to have been afforded the luxury of privacy. Not, he thought, that it was going to do him much good. They'd be off again before nightfall and he had more than enough to do to keep him occupied before the battalion moved out. He looked longingly at the camp beds. Just five minutes' sleep …

He sighed and instead pulled a couple of maps out of his battledress jacket where he had tucked them for safe keeping, and spread them on a rickety table. He was busy studying them when he heard movement outside his tent.

'Come in,' he called. His driver entered with a pile of thick sandwiches on a plate in one hand and a large steaming enamel mug in the other.

'Wads and cha, sir,' he said, handing over his booty. 'I hope corned beef's OK. And I said I thought you'd like mustard too, sir.'

David sank his teeth gratefully into it and nodded vigorously. 'Perfect,' he mumbled indistinctly. He chewed a couple more times and swallowed. 'I hope you've been fed properly, Barnes?'

'I found the NAAFI wagon at the château.' Barnes pronounced it 'chat-oo'.

David suppressed a smile. 'Good. Could you tie back the flaps for me? The light in here is terrible.'

Barnes jumped to it again and David took a swig of his tea followed by another bite of sandwich. He normally only ate corned beef on sufferance, but he was so hungry now it tasted wonderful. As Barnes tied back the tent flaps, the light flooded in along with a waft of fresh air that blew some of the mustiness out. The draught made the map flutter and David weighed it down with his mug and plate. A shadow on it made him look up.

'Come in, come in,' he said to the group of officers gathered outside.

They squeezed in, followed a few seconds later by half a dozen more.

'All here?' The Colonel looked at the assembled men and did a mental roll call. 'Good. Right, well I have been over to Brigade HQ and I now have our orders.' A couple of his officers scratched their necks or ran fingers through their hair. *Nerves*, thought David. Not surprising, considering that this was the first shot at active service for some of them. He took another bite of his sandwich. 'Forgive me for eating,' he said a few moments later when he had swallowed his mouthful, 'but I missed out on lunch.' He had a gulp of tea before carrying on. 'We are to join the Brigade troops here.' He fingered a spot on the large-scale map near the village of Brouay. 'We'll move to the village itself tonight and then we should receive orders at first light as to exactly where they want us to deploy within the Brigade area. We are to be part of an operation to take the airfield at Carpiquet. Once that is taken, then the RAF can move in and give us even more air support. At the moment it is being held by a relatively small force and we don't expect too much opposition.'

'Jolly good,' someone murmured.

'Pretty much my sentiment,' said David. There was some nervous laughter. David carried on with the briefing, giving details of the route they were to take to move up to the front, the exact position of each of the companies at the start of the attack, what artillery and armoured support they would be getting. Around him his officers took notes, marked important places on their own maps, jotted down grid references and radio frequencies and made sure they understood exactly what was going to be expected of each and every man under their respective commands.

'We will move out of the holding area at seventeen hundred hours,' said David. 'Before then make sure the men have eaten and rested. I also want all vehicles and equipment checked.' He saw several of his officers exchange glances. 'Yes, I know this was all done before we embarked at Portsmouth, but I want it done again. Once we get to the front line at dawn we'll be going straight into battle. Jerry won't wait for us to sort ourselves out if we find something wrong at the last minute.' He gazed around at his assembled officers. 'Any questions?' No one spoke. 'Right, well I suggest you brief your men and get any remaining admin squared away.'

As the officers left his tent, a hubbub of murmuring broke out as they discussed the briefing and apportioned various tasks amongst themselves. David finished off his now cold tea and sat at the table to carry on with the business of running a battalion that was going to be in the thick of the fighting before the day was over. He tapped a pencil on the map and wondered what the immediate future held. At the moment he felt quite calm. He doubted that would last once the battalion began moving to the front.

Six

Early Evening, Saturday 24 June 1944

La Ferme de la Source

The last of the cows ambled through the entrance to the Long Meadow and Martine heaved the gate shut behind them. The hinge still wasn't fixed. She suppressed her irritation. She didn't ask her father to do much and yet even the little help she did request never materialised. Perhaps Otto would do it. She made sure the latch was properly in place and walked back up the lane to the farm. Overhead, somewhere behind a bank of cloud, she could hear aircraft droning away and in the distance she could bear the rumble of artillery firing. Was it closer than it had been this morning? She thought it might be. It seemed louder. But maybe it was just the wind direction that made it seem nearer.

The lane Martine was walking along crested a small rise. She stopped and looked over the hedge towards the sound of the guns, but she could see nothing. There was a smudge of smoke on the horizon. Obviously there had been a big fire somewhere towards the coast. Martine looked back at her own little farm – the house, the barn, the stables – and wondered what chance it would have against the firepower of the Allies. For years now she had longed for liberation, for the Germans to be driven out of France, for freedom from their laws and regulations, and, now it seemed imminent, the whole prospect was terrifying. Of course, there wasn't much of a German presence in the immediate area. There were a bunch of soldiers at Carpiquet but she wasn't sure how many, and there were some billeted in the *manoir* in the next village; so, with thousands of Allied soldiers about to appear, would they put up much of a fight? Martine could only hope they wouldn't.

She trudged on up the lane back towards the farm. She still had to wash down the milking parlour and shut the hens up for the night, but when she'd left to do the milking her father had been in the kitchen preparing some vegetables for their supper. That was something, she acknowledged grudgingly as she swished her hazel switch at the marguerites in the hedgerow. She yawned and wondered if Otto would be able to get across to the farm. She wanted to show him the root store. He had to make his mind up soon and perhaps if he saw how perfect it was he might be persuaded.

When she got back to the farm she finished her chores, made sure the hen house was secure and made her way into the farm kitchen. Her father appeared to be making soup and the smell of hot food made Martine realise how hungry she was.

'Is dinner nearly ready?'

'Almost. Cut the bread.'

Martine took the knife and hacked a couple of large hunks off the loaf Then she went to the dresser and took down a couple of bowls.

'I caught that German sniffing around here again today. I've seen him a few times, in the distance. This time he was by the gate to the yard. '

Martine looked up, trying to keep her face a blank.

'I sent him away with a flea in his ear. I told him he's not welcome.'

'Like he'd understand French,' said Martine, putting the bowls carefully on the table. 'He probably doesn't mean us any harm.'

'How do you know? He's snooping to see what we've got that he can take.'

'Ott …' Martine stopped herself 'You don't know that.'

Jean-Paul shrugged. 'Pah.' He took the pot off the range and lugged it across to the big table. 'Besides, I know what the bastards can be like. I know what they did at Verdun. Here.' He slopped the soup into the bowls and handed one to Martine. For a while they ate in silence. The soup was good and warm and filling.

'So,' said Jean-Paul through a mouthful of bread and soup, 'seeing that you're so sure he doesn't mean us harm, does it mean you've spoken to this German?'

Martine chewed her bread, giving herself a moment to think. 'He has tried to speak to me. His French is terrible.'

'I hope you didn't let on that your mother taught you German.'

'Why would I want to do that?' Martine didn't think that would count as a real lie.

'Good.'

'Anyway, what would it matter?'

'The Boche might find a use for you. They might take you away.'

'That's what worries you, isn't it? – the thought of me not being here to run this place for you.' She tried to sound confident and belligerent, but what her father said had rattled her. She hadn't thought about being made to work for the Germans as a possible danger – which it certainly would be if they found out she was bilingual.

'Of course not. I'm just concerned for your safety.' Martine noticed her father wasn't looking at her as he said this. 'And times are dangerous.'

Martine finished her soup and got up from the table. She put her bowl in the sink and went to the larder to fetch some cheese. 'You've noticed,' she said drily as she sat back down again. She cut a lump of cheese off and ate it from the blade of her knife.

'We just need to survive the next few days,' said Jean-Paul.

'Simple really.'

Jean-Paul looked up sharply. 'So don't you do anything foolish like getting friendly with the enemy. There's folk in the village who have heard what they did to some girls in Bayeux for fraternising with German soldiers.'

Martine didn't say anything. Had her father guessed? Had Otto asked for her by name? Surely he wouldn't be that stupid? Or her father that astute? No, he was usually too sozzled. She shrugged and ate another bit of cheese, hoping to imply that nothing could be further from her mind. Then she said, 'What happened to them?'

'Tarred and feathered.'

Martine grimaced. But she'd be all right. No one knew about Otto. No one came to the farm these days, so none of their neighbours would have seen him. Of course, it would be different once he was hiding in the barn. Once the Germans had been pushed back by the Allies and he gave himself up to them, her father was bound to find out. But he wouldn't give her away. No, surely not. Anyway, she'd cross that bridge when she came to it.

'Right,' her father said as he pushed his chair back. 'I'm off out. And if you see that Hun here again, tell him to clear off.'

'I didn't think you wanted me to let on I speak German,' said Martine innocently.

Her father gave her a hard stare and left the room. Martine finished her cheese and began the washing-up. On balance she was certain her father was ignorant of her relationship with Otto. She hoped to God it would stay that way for the next few days at the very least.

Above Normandy

The weather had improved markedly since the morning

and as George flew over the Normandy coastline he could see a column of vehicles, the glass windows of trucks and jeeps glinting and flashing gold, snaking along the narrow roads that led away from a big camp above the town of Arromanches. A battalion on the move, being sent to reinforce the front line, he reckoned. A plume of smoke obliterated a stretch of the landscape as a building burned fiercely in another village just inland. So the French were finding out what war was really like, thought George, just like the Limeys had been finding out for years.

He was flying at around 3,000 feet, just below the cloud. He didn't mind being this low for the time being – he was safe from flak here; but it would be a different kettle of fish when he got to the other side of Bayeux and had to fly over German positions. At the thought of encountering German ack-ack again, his stomach lurched hideously. *Pull yourself together*, he told himself; but it didn't work. The feeling of sickness just seemed to intensify. And it didn't help matters that he knew he was getting very close now to the front line. Just ahead he could see the main road that ran from Bayeux to Caen. It pretty much marked the position of the front. Their briefing had instructed them to fly parallel to the road until they reached the village of Sainte Croix then turn due south, make a dash for Fontenay, attack the OP in the church spire and get back to the safety of the Allied side of the line as fast as possible. Not that George planned to hang about on the enemy side for a second longer than necessary.

He glanced down at the map strapped to his knee and checked the features he could see on the ground against it. Glinting in the watery sunlight he could see a small river running approximately south to north. That was what he was looking for. Yes, and there was the village. Abruptly he banked his plane to starboard and headed over German-held soil. At this speed they should be in and out in a matter of minutes.

Almost the instant they crossed the front line the flak opened up. George could see lines of tracer streaking across the sky. God, he hoped their aim was off. He was terrified of getting hit. Gritting his teeth and fighting the urge to cut and run, he flew onwards. Then he saw the acute angle of a junction between two dead-straight roads and in the corner was the village, and the church.

'Tally-ho,' he said into the mike in his oxygen mask. As he pushed forward on the control column the Typhoon went into a steep dive. George got the church spire in his sights and waited until it seemed perfectly aligned before he pressed the button and fired the first of his rockets. Keeping the plane as steady as he could and ignoring the increasing quantities of flak, he fired until all eight had gone. He could see the rockets exploding around the church, but the spire remained pointing skyward. Damn, he swore mentally. He pulled up out of his dive, feeling the sudden swoop as the negative G changed to positive. At 3,000 feet he levelled off and stooged around, waiting for the other three planes in his section to do their bit. The flak seemed to be concentrating on the Typhoons going in for the attack and George felt relatively safe as he circled. He supposed he must have dropped his guard for a moment, but suddenly he felt his plane judder violently as something repeatedly hit it and then a Messerschmitt shot past. What the ...? Where had he come from? *God dammit.*

'Enemy aircraft,' yelled George into the r/t, adrenalin streaming into his body, making him feel sick and clammy.

'Roger, Red Leader,' said Fred, followed almost instantly by acknowledgement from the other two.

George pushed the throttle fully forward and took off after the enemy. Giving chase wasn't bravado: it was survival – kill or be killed. The Messerschmitt was already turning ahead of George and coming back to attack him again. George could feel his heart thumping wildly and knew that it was only his grip on the joystick that was stopping his hands from shaking. It didn't help matters that the German plane was now coming at him from out of the sun, which was low in the sky. George squinted to try to see better and opened up with the twenty-millimetre cannon. Again the German plane shot past him. George pulled up on the stick and kicked the rudder. The horizon corkscrewed around his cockpit as his Typhoon performed an Immelmann turn. George craned his neck to see where the German had got to. He should be in front of him as he came out of the loop, but even with the sun now behind him George had lost sight of his opponent. Where was the bastard? He scanned the sky again – every nerve prickling, every muscle tense with anticipation. Then, suddenly, bursting out of the clouds above, the Messerschmitt came hurtling towards him. How the blazes had he got up there? Damn, thought George, he wasn't concentrating. He was missing the moves this German was making. If he didn't get a grip, he'd lose this battle. Again George pulled up on the stick and kicked the rudder; no fancy manoeuvre intended now: this was just sheer desperation to live. The enemy plane was lost from view as George jinked and turned this way and that to avoid providing a sitting target. George prayed to every god there was that the German pilot had lost sight of him too. As his plane looped again, he felt it roll dizzyingly. He watched the horizon spin round again until he was back into level flight. He checked for the position of the German once again. He turned his head frantically. Where was he? Where was he? The first one to spot the opposition had the upper hand – no doubt about that. But George was out of luck. He'd lost him again. Then he felt his plane buck and jounce, as if it was going over cobbles. He was being hit again. George reacted this time by diving, but just as he pushed the stick he felt as if he was being hit by a hammer bashing its way up his legs and his side. He knew instinctively what it was. It wasn't just the plane that had been hit.

He'd always wondered what it felt like to get shot. He was surprised he felt as little pain as he was experiencing. It felt more like bruising than anything. He had assumed a bullet wound would be agonising. Perhaps it was shock, he thought quite calmly. He didn't look down to see what the damage was to himself. Better not to know, he thought, but he knew it wasn't good. He could feel warm stickiness pooling beneath him on the leather of his seat and flowing down his leg towards his boot. It was as if someone had spilt a large mug of warm tea over him.

George saw the Messerschmitt again. It was diving down on his starboard side with one of his section in hot pursuit. He almost slumped down with relief. Thank God, the heat was off him for the moment. One of the others was coming to his rescue. He could head back for safety.

George glanced at his instruments and pushed his stick and rudder to bring his kite round on a northerly heading. He wasn't sure if it was him or the plane, but everything felt sluggish and he felt strangely listless despite the danger he was in. He was injured, his plane was damaged, but he didn't seem to care. He knew he should, but instead of being geed up by fear he felt bizarrely detached. He looked at the instrument panel and saw things weren't as they should be. The needle on his altimeter was unwinding – only slowly, but he was descending all the same. He pulled back on the stick in a half-hearted sort of way, but it didn't make any noticeable difference. Then he noted the engine temperature: just as his altimeter was going down, this was rising. His engine was overheating. He knew he should do something, but his brain didn't seem to want to allow him to work out the answer. He felt so fuddled. And woozy. He looked out of the cockpit, as if he would find the answer somewhere else. Below him he could see the Caen-Bayeux road again. The significance of this landmark registered: the front line. Thank God for that. He was almost back behind the Allies. Over the radio he heard whoops of joy as one of his section bagged the German, but George felt increasingly remote from reality. He looked at his instrument panel again. He was down to only a couple of thousand feet. Should he bail out, or land? He still had a horror of bailing out. Even though he'd managed it successfully once, it didn't make it seem any less of a dodgy manoeuvre. Could he limp home even though his plane was damaged and he was bleeding heavily? George wondered which the best option was. God, he didn't know. It was such a tough decision. Eeny, meeny, miny …

'Red Leader, Red Leader, come in, Red Leader.'

George recognised the voice of Fred even though it was distorted by the crackle of the radio receiver.

'Hello, Red One, this is Red Leader,' confirmed George.

'Red One. Are you all right, Red Leader?'

'Red Leader. I've been hit.'

'Red One. How bad?'

'Bad enough.'

'Red One. You're losing height, Red Leader, and heading too far east.'

'Red Leader. I know. Don't seem to be able to correct it.'

'Bail out, Red Leader. Bail out.'

'Roger,' said George. Well, he supposed he better had. It looked as if the decision had been made for him.

He reached up and put his hands on the handles to pull back the canopy. God, he felt tired. He hauled back and as he did a hideous pain shot through his side, making him gasp out loud. 'Jesus!' he exclaimed. His instinct was to drop his hands and clutch the site of the pain, but he managed to summon up the self-control to keep tugging at the canopy. With a whipping roar of wind and engine noise it slid back and locked. George sighed with relief and brought his hands down, ignoring another burst of pain. He unbuckled his harness and then, making sure all the straps were clear, he pushed the stick hard to one side and, as the Typhoon lazily rolled on to its back, George fell clear. He felt himself slide out of his seat and down the slipstream of the aircraft. It almost looked as if the plane was floating up into the sky away from him. He pulled his ripcord and felt the fluttering of the 'chute spiral out of its pack and then the jolt and tug as it cracked open. He looked down to the ground to see where he was likely to land. As he did so, he saw the huge glistening bloodstain all down his right side and leg. He was soaked in the stuff.

'Jesus H,' he whispered. He wondered how bad the injuries were. He'd lost a lot of blood – that was for sure. He felt sick at the thought. Then he was gripped by a further burst of panic. Suppose he landed in some field and no one found him. He doubted, with his leg in the state it was in, he was going to be able to walk. Suppose he just lay in some godforsaken field and bled to death. He didn't want to die like that. Not alone. He was too young. God, he was too young to die. His heart thundered with fear at the prospect.

The ground was rushing up fast now. He had no time to think. He braced himself for landing and shut his eyes as if by doing so it would make the pain of impact on his damaged body less. The jolt to his injured leg made pain cascade through him. It buckled immediately and more pain shot through his arm as he landed heavily on his shoulder. He yelled aloud and collapsed, sobbing, and lay on the ground as the white silk of his 'chute floated down softly behind him. He lay still, waiting for the agony from his leg and shoulder to recede. The ghastly throbbing just seemed to go on and on. He lost track of time and let his eyes shut. He was so tired and cold. He tried to think of something pleasant to take his mind off his injuries, but the pain dominated everything. He drifted into oblivion …

'Hey, bud.' A voice. 'Hey, bud. Are you OK?'

George felt a warm dry hand take his own. He opened his eyes.

'Hey, buddy.' A smiling face with a fag hanging out of the corner of its mouth looked down at him. 'Wanna smoke?' The chap sounded American – but then again he didn't. George couldn't make sense of it. He was just thankful he wasn't German. And who cared? – he was being offered a cigarette.

George nodded. The hand left his and he heard the rustle of paper and then the zip of a lighter. Then – ah bliss! – a cigarette was pushed between his lips. He inhaled and felt the relaxing buzz from the smoke. His brain seemed to begin to function again and the penny dropped: Canadian.

'Thanks.'

'You're welcome.'

The cigarette was removed from George's mouth and then replaced again. He inhaled some more.

'We saw you bail out. We got over to you as quick as we could. Your leg's a mess.'

'I know. I took a hit.'

'Several,' said his saviour drily. 'We've radioed for medics. We'll get you back to a field hospital in no time. Meantime I've got a couple of field dressings here. Just hold still while I try and patch you up enough to move you.' There was a pause. 'Hey, bud, are you American?'

'Sure am.'

'But you're in RAF uniform.'

'Yes.' George just didn't have the strength to explain. He shut his eyes and thought that perhaps he wasn't going to die after all. At least, he thought that until they moved him.

Carpiquet Airfield

Otto was again on his gun position. They'd been stood-to for a couple of hours now, but nothing had come their way. In the distance they heard the sound of bombing, but it had been several kilometres away. It was difficult to keep one's attention focused for this long but they scanned the skies for any sight of enemy aircraft and tried to keep their spirits up with talk of what they would get up to if they ever got some leave.

'Shh,' said Otto. He thought he'd heard something. He looked towards the western horizon, squinting against the low sun.

'What are you hearing?' asked Dieter.

There it was again: the rising and falling whining of an aircraft engine being pushed to the limits. A mass of cloud drifted over the sun. Otto took his hand away from his face and was able to have a proper look now he wasn't half-blinded. There it was: two planes chasing each other around the sky. 'Over there,' he said, pointing.

His pals on the anti-aircraft cannon followed his finger and smiled when they saw that it was one of their planes chasing the enemy Typhoon. Then a trail of dark smoke appeared from the Typhoon; but, just as it did, another enemy plane joined the battle and the Messerschmitt had to break off in order to try to keep himself out of danger. The four men on the cannon watched, fascinated, as the Typhoon flew on a vaguely easterly heading. They saw it roll on to its back and then a minute speck appear as the pilot dropped out followed by the billowing, blossoming of his parachute opening. However, the pilot must have kicked the rudder marginally as he exited, as the plane, still upside down, assumed a slightly different heading. It was still descending slowly, still upside down, but now on a heading that was directly towards them. It seemed unlikely, given its descent path, that it would get as far as the airfield; but between them and the plane lay Martine's home.

Otto found himself willing it to explode in mid-air, to change course, to nosedive suddenly – anything but carry on as it was. But the plane continued steadily, trailing its line of smoke until it disappeared behind a low rise. There was a pause of around a second, then a fat plume of thick black greasy smoke rose into the sky. A couple of seconds later they heard the detonation.

'*Scheisse*,' said Dieter turning away in disgust. 'The pilot got out.'

Otto tried to smile in agreement, but his whole being was taut with worry. There was no way, at this distance, that he could tell whether or not the plane had landed on La Ferme de la Source, but it must have been close. Please God Martine was OK. He had often contemplated his chances of surviving the war, but since he'd met Martine he hadn't considered the possibility that she might be a casualty.

La Ferme de la Source

Martine went to the pump to fill the bucket with water. The bowls in the sink weren't going to wash themselves and she still had some laundry to do. Not that she could do anything for their clothes but rinse the worst of the dirt out. Without soap she could get nothing clean. In some ways Martine was glad her mother was dead. She would have been horrified at the way they were reduced to living – everything grubby, the house a shambles, no time to go to mass and meals barely more than bread and cheese because Martine didn't have time to cook and her father was often too drunk to. Martine remembered when the times had been good. When her mother had been alive the house had gleamed and shone with love and attention. Martine's clothes might have been shabby but they were spotless, and there was never any excuse for missing confession or mass. And the best thing was the kitchen –

always filled with the smell of stock simmering on the range or a *tarte aux fruits* cooking in the oven, and bunches of herbs hanging to dry above the window, and her mother bottling fruit or stuffing pigeons or ... Martine stopped herself. What was the point? Life was never going to be like that again. She couldn't imagine ever being looked after so wonderfully again: someone heating up water for her to wash in, someone standing behind her brushing her hair, turning back her bed and slipping a hot brick into it to warm it ... life for her was going to be a drudge; she had better get used to it.

Angrily she pumped the old lever rhythmically as if she could wash away the memories with the spurting water. Slowly she was aware of another noise than the splosh of the water into her bucket and the squeak-squeak of the pump handle. She could bear the drone of an aircraft and it was quite close. She turned her head to look and saw the odd sight of an aircraft, on its back, dark smoke streaming from it, heading straight for her. Martine stood transfixed, her mouth agape; then suddenly she flung herself flat on the cobbles of the farmyard and covered her head with her arms. Petrified she waited for the impact as the noise grew deafening, and then, hearing a sudden deepening of the pitch of the engine note, she knew it had passed overhead and had missed the farm. Almost instantly she heard the blast.

Martine jumped to her feet and ran round the back of the farmhouse. In the wood on the hill behind the farm the wreckage was burning intensely. Martine stared at the scene. If the pilot had been in the plane, he was surely dead now. Martine crossed herself and watched the embers and smuts from the fire rise into the sky and the smoke billow and drift over the countryside. Thank goodness it had been so wet recently; the fire was unlikely to spread.

With a shock Martine realised she was shaking violently. It had been a near thing. Their farm had so nearly been destroyed. What did clean clothes or a warm bed matter compared to being homeless or destitute. For the moment she had a home, but for how much longer? She leaned against the wall of the cottage, feeling quite shocked. So this was what it was going to be like when the war finally reached her corner of France. Or was it going to be worse?

Orchard Cottage

Gwen was tired when she got in from a day at the dockyard canteen, but Jasper was delighted to see her and Gwen rewarded him with a couple of dog biscuits. While he was chomping down those, Gwen had a look to see what Mrs Viney had left her for her supper. There it was, ready for her to cook; the potatoes were peeled and the carrots pared and sliced and all Gwen had to do was boil them up and dish them out. A note on the kitchen table in Mrs Viney's neat but childish hand told Gwen that there was a slice of ham in the larder. Gwen looked at the plate and thought she had rarely contemplated a more unappetising meal.

'But beggars can't be choosers,' she sighed as she moved the saucepans on to the hotplate on the range. She stoked the fire up then slipped up to her bedroom to hang up her uniform and change into something more comfortable. Expecting George later, she touched up her lipstick and ran a comb through her hair, but only to make herself presentable, not attractive. She had made up her mind she had to do something about their relationship. She was praying George would understand But it would be too bad if he didn't. Gwen was determined that she had to end their affair and return to being faithful to David. Of course, she knew she would always know about the adultery, but he need never be aware of it. In time it would fade into the background. As long as David never had an inkling, all would be well. She checked her appearance in the looking glass and made a promise to herself that he'd never find out from her.

By the time she returned to the kitchen, both the potatoes and the carrots were on the brink of simmering. Deciding that ham and boiled vegetables were just too depressing, she picked some parsley from the garden and made a parsley sauce to accompany it. When it was all cooked, she loaded up a tray and took it through to the sitting room. Putting the tray on the table, Gwen switched on the wireless and then sat down to enjoy her supper.

As she ate, she listened to the news full of gung-ho stories about 'our gallant soldiers making advances into France' and 'overjoyed French citizens greeting the Allies', but she also kept an ear cocked for the noise of a motorcycle coming up the lane. The news finished, her plate was empty and still no sign of George. Gwen took her tray back to the kitchen and washed up her plate and cutlery; then she went and put up the blackout in her bedroom. From the sitting room, the strains of a big band playing dance music on the wireless reached her, but still there was no sign of George's motorbike. Gwen tried not to worry; there could be a number of reasons for his absence: he'd been sent to raid somewhere much more distant than he had been of late; he'd had problems getting off the station; his motorbike had broken down; he had run out of petrol … the one possible cause for his absence that Gwen was deliberately avoiding was that he'd been shot down. But lurking in the back of her mind was the knowledge that it was a possibility.

She called to Jasper. It was time for his evening walk. If she took him down the lane, George would have to pass her if he came to visit. Jasper waddled towards her, the stump of his tail wagging vigorously. Gwen grabbed her mackintosh off the hat stand in the hall and let herself and the dog out of the house. As she ambled along the country lane, she scanned the sky for any sight of a returning aircraft, but there appeared to be nothing. Gwen stopped and leaned on a gate to a field and regarded the view off the downs to the sea beyond. Somewhere in the distance was Thorney Island and further still was France. And somewhere out there, somewhere near the invasion beaches, was the man she loved.

That thought brought her up short. It made her realise once and for all that she was only fond of George. It was David she really loved. Yes, she was concerned that George was safe somewhere, that he hadn't been shot down, but she wasn't really worried about him – not like she was worried about David. She worried about George as she might about any young man she was acquainted with who was fighting the war. Now she knew David had gone across to France she knew she would be losing sleep over him, listening to every news bulletin and dreading the sight of the telegram boy. No, she mustn't think of the worst that might happen. She must look on the bright side. She'd go mad if she spent the next few weeks and months expecting bad news.

The wind suddenly whipped around her ankles. With no stockings on it was chilly. *Time to go home.* She called Jasper to follow her and slowly walked up the lane again.

Returning to the sitting room Gwen got out her writing paper to write to David. As always she tried to keep her letter light and chatty. This time she told him about her journey into work and her encounter with Big Bertha.

"I think we ought to enlist her and send her over to you," she wrote. *"I am sure that if we deployed her the Germans would find our Big Bertha just as scary as the Parisians found theirs in the last war."* Gwen stopped writing and sucked the end of her pen thoughtfully. She looked over the page or two she had covered with her elegant writing. Beginning a new paragraph she wrote several lines about her worry that he was keeping safe and

that conditions weren't too tough. *"I know you'll make light of the hardships but do tell me if there is anything I can send to you that might make life a little more bearable. As always I send you all my love and my prayers that you will keep safe from harm. Surely this wretched war can't last so very much longer? I wish the Jerries would realise that we've got them on the run and they should give up right now.*

I love you, my darling, and can't wait until you are safe again at home with me. Hugs and kisses ..."

Gwen thought she heard a noise and cocked her head to listen better; but no, she was mistaken again. She finished her letter off, addressed an envelope and found a stamp. Putting it by the front door ready to post in the morning, she glanced at the hall clock. It was getting late. Gwen sighed and accepted that George probably wasn't going to make it tonight. She returned to the sitting room, collected her library book, switched off the wireless and the light and made her way up to bed. She'd have to tell him tomorrow that it was all over between them, she thought, as she sleepily got undressed.

Seven

Nightfall, Saturday 24 June 1944

South-east of Caen

Peiper looked at his watch and the colour of the sky. It was dark enough. With the nights so short at this time of year he couldn't afford to wait any longer. He wasn't going to risk having his tanks caught out in the open in daylight a second time. How humiliating it would be if this section of his battalion was wiped out before they had the chance of engaging the enemy. He gave the order for his men to move out. The air began to throb as the huge Maybach V-12 engines roared and then even the ground vibrated as fifteen tanks, each weighing in at well over forty tonnes, began to graunch their way out of the wood towards the road that ran along the Bourguébus ridge. Interspersed amongst the column of tanks were soft-bodied vehicles carrying supplies, spares and signal equipment. As the lumbering Panzers turned on to the metalled road, their steel tracks squealed hideously and the engine note changed as they were able to move up several gears to attain an impressive show of speed. The narrow road wasn't suitable for them to reach their full potential of over fifty kilometres an hour, but Peiper, leading the column in his command tank, estimated they were moving at well over twenty. At this rate they should easily reach Carpiquet in just a few hours.

From time to time the tanks passed through silent, dark villages. As they roared and squealed through the streets,

Peiper was aware of shutters opening a chink and of pairs of eyes watching and noting their progress. Although he tried to ignore it, there was a palpable feeling of malevolence emanating from these hidden watchers. Well, they'd change their attitude when the enemy had been repulsed. Once the French realised they were part of the thousand-year Reich forever, they would stop thinking of the Germans as their enemies but as their guardians.

The tanks ground on, leaving scarred and pitted road surfaces to mark their passing. They crossed the main road from Caen to Thury-Harcourt and just a couple of kilometres further on they reached the Orne.

The bridge was battered but in one piece. Peiper breathed a sigh of relief. The convoy stopped and Peiper climbed down from the hull of his tank as the battalion – or the part that had been on the first train from Paris – prepared to cross. The structure looked none too safe: one of the parapets was missing, a chunk of roadway had been blown to bits, leaving a large pothole, and the central pier must have received a direct hit from some sort of rocket, as a quantity of stone was missing from one side. Peiper's sergeant major inspected the structure and walked over it. He stopped when he reached the far bank and examined the bridge from the other direction. Peiper walked over and joined him.

'What do you think?' he asked his subordinate.

'Well, sir, it's not ideal. I am concerned about that pier.'

Peiper went to the middle of the bridge and leaned over the remaining parapet to get a better look at the damage. There was a lot of masonry in the water, and the river, swollen by the rain of the recent foul weather, was foaming round it. Peiper looked at the structure of the bridge, trying to assess whether it would be strong enough to take the weight of a forty-four-tonne Panzer.

'We'll send the service vehicles over first,' he said,

making a decision. After all, where was the next bridge that was intact? His priority was to get to Carpiquet, and if that necessitated taking risks, then so be it. 'Get all the men to dismount with the exception of the drivers. We'll send the tanks over one at a time once everything else is across.'

The sergeant major had another look over the parapet. 'No possibility of fording the river, sir?'

Peiper shook his head. The banks weren't steep. There would be no problem getting the tanks in and out of the water, but the river looked dangerously deep. And the current's strength was an unknown. 'Not a chance. Just listen to the way the water is roaring down. It would be much more dangerous than taking our chances on the bridge.'

Beneath them the black water, swollen by the recent storms, churned and foamed as it thundered between the bridge's stone piers and rushed towards Caen and then the sea. The sergeant major took a last look at it and strode back to the eastern bank to get the men organised. Peiper paused for a minute, wondering if he had made the right decision. They would soon find out.

The trucks and Volkswagen personnel carriers crept gingerly over the bridge one by one. The sergeant major and Peiper kept a close watch on the structure as each crossed, checking for any failings in the stonework, and falling masonry, and cracks appearing. When the last one crossed and the soldiers had walked over, Peiper gave the order for the first of the tanks to move. As it approached the bridge, Peiper flagged it down and leapt up on to the hull. He knelt down and yelled into the driver's ear over the roar of the engine: 'Keep to the right-hand side,' he ordered.

The driver nodded and waited for his commanding officer to jump clear before he nudged the lumbering brute into first gear again. Tracks squealing on the metalled road, it ground off, keeping over to the side directed. Slowly it crawled over. The bridge held. Peiper breathed out and relaxed, thankful that his decision hadn't been proved wrong – he'd lost enough equipment and men from the raid; to lose more now, from a decision that might be judged to be reckless, would risk disapproval from the highest level. Well, so far so good; he just had to hope now that the bridge would hold up long enough to get everything over.

It did. As Peiper clambered on to his command tank once more he glanced at his watch. It was two in the morning already. They would be pushed to get to their destination before dawn if anything else held them up. They were probably only about ten kilometres from their destination, but there was a maze of narrow lanes to navigate between where they were and the airfield, and the nearer they got to it the more vulnerable they became to the enemy heavy artillery.

But Peiper kept his worries to himself. No point in risking demoralising his troops.

Eight

Night, Sunday 25 June 1944

Brouay Village

'Right, Mr Brown,' said David as they came to a halt on the outskirts of what had once been a pretty French village. 'I want the men to deploy and dig in. We're to wait here until we get orders as to exactly where Brigade wants us.' He was about to continue, but a troop of artillery, deployed at the edge of the settlement, opened up and the deafening noise made him jump. The bombardment continued and, with no sign of a let-up, he had no choice but to try to yell over the racket. Around them the sky was lit with hellish flashes of orange and red and in the distance they could see the shells exploding in brilliant incandescent-yellow bursts. The raw power of heavy artillery never failed to impress him, even when it was just live-firing on the ranges, but watching guns being fired in anger, at real live targets was beyond awe-inspiring. He watched the spectacle for a second or two before bringing himself back to the deployment of his own troops.

'When they've dug in,' he bawled into Mr Brown's ear, 'they can get what sleep they can. I want the usual pickets and sentries posted.'

Mr Brown nodded and went off to pass on the order as quickly as he could. David looked about him. The village was a wreck: roofs were destroyed, windows blown out, doors hanging off hinges, shell holes in the road and rubble everywhere. He wondered what had happened to the inhabitants, poor bastards. Certainly they had abandoned the place. There wasn't a sign of life in any of the houses.

The barrage stopped. The sudden silence was astonishing, though David's ears still rang. He moved amongst his men, having a word here and there, as they wielded their entrenching tools and spades. They knew the form and many were busy getting dug in before the orders had been passed down to them. It was as much to do with self-preservation as anything else.

He reached the church at the northern end of the village. It stood on high ground and, despite the darkness, from the graveyard David was able to make out the lie of the land. The hedges were darkest black, but between them the fields were battleship-grey, rippling with lighter and darker shades as the wind blew across them. It was perfect country for defence, with thick hedges neatly dividing all the fields mostly now filled with waist-high crops. The enemy might be lurking anywhere around them, just waiting for the order to emerge and attack. *This is not going to be easy ground to win*, he thought.

By now his ears had stopped ringing and he was attuned to the noises of the night: the rustle of small creatures in the long grass in the untended cemetery, the distant shriek of an owl, the creaking of branches and the swish of the wind through the leaves. As he listened, he recognised the sound of his men digging away in the village; and in the distance, right over towards Bayeux, came the faint boom of another action involving the gunners. An aircraft droned overhead – One of theirs or one of ours? he wondered – and not far away he could hear a cow lowing. In the distance a flare flashed into the sky and drifted down. Below he saw machine-guns open up, the tracer dotting an arc across the horizon with neon intensity. Then the guns by the village opened up again and once more everything was shattered by the hellish cacophony.

On his return to the village centre he was met by Mr Brown.

'There's a slit trench by this house for you, sir. I've posted sentries too,' he bellowed over the racket.

'Thank you, Mr Brown. I suggest you try to get your head down for a couple of hours.'

Mr Brown raised an eyebrow and then saluted. 'Sir.' He marched off.

David doubted that Brown was going to sleep. It was much more likely that he was going to take a turn round the village and reassure some of the younger soldiers who had yet to see battle.

David jumped down into his trench and pulled his pack and webbing in after him. He squatted down in the narrow confines of the hole and pulled a blanket out of his bed roll and put it round his shoulders. Leaning on his pack, he shut his eyes. As he did so, the barrage stopped. *Peace*, he thought.

The first shell must have exploded only forty or fifty yards from his position. He saw the flash from behind his closed eyelids and had his eyes open just as the blast wave hit him. The concussion, even in the shelter of his trench, was like a physical blow. A second or two later earth and small stones showered down on him, rattling off his tin hat and spattering his uniform. The second shell dropped about the same distance the other side of him and then the explosions came thick and fast. The enemy were trying to exact retribution from the gunners nearby, but the shelling was not aimed at a precise target and David's men, in barely adequate positions, were bearing the brunt.

David crouched as deep as he could in his shallow shelter, feeling his insides churning, partly from sheer fear and partly from the constant thundering vibrations that shook everything. He was aware that he had gone beyond crouching and was now cowering, but self-preservation is a difficult instinct to ignore. He knew, from Dunkirk, what effect a high-explosive shell can have on the human body and, as he lay curled like a foetus, his hands clasped over his head, he hoped that, if he was to be unlucky, he got a direct hit. Being blown to bits in a second was vastly preferable to having shrapnel from a bursting steel shell case rip flesh off his bones, flay skin off his limbs or tear him open and allow his guts to spill out. He'd seen it happen to too many soldiers to have any illusions about the kind of injuries that might await him. Better by far to find instant oblivion. But the shells continued to miss him, though once or twice a particularly close explosion would fire another shot of adrenalin into him and for a moment he was aware of his heart lurching and his guts clenching. But each time the fear was less pronounced, his feeling that his luck was going to hold grew stronger. The pounding seemed to go on and on and the air grew unpleasant with the smoke and dust and smell of explosives. David, crouching in his slit trench, lost track of time.

When the shelling ceased, the yells began. David sat up in his trench and took several deep breaths to steady himself. It wouldn't do to look rattled in front of the men. Feeling extremely shaky, he crawled out and stood up. He could see from the shell splashes that some of the shells had landed almost lethally close. His life had been spared because his death just hadn't been pulled out of the lucky dip – *or should that be unlucky dip*? he thought grimly. Around him other figures were appearing, with grimy faces and mud-streaked battledress. The village street was lit up with the eerie light of a couple of burning vehicles. David didn't want the flames to attract more attention to their area while they were trying to sort out the casualties and the damage from the last attack.

'Get water and douse those,' David ordered a couple of passing squaddies.

They rushed off to deal with the fires. Another figure approached David through the swirling smoke. The soldier halted and saluted. David was unsure who it was, as the face was a mask of blood.

'Sir.'

'Mr Brown?' The figure acknowledged he was right. 'Get yourself to a medic. You're injured.'

'Looks worse than it is, sir. Just rather a lot of blood.'

Mr Brown was obviously determined to soldier on for the time being. David reached for his web belt and pulled a field dressing from a pouch. 'Here, take this.' The RSM took off his helmet and clasped it between his knees. With his head bare David could see there was a nasty gash across his forehead. Mr Brown pressed the thick pad of lint against his head and tied the bandages. Then he put his tin hat back on again. It had to go at an incongruously jaunty angle because the dressing prevented it from sitting square.

Around them the soldiers were already organising themselves into stretcher parties and, using whatever came to hand as makeshift litters, ferrying the wounded into the shelter of one of the less badly damaged houses, though after the latest barrage there was precious little standing. One or two of the men were carrying shapeless lumps wrapped up in blankets. David didn't look too closely at those.

'I'll get the platoon commanders to report to me with casualty figures,' said Mr Brown.

'We haven't even gone into action yet,' said David quietly, shaking his head. He bit his lip and pushed his shoulders back. Already he'd lost soldiers. He had to stand tall for the sake of his men, but the fact that some of his chaps were already dead made him feel as though he had failed them. They were his responsibility. They trusted him to lead them wisely and now some of them were dead, others dying and more maimed for life, while he was unscathed.

'Baptism by fire for some of the lads,' said the RSM. 'I didn't see any of them panic, though.' He paused. 'Shows the training worked.'

David felt comforted by this observation. Perhaps he had done all that could have been expected of him. After all, this was war, not some tin-pot exercise on Salisbury Plain.

'Thank you, Mr Brown.'

He strode off to make sure the men were stood-to, all hope of a couple of hours rest abandoned. Then he went to the casualties. Along the wall at the front of the house – or what was left of it – was a line of bodies covered in blankets. About twenty, he reckoned. He stepped through a hole in the wall and saw dozens of men being tended by the battalion medic and a dozen or so soldiers in the light of several hurricane lamps hanging from two joists that were all that remained of the upper storey. The air smelt of vomit and other bodily odours, and noise of low moaning and groaning provided a constant backdrop of sound.

'Hello, sir,' said a familiar voice near his elbow.

'Sergeant Viney?'

'That's right, sir. The doc reckons I've caught a Blighty one. I'm not going to see much of France, am I?' The sergeant was trying to sound cheery, but the pain in his eyes and the perspiration beading his forehead told a more accurate tale.

'We'll get you back to the coast and some proper treatment just as soon as we can, Viney. We don't want Mrs Viney worried, do we?'

'That would never do, sir. She gets in a right two-and-eight when things go wrong.'

'We'll try and make sure that doesn't happen.'

'Thank you, sir'

David, wondering why on earth Viney should feel the need to thank him for this, patted his subordinate's shoulder and moved on, exchanging a word of comfort here and one of encouragement there. He reached his medical officer.

'How is it?'

The doc handed over a roll of bandages to one of his orderlies and indicated to the Colonel that he should follow him outside. Once in the fresh air he pulled a packet of Senior Service out of his pocket, offered one to David, who accepted gratefully, and then flicked his lighter. David inhaled and watched the doctor light his. He took a deep drag and exhaled with his eyes shut, relishing the moment of relaxation.

He said, 'Could have been worse. There are a couple of the injured who I don't think will make it, but the rest …'

'Sergeant Viney?'

The MO thought for a moment. 'Viney, Viney … oh yes. Probably not fatal. They may be able to save his leg at the field hospital.'

'Oh.' David felt a stab of sorrow. Viney was a good man. It would be tough on him and his wife if he ended up as a cripple. He turned away. Fatigue, the suddenness of the attack, the sight of friends wounded made him feel rather emotional. That would never do. He swallowed and turned back. 'Right. Well, get the field ambulances organised as soon as possible.'

The doc nodded. 'We're getting the worst cases sent back to the field hospital tonight. Some of the other chaps can probably be patched up and will be back with us by next week.'

'Good, good.' David nodded, feeling like a liar. As if these guys hadn't been through enough already, they were expected to face the possibility of it happening all over again. Perhaps Viney was one of the luckier ones after all. It looked as if he was likely to be out of the whole push permanently.

Otto picked up his gun from where it was slung over the chair by his bed, walked out of the dormitory and headed towards the latrine block. Like the other soldiers around him, he had been sleeping on top of his cot fully clothed. With the situation as it was, there was no point in getting undressed, as the order to stand-to could come, and often did, at any time. If anyone had watched him leave the blockhouse, there was nothing about him that would have raised any suspicion – Otto was apparently going for a pee in the middle of the night, as they all had to from time to time – and standing orders dictated that personnel should carry their personal weapon with them at all times.

Once Otto got to the latrine block he didn't enter it but slipped into the shadows behind it. He gazed out over the surrounding countryside. It was moonless and, although it wasn't completely overcast, the night was as dark as he could have wished for. Like David, seven kilometres away, he could make out vague details of the surrounding fields, but Otto wasn't assessing the lie of the land; he was checking for any troop activity. Suddenly the horizon was lit up by artillery fire. The flashes from the muzzles and exploding shells not only lit up the distant skyline but reflected off the clouds above, making them glow orange as if they were strange, misshapen vessels containing huge celestial fires. About twenty seconds later the crash of the guns reached him followed by the detonation of the ammunition. After about half a minute the bangs and crumps became indistinguishable; there was no telling what roar or report belonged to which flash. It was like watching some sort of mad thunderstorm. Fascinated, he forgot he was there to make a decision about his future and watched for a while. The firing from that gun position stopped, then the shells started flying in the other direction. He could clearly see the muzzle flashes; then, further away to his right, he could see the shells exploding. At this distance and with no knowledge of whose forces were positioned where, Otto had no idea who was firing on whom. What he did know was that the battle was edging ever closer to Martine's farm. This could only be taking place a matter of a few kilometres behind La Ferme de la Source.

He had been down there at lunch time to try to talk to Martine again to discuss with her the implications of him deserting, but had only encountered M. Bracque. He hadn't understood what had been said, but the message had been clear enough: he wasn't welcome. Taking the hint, Otto had scarpered. But, since then, that plane had crashed and now Otto didn't know if he still had a girlfriend let alone a place to hide. One way or another he had to find out if Martine was all right, but if he reached the farm tonight, and if he found out she was still alive, was he going to come back here?

Which brought him back to the reason for sneaking out of the dormitory. Firstly he wanted to establish just how close – or far – the front line was. He needed to know what his chances were of accidentally running into the fighting on his way over to Martine's place. It had been all right at lunchtime, but goodness only knew what troop movements had taken place since then. Besides, it was much easier to judge where the main action was at night. The muzzle flashes from the guns became really obvious once night fell.

If he was going to take the risk, he had to take it tonight. All along he'd told himself that when the right moment presented itself, when the front reached that critical point, he'd walk out of the camp and hide at her farm. Well, now it had. That was the plan. Now that he was in pitch darkness, alone and apprehensive, the plan didn't look so feasible. Doubts crowded into Otto's mind. What if the enemy got pushed back? Supposing the invasion faltered? There was any number of things that could go wrong. If he carried out his resolution and it was a disaster, he might be putting himself and Martine in terrible danger. He watched the artillery exchange rage and tried to pluck up courage to go, but there was too much at stake.

Another noise caught Otto's attention and brought him out of his troubled thought process. It was another low, thunderous rumble. It was intermittent, coming and going with the wafts of breeze that rippled across the huge grassy expanse of the airfield. He listened, perplexed. *Aircraft? No.* Then recognition dawned. *Tank engines. Panzers.* The SS tank regiment that they had heard the rumours about was arriving. Otto breathed out slowly. This was going to make things different. Well, he thought, it was as if God had made the decision for him. Once the SS and their Panzers arrived at Carpiquet there was no telling what life would be like. One thing was probably certain: his chance of slipping through the fence because of almost non-existent sentries would become unlikely. If he was going to go, it was now, or never.

Otto walked back behind the latrine block again and from there headed towards the perimeter. He walked slowly and carefully, not wishing to stumble, nor to blunder into the wire fence. He strained his eyes to try to make out the more substantial posts that supported it. Ah, there it was. He looked up and down the wire as far as he could in the darkness. There didn't seem to be any sentries patrolling in his area. Carefully he lifted the lower edge of the wire and pushed his gun underneath. There was a dip in the ground here where the wire didn't quite touch the earth below and Otto's frequent forays after dark to Martine's had increased its depth. Taking his forage cap off and stuffing it in his pocket. Otto wriggled under on his belly. Once on the other side he got on to his knees, brushed himself off and then pushed clods of earth back into the dip. After a couple of minutes work he felt no one would be able to tell he had passed that way. Picking up his gun and shoving his cap back on his head, he set off at a brisk walk across the neighbouring field towards the village and Martine's farm beyond that.

La Ferme de la Source

The guns opening up roused Martine out of her exhausted sleep in an instant. She lay for a terrified second on her bed before she leapt out and threw open the shutters to see how close the battle was. Across the horizon the explosions flashed. Martine gazed at the scene and tried to judge the distance. She reckoned it was all happening around Brouay or Putot – not the first time either of those villages had been fought over in the last few days, if rumours in the village were to be believed. It seemed unlikely that the German and Allied positions would change dramatically before daybreak, nor that the gunfire would get closer; so Martine closed the shutters once again and returned to herbed. She was getting blasé about the guns. The first couple of days after the invasion she had jumped at any kind of gunfire and hurried for the cellar, but now she had worked out that until the guns got significantly closer, they were not in any particular danger. She rolled on to her side and pulled her pillow over her ears but, with the racket raging outside, sleep was going to be difficult. The barrage stopped. The silence was wonderful.

'*Bon*,' muttered Martine as she snuggled into a more comfortable position and then, '*Merde alors,*' as the firing restarted. Angrily she threw back the covers. This was impossible!

Shoving her feet into a pair of clogs, she pulled an old woollen sweater over her pyjamas and went downstairs. She made sure the shutters were still closed tight before she lit the lamp on the table. As the mantle heated up and she adjusted the wick, the kitchen was filled with a warm golden glow. She took a pan down from the rack over the range and then went to the larder to pour a dipper of milk from the crock into it. A cup of warm milk might make her feel sleepy enough to nod off again despite events down the road. She put the pan on the range and shoved a few sticks into the fire. The ashes still glowed red-hot and they caught immediately. She stoked it up and then sat down in the old wooden armchair to wait for her drink to warm through. She was so tired she ached and the prospect of another hard day's work after a broken night made her want to weep. She looked across to the pan. The milk was fizzing and bubbling at the edge. She slid the pan off the heat and poured the warm liquid into a mug. Sitting in the chair, bathed in the warmth from the range and clasping the warm mug in both hands, she began to feel the tension leave her body. The guns fell silent again. She sipped the drink; she relaxed; her eyelids drooped; her milk went cold …

The banging on the back door woke her with such a start that the mug flew out of her hands and shattered on the flagged floor in front of her feet.

'*Merde*!' she exclaimed, looking at the pool of milk and pottery. '*Qui est là?*' she yelled, fear making her voice shrill.

'Martine, it's Otto.'

'Otto?' She ran to the door, her clogs clattering, and pulled it open. Outside, dawn was breaking. Watery, grey light was struggling through scudding clouds. She shivered. *Zut,* it was cold for a June day. She threw her arms around him and kissed him on both cheeks. 'Come in, come in. I'll make you coffee. You must be hungry. What are you doing here at this time?' she babbled.

Otto ducked through the low door and then pushed it shut behind him. 'Ssh,' he said. 'I can only answer one question at a time.' He leaned his rifle against the deal table and plonked himself down in the chair by the fire. He looked worn out. His eyes fell on the broken mug on the floor. 'I thought you would be up at this hour. I frightened you?'

Martine explained about the warm milk. 'I never meant to fall asleep. I was so tired.' She stroked Otto's cheek. 'Like you are.'

Otto smiled. 'Soon the war will pass over us and after that we can have as much sleep as we want.' He clasped Martine's hand and kissed it. 'Not long now, *Leibchen*.'

Martine smiled at him. 'You must have some breakfast and then you must go to the root store. We can't risk anyone seeing you until it's safe. You got away all right, didn't you?'

Otto shrugged. 'I had to come today. The SS were coming in the front gate when I crawled under the fence at the back,'

'But they didn't see you.'

'Obviously not; they'd have shot me if they had,' he said lightly.

Martine shook her head angrily as she took the day before's loaf out of a crock. 'For God's sake, it's no laughing matter, Otto.' She cut off two large hunks of bread, split them and put them in the oven to toast. 'How many SS have arrived?' She put a pan of water and another of milk on the hob to boil and spooned the brown dust that passed for coffee grounds into a jug.

'I didn't hang around to count. We were told to expect a whole regiment.'

'Is that a lot?'

Otto nodded. 'I'll say.'

Martine felt a swoop of fear. Thousands of British and Canadians were on one side of the farm and thousands of Germans were on the other side. What chance did she and Otto have in this mess?

'We need to get you hidden,' she said, getting to her feet. 'Watch the bread; make sure it doesn't burn. I'm going to get dressed.' She disappeared up the stairs and reappeared a surprisingly short time later in her work clothes, pulling on a sweater. Otto had the *tartine* on the table and was spreading a piece with butter.

'Water's nearly boiled,' he said. 'You eat this. I can make coffee.'

He pushed the *tartine* across to Martine, who took it gratefully. While she chewed the hard bread, she buttered the other piece for Otto as he poured the boiling water into the jug. A bitter smell filled the air, which might have had a hint of coffee within it if you had a good imagination. A couple of minutes later the milk had boiled too and Otto divided it between two large bowls, then poured the coffee from the jug through a sieve and into the hot milk. Martine tentatively opened the shutters a crack. It was getting light. She blew out the lamp and pushed the shutters right back.

'We need to hurry,' she said. The pair ate and drank quickly, not wasting time with talk. As soon as they had finished, Martine rinsed the bowls in cold water and put them back on the shelf – she didn't want any evidence of a visitor, should anyone come prying. Not that it was likely, she reasoned, but now was not the time to take any unnecessary chances.

'Come on,' she said as she led the way across the yard to the barn. She took Otto to the far corner and indicated that he should help her move the farmyard junk that she had carefully pushed back only the day before. With two of them working together it took only a few minutes to reveal the trapdoor. Otto bent forward and heaved on the ring. He looked into the hole.

'Not bad, not bad,' he murmured. He slung his rifle over his shoulder and swung himself down the ladder, jumping the last couple of rungs. There was a pail of fresh water, several cans of food, a tin-opener, some candles, a box of matches, two blankets and an empty bucket.

'You will need to be careful about lighting that candle. You don't want to make the air bad.'

'I probably won't use it. But it's nice to know I have it. You have thought of everything,' he said looking up at her …

'I don't know how much I will be able to get to see you over the next few days.'

'I understand.'

'I don't want to draw attention to this place. The more I move stuff back and forth the more likely it is Father might notice.'

Otto nodded. 'I'll be fine.' He tried to sound bright and cheerful. He didn't want Martine to sense his angst. The idea of being shut below ground, in the dark, appalled him, but he would be able to bear it if it meant he could be with Martine for the rest of his life.

'If I do get the chance to come and see you, I'llknock on the trapdoor like this.' She knocked out the rhythm of the first few bars of the Marseillaise and hummed the tune so he would realise the significance of the beat.

Otto repeated it. 'Like that?'

'*Ausgezeichnet* –excellent.' She paused, then clambered down the ladder to be with him. Otto caught her by the waist, supported her till her feet touched the ground, then drew her to him and kissed her long and tenderly.

'Now you must go. You have milking to do. You must put me out of your mind until the British get here.'

Martine leaned against him. 'This is going to be so hard.'

Otto nodded and rested his chin on the top of her head. 'We must both be brave. You especially. It will be hardest for you.'

Martine nodded. She kissed him again and then made her way up the ladder. At the top she blew Otto a last kiss before she shut the trapdoor and began to drag the farmyard junk back into position to conceal it. She scuffed her feet across the marks left in the dirt floor to conceal them and then turned her back on the barn.

'*Je prierai Dieu de tu protéger, mon ami,*'' she whispered as she left the yard.

In the dark, Otto lit a candle and gathered the items Martine had placed for him around where he sat, propped against one of the earthen walls. He wrapped himself in a blanket and folded the other up to be used as a pillow if he decided to lie down. Once he was sure he knew where each item was, he blew out the candle. The darkness was absolute. Otto stretched his legs out in front of him and shut his eyes. Sleep would pass the time. There was nothing else to do.

Up in his room, Jean-Paul, woken by the need to take a leak, had been climbing back into bed when he had seen Martine leave the barn. That girl had been in and out of it in the past day or so. He wondered what she was doing. Why on earth did she need to go in there when she was supposed to be getting on with the milking? It wasn't as if they used the place much in the summer – well, not now the horse had been taken and it wasn't stabled in there. As far as Jean-Paul was aware, there was nothing in the barn at the moment apart from some old machinery, a few bales of hay and straw and a pile of junk. He decided that he'd investigate later on. Yawning, he returned to his bed to sleep off the last of the previous night's calvados and *cidre bouché*.

Nine

Morning, Sunday 25 June 1944

Orchard Cottage

Gwen woke up with the alarm clock. Despite the fact that it was the weekend and she didn't have to go to work, she had too much to do to lie in bed. She reached out and flicked thesnib to shut off the bell and instantly heard scrabbling paws at her door.

'All right, Jasper, I'm coming.' She thrust her feet into her slippers, hauled her dressing gown over her shoulders and opened the door. Jasper was overjoyed to see her.

'Silly old mutt,' said Gwen, fondling his ears as he went into ecstasies at the attention – his eyes half-closed, his tongue lolling, the stump of his tail wagging so hard his whole rear end moved like a pendulum. Gwen pottered downstairs, stoked the range, fed Jasper and made herself a cup of tea; then she took a packet of Craven 'A' from her dressing gown pocket and lit up. As she blew out a long plume of smoke, she sank into the comfy old Lloyd Loom chair in the corner. It was then she spotted the note behind the sugar basin:

"Dear Mrs Clarke,
I told the grocery boy about putting it on the
account. He promised to tell Mr Goodbody. The
laundryman came. I gave him the l/6d and also the
laundry from the back bedroom. I'll see you again
on Monday.

Yours, Nan Viney."

Damn, she'd forgotten all about the laundryman. Good for Mrs Viney for paying him. Then a ghastly thought struck her: had Mrs Viney changed her sheets? Hastily, stubbing her ciggie out in a saucer, Gwen gathered up the trailing skirt of her gown and raced up the stairs. In the back bedroom was a neat pile of used sheets and pillowcases. A cold, clammy feeling sank leadenly into her stomach. Gwen was always careful to make her own bed and change her own sheets. There was no way she wanted Mrs Viney to see any evidence of her liaison with George. And Mrs Viney was no fool. Quickly Gwen shook out one of the sheets and cast an eye over it. Nothing. She checked the other one. Slowly she sat on the edge of the bed, clasping it on her lap. *Damn, damn, damn.* If only she had remembered that the laundryman had said he was coming earlier than usual. If she had just left out a note to Mrs Viney and told her not to bother with the bed. If only, if only …

Well, all the 'if onlys' in the world weren't going to put the clock back. Gwen wondered what she should do. She could ignore the whole matter – what did the aristocracy always say? Never apologise, never explain – was that it? Or did she make up some excuse about having had a married couple drop by and let them have the double bed? Would Mrs Viney believe her? Gwen grimaced as she slowly folded the sheet up again. It seemed unlikely. Perhaps it was better to ignore it.

One thing was certain, though: her resolve to end things with George was now absolute. If Mrs Viney had guessed something, Gwen wasn't sure how she was going to be able to explain things. Or *if* she should. Perhaps she'd be better ignoring the issue. Gwen felt a flutter of panic as she considered her options and realised she didn't have a clue how to handle the situation. If George came round again, she'd have to …

But that was it … *if* George came round again. It wasn't like him not to make an appearance or phone to say he'd been held up. She wondered what had happened. It was probably nothing, she reasoned. There were a dozen things that could have got in the way of his nightly trip to see her. In the circumstances it was probably a blessing – gave her a chance to work out exactly what she would tell him so that he would have no doubt she meant what she said.

Putting the neatly folded sheet back on the bed, she returned to the kitchen and lit another ciggie to calm her ragged nerves.

44 Selkirk Street, Havant

Nan Viney sat at the table in the window of her neat terraced house, sucking on the end of a pen. Curled up on the chair next to her was a large fluffy ginger tom that answered to the name of 'Tibbs'. Every now and again Nan's hand moved across to stroke him and when she did she was rewarded with a few deep, wheezy purrs.

'I don't know, Tibbs,' she said to him as she fondled his ears. 'Does Bill want to be bothered with this?' She sighed and looked at what she had written so far:

"My dearest Bill,
I hope this finds you as it leaves me. I am well at
the moment. The weather is shocking, rain almost
every day. I saw a newsreel about the invasion at
the cinema last night. It looks as though you are
having bad weather too. I thought it was supposed
to be hot abroad."

Well, she thought, *that was all right*; but it was what she wanted to put next that bothered her. 'I don't know,

Tibbs,' she said again. Tibbs stretched out a paw and rolled over slightly to present the other ear for scratching. 'If she were my daughter I'd give her a piece of my mind, that I would. If her mother was here, I expect she'd do the same.' Nan didn't rightly know what to do and, although she didn't want to burden Bill with the problem, she needed to ask advice from someone.

Trouble was, Nan thought, she wasn't sure she wanted to go on working for Mrs Clarke if she was going to be carrying on like she was no better than a common streetwalker. She liked Mrs Clarke, though – that was the problem. She had always thought her boss to be a lovely lady, but now she knew different. And she didn't think her Bill would like the idea of her working for a woman like that either. What Mrs Clarke was doing was downright wicked, what with her hubby over in France. Mind, this carry-on must have been going on for some time, while he was still in the country, but that didn't make things any better – worse if anything. If the Colonel knew, he'd put a stop to it and no mistake. He'd tell Mrs Clarke what was what. She sucked on her pen again and worked out what to say next.

'I think there's something you should know,' she wrote laboriously:

"The Colonel's lady is having an affair. I don't know who with but I know for definite she's seeing someone. Don't ask me how I know, but I do."

Nan sucked her pen again and then underlined 'seeing' and 'how'.

"I know it is none of my business, but I know how much you respect the Colonel and I want some

advice. Also I am not sure I want to go on working for her when I know what she is getting up to now the Colonel is out the way. Do you think I should hand in my notice? Or maybe you think I should say nothing. I know it is none of my business, but what she's doing isn't right."

There – she'd told him. Nan felt better already.

"I hope they're feeding you properly and make
Sure you don't catch cold. Tibbs and I miss
you something terrible and hope you come back
safe and well soonest.
Your ever loving wife, Nan."

Nan sat back in her chair feeling quite worn out with the effort of writing. She read through the letter again. *Good*, she thought. She eased herself out of the overstuffed chair and went over to the chest to fetch an envelope. She addressed it carefully and tucked the flap in; she never sealed envelopes, ever since she gave her tongue a nasty paper cut when she'd been a child. That sort of experience stayed with you for life and Nan shuddered very slightly as she recalled the awful stinging pain and the subsequent gouts of blood that had flowed. She put the letter in her bag ready to post. She'd do it on her way to Mrs Clarke's tomorrow.

'Right then, Tibbs. Nice cup of tea – that's what I need now,' and, feeling satisfied with a job well done, Nan went into her kitchen to put the kettle on.

RAF Thorney Island

'Come on, Wilf,' said Fred. 'Let's get it over with.' He looked around George's bedroom and put the cardboard box he'd been carrying down on the bed. 'Do you want to do the chest of drawers while I clear out his wardrobe?'

'Might as well. What are we doing with Air Ministry stuff?'

'I thought we could pile it on the bed and someone from Stores can come and get it.'

'Old George doesn't seem to have much, does he?' Wilf was fingering a photograph of an older couple standing in front of a big house with a wide porch, squinting into the sunshine, a Labrador sitting at their feet. 'Suppose these are his parents.'

Fred glanced at the picture. 'Imagine so. Let's hope all this just has to sit in store for a bit till we hear that George is OK, and we're not asked to send it all back to them. Gawd knows how it will get shipped across to the States.'

'But you're sure he bailed out.'

Fred shrugged as he began taking clothes out of the cupboard. 'I think he did. I told him to get out, but I didn't see him jump. So "I don't know" is the honest answer. I saw the plane crash, though.' He made a graphic turning, plunging gesture with his hand. 'Whoosh, bang.'

Wilf finished clearing George's stud box, photograph and hairbrushes off the top of the chest of drawers. He put it all in the box, then opened the top drawer. Lying on the neat piles of underpants and vests was an envelope. Wilf picked it up and read the address. *"Gwen Clarke, Orchard Cottage ... "* This must be to his bint. So that's why he was never in the mess in the evenings.'

'Give it here,' said Fred, leaning across and flicking it out of Wilf's hand. 'My, my, the sly old dog. She must be a hot bit of stuff for him to have trekked over there every evening. That's quite a hike. What do you reckon – we ought to deliver it personally?'

'But it's miles away. Anyway, we don't know what it's about. He might have changed his mind about sending it to her. It doesn't have "To be delivered in the event of my death" or anything like that written on it, does it?'

Fred looked at the back of the envelope. 'No. But it is addressed to her. I think she should get it. What else are we supposed to do with it?'

'Leave it be until we know one way or the other about George,' said Wilf without hesitation.

'But don't you want to see what George's popsie is like?' Fred grinned. 'Just think, she may need consoling.'

'And what about George?'

'What about him?'

'It's hardly Queensberry rules, is it?'

'What would he know about Queensberry rules? He's a Yank.'

Wilf considered the logic of this statement. Fred continued before he could refute the reasoning, 'All I'm going to do is deliver the letter and tell Miss Clarke what I know about George.'

Wilf didn't look convinced. 'And you've just told me you don't know much at all.'

'Come with me if you don't trust me.'

'How? How are we going to get there?'

'We'll use George's motorbike.'

Wilf thought for a minute. 'I'm not sure he's still got it. I haven't seen it for weeks.'

'That's because he hides it in the bushes at the back of the airfield. He can't be bothered with all that malarkey of booking in and out.'

'How do you know?'

'He told me.'

'So whereabouts is it?'

'Dunno, but we need to find it anyway,' said Fred. 'We may have to return that and all to his parents.'

'What a little ray of sunshine you are.'

Carpiquet Airfield

Jochen Peiper was supervising new arrangements at the

airfield. In front of him stood Major Hoffmann, the previous commanding officer whom Peiper had just relieved of his duties.

'I don't care whether you think the resistance is active or not in this area,' Peiper reiterated coldly. 'I think it is, or will be soon, and as I am now in command I am ordering you to draw up proper duty rosters for sentries. You will have these sentries posted every hundred metres around the perimeter.'

'But I have so few men ...' the major protested.

Peiper shook his head and sneered. 'Then they will have to work a bit harder, won't they? – go without a few hours' sleep.' He looked at the portly officer in front of him. When had this joke of an officer gone without anything? He knew the sort that was stationed here: the sick, the lame and the lazy, and this idiot was probably all three. And greedy, he added mentally, eyeing his subordinate's rotund belly. No wonder the enemy had managed to invade with such ease. This shambolic outfit wouldn't have been able to prevent a kindergarten from landing on the beaches. Well, this posting wouldn't be such a sinecure now. Not now he was in charge.

'How many men have you?'

'One hundred and thirty-seven,' said the major without hesitation.

'Then I want to see all one hundred and thirty-seven on parade in an hour.'

'Yes, sir. Seig heil: The major threw up as smart a Hitler salute as he was capable of executing and strode off.

Peiper watched him go. This man was an insult to the uniform he wore. He called to his adjutant and began to issue orders. 'I want you to set up a briefing room in that block over there,' – he indicated a three-storey brick structure that was the least badly damaged of the office buildings. 'I'll need maps of the area and I want you to get hold of Division HQ and find out what the latest enemy positions are. I imagine things have changed in the time it has taken us to move here.'

'*Jawohl.*'

'And tell all the officers I want to see them in two hours. In the meantime organise the mess hall to prepare food for all our men. I want everyone to have a hot meal. If the cooks complain about insufficient rations, tell them to requisition supplies from the local farms.' Peiper looked at the gently rolling landscape that surrounded the flat expanse of the camp, at the lush green of the pastures and at the height of the standing wheat. 'I doubt if the people here have wanted for anything over the past few years. They can go short now if necessary.'

Captain Kowal nodded. It was the same everywhere; the local farmers would squirrel away more than enough for their own needs while the people in the towns and the soldiers starved. If there was a problem with feeding the extra troops that had suddenly arrived in the immediate area, he was sure they would be able to unearth more than enough rations to cope. Kowal ran off to get things organised.

Peiper looked at where his men were largely grouped, in an area in front of the main gate. He could see that, despite the fact that they were all tired from their loss of a night's sleep, they were all busy making sure their tanks were in first-rate condition for the battles ahead. Most of the men were in black SS coveralls and were tightening the tank tracks, cleaning the gun barrels, greasing the engines, clipping together machine-gun rounds and performing all the general routine maintenance these beasts required on a day-to-day basis. Peiper was pleased. This was exactly how his battalion should function. It was exactly like the way any unit should function, and if he had the time it was how he would make Hoffmann's shambles work.

Despite his satisfaction that his men, at least, knew how

to behave like professional soldiers, he was concerned that he had less than a third of his men with him. God alone knew where the other two train loads had got to. In all likelihood they were still stuck in Paris – or worse, had been shunted off to some godforsaken siding somewhere in France. With a full complement of over seventy tanks they could seriously hope to turn the tide of the enemy advance, but he had less than twenty. His resources were hugely depleted and, while he knew he and his men would do their best, they couldn't hope to achieve the same results.

Peiper strode over to his men and chatted to them as they worked, raising his voice from time to time to be heard overthe clang of sledgehammers on tank-track links. Peiper had been with many of them as they had fought through Poland and Russia. They had celebrated victories together and suffered some defeats and he trusted them as much as he knew they trusted him. He moved amongst his men, exchanging words of encouragement, an occasional cigarette and some light-hearted banter, until Kowal came jogging over to tell him that Major Hoffmann had got his men on parade.

Peiper looked across to where they were lined up on the edge of the pockmarked runway. 'I suppose I had better have a look at them,' he said without enthusiasm. He walked the several hundred metres to where Hoffmann's men waited.

Hoffmann strode up, his paunch making him waddle rather than march.

'One hundred and nineteen men ready for your inspection, sir,' he reported as he halted and saluted.

'Ithought you told me you had one hundred and thirty-seven men,' answered Peiper, cocking his head and narrowing his eyes.

'Yes, sir, but there are ten men in the kitchens preparing food for your troops, sir, plus the guard detail on the gate.' Hoffmann sounded flustered.

'How many?'

'One NCO and six men.'

'So who isn't present?' Peiper asked, letting just a hint of menace slip into his voice. He paused as he allowed Hoffmann to do the maths. He could see the man's lips move as he added up the numbers. 'That's right,' Peiper encouraged him silkily. 'One hundred and nineteen plus ten … one hundred and twenty-nine … plus one, plus six … I make that one hundred and thirty-six. So' – another pause – 'I'll ask again: who is missing?'

'*Einen moment, bitte.*' Hoffmann scurried off to talk to one of his junior officers. Peiper watched impatiently as there was a hurried discussion. A few moments later Hoffmann returned, licking his lips nervously. 'We don't know, sir.'

'Well, Hoffmann, may I suggest you find out, and when you have, come and tell me. Right, get these men back to their duties.'

'But don't you want to …'

Peiper's look stilled Hoffmann into silence. 'Don't *ever*,' he said quietly, 'query an order of mine again. Understand?' Hoffmann nearly stumbled in his haste to get back to his own men and stand them down. Peiper shook his head contemptuously and returned to the company of *proper* soldiers.

As he walked back to his own men, Kowal approached again. 'Sir, I have a set of maps of the area. And a dispatch rider is being sent from Division with our orders.'

'Thank you, Kowal. Send him to me as soon as he arrives.' *Good*, thought Peiper, the sooner they found out what they were supposed to be doing the sooner they could get at the enemy. 'In the meantime make sure the men get fed and get a chance to sleep. I imagine we'll be engaging the enemy in the very near future.'

Ten

Afternoon, Sunday 25 June 1944

A Field Hospital near Arromanches

George was lying in bed, his right leg in plaster, his chest and left thigh heavily bandaged, his right arm in a sling. He ached all over but he was safe and warm and alive and, very importantly, out of the action, so he felt more relaxed than he had done for weeks – months, possibly. He was half-asleep and his eyes were shut, though he was aware of various noises going on around him. It had all been rather weird to start with, as he hadn't had a clue where he was. The feeling of missing a bit of his life was quite disturbing. He remembered bailing out and landing and had vague memories of a Canadian giving him a cigarette, but after that it was all a bit of a blank. As he lay between crisp white sheets and thought back, a vague memory hovered at the edge of his mind of a couple of other Canadians arriving and trying to move him. That was where his memory came to a full stop. George reckoned he might have passed out.

And now he was here, wherever 'here' was. Obviously it was some sort of casualty station. Above him he could see green canvas and he could smell crushed grass, but where exactly this place was he had no idea.

'How are you feeling?' asked a calm female voice.

George lazily opened his eyes and yawned. A pretty nurse in khaki battledress trousers, blouse and a white starched cap was standing beside him, looking down. 'I have felt better, if I'm honest.'

'Are you in pain? I could give you something for it if you are.'

'I ache a bit.'

'Bearable?'

George nodded.

'That's good then. What about anything else? I could get you some food or something to drink?'

'A large Scotch would be welcome.'

The nurse laughed. 'You boys are all the same. Tea, coffee or water.'

George attempted to shrug and grimaced as pain shot though his shoulder, up his neck and exploded in his brain. *Not a good thing to try and move*, he noted. 'In which case,' he said, 'I'll have tea. One sugar,' he added.

The nurse turned to go and fetch it.

'Nurse?'

'Yes?'

'What's ...' George stopped; he didn't want to sound like a drama queen. 'I mean ...' No, that wasn't going to sound right either. 'How bad ...'

'You want to know what injuries you received,' she interrupted.

'Yes, I do rather.'

'Well, as you have probably gathered, nothing very life-threatening.'

'*Very* life-threatening?' This wasn't what George wanted to hear. Even slightly life-threatening was scary. His fear must have registered on his face.

'Life-threatening at all, perhaps I should have said.'

George let out a heavy sigh of relief.

'We should have you properly patched up and on a ship back to England in no time. We had to take several bullets out of you, your leg is a bit of a mess but probably nothing we can't fix, and you dislocated your shoulder.'

'Is that all?'

'Enough, I would have thought. Now if you want some tea, you had better let me go and get it.' She smiled engagingly at her patient and walked briskly down the tent. George managed to turn his head just enough to be able to admire her bottom as she walked between the beds to the tent entrance.

Once she was lost from his view he turned his attention to the occupants of the other beds. There were another four in the tent that he could see, three opposite and one to his right and presumably one the other side of him, but he couldn't be bothered to turn his head. Each of the beds he could see contained another casualty.

'She's rather delectable, isn't she?' said a slightly muffled voice from the bed immediately next to George.

He swivelled his head slowly and carefully so as not to aggravate his shoulder and saw a young man with a heavily bandaged face looking back at him.

'Oh, I hadn't noticed,' lied George.

'Then you're the only man around here who hasn't. When Nurse Armitage was reeling off your injuries, I didn't hear her mention you'd lost your sight.'

George smiled. 'No, well ...'

'I'm Max Fairweather, by the way. Can't offer to shake your hand and all that; can't get out of bed.'

'Neither can I, so we'll take the will for the deed, shall we?'

'What happened to you?'

'Shot up and bailed out. You?'

'Trod on a land mine.'

'Oh God.' George realised the significance of his new acquaintance being bed-bound now. 'I'm sorry.'

'Don't be. I'm still alive and the delectable Nurse Armitage has to give me bed baths. Everything has its compensations. '

George wasn't sure about that;

'Besides which,' Max continued, 'it means I have

survived. For you, Tommy,' he said with a pantomime German accent, 'the war is over.'

'It's one way of looking at it.' George was still unconvinced.

'Here you are.' Nurse Armitage was back with a feeding cup. 'Not very dignified, I know, but if I try to sit you up I'll probably hurt you. Now then,' she said as she sat on the metal-and-canvas chair by George's bed and slipped her arm under his neck, 'let's see if you can raise your head just an inch or two.'

Her arm might have been under his neck but her left breast was pressing firmly against his right shoulder and just inches from his face. Perhaps Max was right after all – about life having its compensations.

With her support George managed to get his head off the pillow; he was completely oblivious as to whether his shoulder was causing him discomfort, and all his senses seemed to be concentrated on feeling the warm swell of Nurse Armitage's breast through the khaki fabric of her uniform. He took the spout of the cup on his lips and sucked for the tea. *Nectar*. Like Baby Bear's porridge in the fairy story, the tea was just right and he gulped it greedily. He was parched. He finished it in next to no time and, as he did so, he realised he'd made a mistake. As soon as the cup was drained, Nurse Armitage let his head rest gently on the pillow again and she withdrew her arm – and her breast.

'I'll come back and see you again in a little while,' she promised as she left.

'Do,' said George dreamily. Gosh she was a corker – even prettier than Gwen. If he was going to get out of his relationship with Gwen, this might be where he could rebound to.

'Told you there were compensations,' said Max.

At first light David's battalion had moved out of Brouay into the nearby countryside, away from the artillery troop that had caused the Germans to retaliate. They had found shelter in a wood just to the south of the village and had moved in there under the trees. There they had dug slit trenches, rigged up camouflage netting and generally made themselves as comfortable as they could. David had managed to grab a few hours' sleep before writing letters to the next of kin of the two officers and the fifteen men who had died the night before, and making sure that arrangements had been made for the proper burial of the bodies. Then he checked that the injured were being evacuated back from the front and saw to various other bits of battalion admin that didn't stop just because they were at war. By the time he had carried out all his duties it was time to report to Brigade for a briefing.

As he and his driver drove away from the wood he wasn't sure what he felt more: tired or scared. He'd only managed about three hours' kip last night and the night before, when he'd been on the landing craft. Wearily he wondered when he would manage to get his head down. But he knew that what was keeping him going was adrenalin – that and copious quantities of coffee.

The countryside they drove through was a bizarre selection of contrasts. On either side of the road for several hundred yards everything would be entirely normal: fields full of wheat and barley, cows grazing, prosperous-looking farmhouses, orchards laden with ripening fruit. And then the next village they came to would be a bombed and smoking ruin – shell holes in the roads and wrecked buildings, surly locals trying to rescue what few possessions they had that weren't smashed to pieces. Then after another hundred yards things would look completely normal again. Of course, even when things might look superficially normal there were other indications: David noticed that the smells of rotting flesh and burning buildings were almost constantly present. The armies might be scrupulous about burying their own dead, but dead livestock was left to rot – and there was plenty of that around.

A few minutes later Barnes pulled up outside an imposing farmhouse.

'Here we are, sir,' he said as he yanked on the handbrake.

'Thank you, Barnes. I suggest you find yourself a cup of tea and take a nap for a few minutes. I think we may be busy tonight.'

'Righty-oh, sir.'

David got out of the jeep and stretched, then walked into the shadowy gloom of the building. Through a pair of double doors to his left he could see trestle tables and several men gathered. He pushed one of the doors open wide and walked in.

'David! Good to see you.' A tall silver-haired man strode towards him, a hand outstretched.

David saluted and then grasped the offered hand. 'Brigadier.'

'I gather you had some trouble with the Hun last night.'

'Seventeen dead and twenty-one injured. I lost two officers.'

The Brigadier sighed and shook his head. 'Dreadful, dreadful. My signals officer was killed last night – hit by a shell as he returned from the shower unit. What bad luck was that? A good man, like your men were, no doubt.' There was a moment of silence as they both considered the shocking waste of life that was happening on a constant basis. 'Right, to business. Come over here.' He walked towards a large-scale map laid out on a table. They passed another staff officer as they went. 'Tea, David?'

'Coffee, please.' David was desperate for anything that

might keep him awake.

The Brigadier turned to his staff officer and asked him to organise some refreshments. He stood in front of the map and David saw the clear line drawn across the map denoting the front line. It curved and waved, but it ran across the Calvados region of Normandy about ten miles in from the sea.

'We took Le Mesnil-Patry last week.' The Brigadier pointed to a tiny village, about the same size as Brouay and about a mile to the south-east of it. It was in one of the wavy bulges on the line. He saw David reaching for a notebook in his breast pocket. 'Don't bother to take notes. I've had the clerks type up all the grids and unit locations. You'll be given a copy before you go.'

David put his notebook back and re-buttoned the pocket.

'Now we're in a bit of a stalemate. We're planning a big operation starting tomorrow – Op Epsom, which has the objective of completing the envelopment of Caen – and we'll need your boys particularly. This is where we want your chaps to come in. I want your battalion to move up to cross the start line, here' – he pointed to a dotted line joining Le Mesnil-Patry with another nearby village – 'at oh four hundred hours tomorrow. It will be a brigade attack supported by six regiments of field artillery. There was a rumour that another German tank regiment was moving up, but we've been told not to expect them to join the party after all. Our intelligence tells us that with your battalion and the other reinforcements we should easily be able to overcome the opposition in this area. Once we have, we should get a clear run through to the airfield. And once we've captured that …'

'There's somewhere for our planes to operate from,' David finished.

'Precisely.'

'Good show,' said David, trying to display an

enthusiasm he didn't feel. The coffee arrived and David took the steaming mug gratefully. He examined the map carefully as he sipped the hot drink.

The Brigadier went on to detail where he wanted each of David's companies to be at the start of the proceedings, and what other support they could all expect. David knew he was going to get written orders but still had to concentrate hard on what the Brigadier was saying in case there was anything else he ought to know. However, it all seemed fairly straightforward, textbook stuff. 'There will be an extensive air bombardment beginning at oh three hundred hours. We've been promised several hundred Flying Fortresses, which should make the Hun keep their heads down.'

'Good show,' repeated David, again with forced enthusiasm. He was too tired to think of a different way of expressing his false approbation. He was reminded of the promised effects of bombardments in the Great War, which had invariably proved completely mistaken when it had come to the moment for the men to go over the top. Now, though, was not the time to voice such cynical doubts.

'I want your men to take this objective here.' The Brigadier pointed to yet another dot on the map. David leaned forward to look at the patch of ground his men were going to have to risk their lives for.

'La Ferme de la Source?'

'Is that what it's called? Well, anyway – whatever the place is, it occupies a useful piece of ground and that's where your battalion is to end up if all goes according to plan. Meantime, you and your men have got some time to make sure they're well rested, fed, watered and their kit is in tip-top condition.'

'Thank you, sir.' David drained the rest of his coffee and put his mug down on the table.

'Don't forget to pick up your orders on the way out.

Goodbye and good luck.'

David saluted as he left. He would rather luck didn't play too big a part in the next day's events. He was rather hoping the planning would be the key. Well he'd find out soon enough.

La Ferme de la Source

Martine had finished the afternoon milking and looked longingly at the barn as she passed it taking the cows back to the field. She would have loved to pull away the junk, yet again, from the trapdoor and talk to Otto, but she was well aware of the danger of drawing any attention to his hiding place. If only they had some way they could communicate with each other without all the rigmarole of uncovering the trapdoor, but it was impossible. Taking her eyes off the barn and focusing on her small herd, she opened the gate to the yard and encouraged the beasts to make their stately way back to the pasture.

As they walked through the lush countryside, the guns opened up again. *Definitely closer*, she thought. She glanced around nervously, wondering what the target was, or indeed *where* the target was? Her ladies, however, seemed completely unperturbed by the sudden noises and swayed sedately down the road as if nothing unusual was going on at all.

Jean-Paul had seen his daughter pause outside the barn and stare at it for several seconds. What was it with the girl and the place? She was up to something and he wanted to know what it was. Well, he had a few minutes now while she took the cows back to the field. Besides, when she returned she had the dairy to clean down. He probably had nearer to half an hour to find out what she was up to. He'd been thinking about her behaviour all day, while he'd waited for an opportunity to have a good snoop round. He'd formed a suspicion that she might be mixed up with the Resistance. It was the only solution he could come up with. Perhaps she was hiding equipment or weapons for the Maquis. If she was, he'd put a stop to it. He didn't want trouble – not at his farm; there was no way a daughter of his was going to jeopardise them or it.

Muttering angrily to himself, Jean-Paul stamped across the yard and went into the cool, dusty gloom of the big barn. He allowed himself a couple of seconds for his eyes to adjust to the difference in light and then he looked around him. It all looked the same. So what was it she had been getting up to in here? He began to walk around the big airy space. He knew in his bones that something had been going on here, but what? He went over to the last of the previous year's hay but, judging by the cobwebs that were spun from the corners of the bales to the beams and rafters, nothing had been moved there for months. The old stall the horse had been housed in, till it had been taken away, looked equally derelict and abandoned. And that pile of junk ... Jean-Paul wandered closer.

Well, well, well, he thought. The beaten-earth floor around it was scuffed and marked. Someone had been shifting it around and it didn't take the intellect of a scientist to work out who. Then another thought lit up a recess of Jean-Paul's brain. *The old root store!* What had that minx Martine got hidden down there? With any luck it might be something useful. He began to drag away the junk and scrap that was piled up.

'Father. Father what are you doing?' Martine ran into the barn and grabbed at his arm. The note of near panic made her voice shrill.

Jean-Paul swung round. 'Why aren't you in the dairy?'

'Because I heard someone in the barn. It could have been looters or anyone. So come on: what are you doing?'

'Isn't it me who should be asking you that question? What have you been up to? What has been going on behind my back?' He stared at her belligerently. 'I want the truth.'

Martine looked him in the eye, her chin up. 'Nothing. Oh, apart from running the farm without a scrap of help.'

'Don't you get cheeky with me, my girl.' Jean-Paul moved away the old mangle and a couple of buckets, grunting with the exertion.

Martine paced back and forth nervously. 'Leave that mess alone. You'll hurt yourself moving it on your own.'

'I doubt it. I see you managed to shift it.'

'I didn't.'

Jean-Paul took a step towards his daughter, his hand raised, but Martine didn't flinch. Jean-Paul sighed and lowered his hand again. The girl had courage – he'd give her that.

'You've got something hidden in the root store; what is it?'

'Nothing.'

Jean-Paul shook his head and returned to calmly moving away the pile of useless items.

'Please, Father, don't.'

Jean-Paul paused and turned. 'So you admit it: there is something down there.'

'It'd be better if you knew nothing about it.'

'This is my farm, young lady, and don't you forget it. What goes on here is my business.'

Martine longed to make a sharp retort about the only business that he had conducted for months had been down at the café in the village, but she bit it back.

'Trust me, Father, you don't want to know,' she pleaded instead.

Jean-Paul gave her a hard stare and moved away the last few items; then he bent down and scrabbled for the heavy iron ring. He pulled it up and let the heavy trapdoor fall back with a dull thump against the wall of the barn. Slowly he moved forward so he could peer into the pit. When he saw what was down there, he reeled back.

'Good God Almighty!' Jean-Paul had never experienced such a spasm of rage and disappointment all rolled into one devastating emotion. Slowly he turned to look at Martine. She was pale with fear. 'You're harbouring a German?'

She didn't answer.

Jean-Paul took a stride so he was right in front of her. 'A German? Hiding on my farm?' he shouted, spittle spattering his daughter's face, he was so close and so incensed. 'What the hell are you doing that for?' Jean-Paul raised his eyes to the dusty rafters above as if he would gain some insight or wisdom from them. 'This is the man who's been hanging around here. I knew he was up to no good. What has he persuaded you to do?' The last thing that Jean-Paul wanted to believe was that his daughter had voluntarily got herself into this situation with the enemy.

Martine took a deep breath. 'I knew you wouldn't understand. That's why I didn't tell you.'

'Tell me what?' Jean-Paul's voice was almost falsetto with rage.

'I'm going to marry Otto. I'm hiding him here because I want to be sure he's going to survive the war.'

Jean-Paul staggered. 'Marry?'

Martine nodded. 'I'm twenty-two – why not?'

'But … but …

'But what? You can't stop me.' Martine was beginning to lose her temper too.

Otto appeared at the top of the ladder into the root store.

'Don't get involved,' said Martine in German.

'What did you say?' asked her father.

'Nothing that concerns you.'

'Don't you dare talk to me like that.'

'I am not a child any more. I'll talk to you how I like.'

'Not while you live on this farm.'

'And who will do all the work if I leave? When was the

last time you did anything around this place? Huh? Tell me that?'

Otto's head had swivelled from one angry face to another as he tried to keep track of the conversation and perhaps gather what was going on. As he saw Jean-Paul step towards Martine once again with his hand raised, he slowly and deliberately unslung his rifle from his shoulder and cocked it. The sharp metallic click brought the warring couple up short. Both pairs of eyes instantly turned and stared at him.

Martine shook her head. Quietly she said, 'That won't be necessary.'

'I'm not going to let him hurt you.'

'He won't. It's all bluster.'

Jean-Paul narrowed his eyes. 'Talk in your own language, damn you,' he said.

'You should have learned German while Mother was alive,' said Martine, switching languages without thinking.

Jean-Paul spat by way of an answer.

'Otto only has to stay here for a day or two. As soon as the front line has passed us by he's going to give himself up to the Allies. He'll be a prisoner till the end of the war but he'll be safe. What happens after that is up to you.' Martine saw the curious look on Otto's face and rapidly translated what she had said for his benefit.

'How do you mean "up to me"?' asked Jean-Paul.

'If you don't make Otto welcome, I shall go and live with him in Bavaria. You'll never see me again.'

Jean-Paul looked like a defeated man. 'You wouldn't, would you?'

Martine just stared at him and then moved sideways to stand next to Otto. She slipped her hand into his.

Jean-Paul dropped his gaze and then walked out of the barn.

Martine sagged against Otto. He put his arm around her protectively and gave her a hug.

'That was awful. That wasn't supposed to happen,' she said, blinking back tears.

'He knows now. It was bound to happen sooner or later and it was always going to be difficult.'

Carpiquet Airfield

Peiper leaned over the large-scale maps of the area and tapped a pencil thoughtfully against his teeth. He was studying the terrain to the west of the airfield and trying to work out where he could most effectively position his tanks to prevent it from falling into enemy hands. Strategically the airfield was of huge importance and the orders he had received from Divisional Headquarters reflected it.

So ...he thought long and hard as he studied the map and tapped his teeth some more. Given the fact that he had only a quarter of the tanks he should have, what should he do with them to obtain the best use? Peiper walked round the map as if looking at it from a different angle might give him inspiration. He'd marked on it the enemy positions that intelligence had come up with. Not that he had any way of knowing if they were right or wrong, but he had nothing else to go on. It seemed the main opposition that he had to contend with was an infantry brigade based around the village of Le Mesnil-Patry. Peiper looked at the contours on the map. The land sloped away very gently to the south-east of the village and then rose again to a wooded hillside just the other side of a small farm. If his tanks stationed themselves in this wood, they would have clear lines of fire to where the brigade was based, but they themselves would be hidden from view. It would mean leaving the airfield unprotected except for the shambolic Hoffmann and his men, but that couldn't be helped. It would be better to take the battle to the enemy and act like heroes than to wait like dogs.

Besides which, they would have better cover and fields of fire.

'Kowal,' he called.

The sound of a chair scraping back came from the next room. His adjutant appeared in the door.

'Sir?'

'I want all company commanders here in ten minutes.'

'*Jawohl*, sir.'

After Kowal had left, Peiper made some notes from his map and worked out a route that would be safe for them to use when darkness fell.

His company commanders filed into the office some minutes later.

'Good afternoon, gentlemen. I trust your men have been fed properly.'

'I'll say one thing for this place: they eat well,' said one of Peiper's subordinates. 'Proper meat on the plate.'

'Good. Glad to hear it.' Peiper had had to make do with dry bread and soup for lunch while he worked on his plans for his regiment's deployment. Swiftly he outlined his plans and pointed out the enemy positions. His officers nodded in agreement as Peiper explained the thinking behind his proposals.

'So, we will move out of here at dusk and move into position in the woods behind this farm.' Peiper tapped the map with the point of his pencil, then bent forward to read the name: 'La Ferme de la Source.'

Eleven

Evening, Sunday 25 June 1944

Orchard Cottage

Gwen was pottering around in the garden, tidying up the battered roses and re-staking some plants that had been beaten down by the recent rain and gales, when she heard the sound of a motorbike coming up the hill towards the cottage. *George.* He was all right after all! Despite her intentions to finish her affair with him she felt a surge of relief that he was well and safe, which completely submerged her earlier feelings of guilt and worry about her behaviour. Jasper heard the machine too and raced round to the front of the house, barking and wagging his tail. Gwen dropped her ball of twine and the canes she was carrying and shot into the house through the back door. George mustn't catch her looking such a mess. She almost ran into the downstairs cloakroom and checked her appearance in the minor over the basin. What a fright, she thought. She took a hanky out of her pocket and licked it before rubbing a smudge of soil off her cheek; then, as the doorbell rang, she ran a comb through her hair. Too late to run upstairs and get her lipstick, but at least now she didn't look like some sort of street urchin. She ran to the door and opened it, but her words of welcome stuttered into silence when she realised she was looking at two complete strangers. She looked beyond them – yes, it was George's motorbike she'd heard. There it was parked in the drive. So what the hell were these two doing riding it?

'Miss Clarke?' said the taller of the pair.

'Mrs,' corrected Gwen automatically. She saw his eyebrow lift a fraction. 'Can I help you?'

'We've ...' The taller man stopped and looked at his companion. The pair of them looked desperately uncomfortable. 'I say, do you think we might come in?'

Gwen felt as if a cold lump was sinking slowly down her body. This was bad news. She knew it. And it was about George. But how the hell did they know to come and see her? A ghastly thought struck her: had George been bragging about their affair in the mess. *Surely not. He wouldn't ... would he?* She opened the door wide and stood to one side to let the two men pass.

'Go into the drawing room,' she said. 'It's the door on the left.' She shut the door and leaned against it for a second or two to compose herself before she followed her guests.

'Gwen Clarke,' she said, holding out her hand. 'But apparently you already know that.' The tall chap took it and shook it.

'How do you do, Mrs Clarke. I'm Fred Daventry and this is Wilf Turner.' Gwen shook Wilf's hand too and then gestured that they should all sit down.

'So,' she said brightly, 'what can I do for you?'

Fred pulled an envelope from his inside pocket and looked at it before leaning forward and passing it to Gwen.

'Where did you get this?' she asked, but in her heart she knew the answer.

'Wilf and I, well ... George had a tangle with Jerry over France yesterday. We had to clear out his room this morning. We found this.'

Gwen looked at the carpet and turned the envelope over in her hands. She was surprised how calm she felt, but she supposed she had been preparing herself for bad news since the night before, and her worst fears had been confirmed when she'd seen Wilf and Fred at the door.

'What happened?'

'To be honest, we're not entirely sure. We were all on a sortie over France and he got shot down. What we don't know was whether he managed to bail out or not.'

'We know the plane crashed. We saw that,' interjected Wilf. 'But no one in the section saw a 'chute.'

'You think he's dead then,' said Gwen.

'We don't know. He may not be. He's been posted as missing for the time being. You know how it is.'

Gwen did, only too well. There were plenty of stories about airmen who had been reported 'missing, presumed dead', and who had turned up days or even months later. But then again, there were plenty who hadn't.

'And we don't know which side of the front line he landed on if he did get out,' continued Fred. 'Either way, it's such chaos over there at present it may be some weeks before we find out ...' His voice petered out.

'... if he's dead or not,' completed Gwen for him.

Fred nodded slowly. 'We just thought you ought to know.'

'Thank you. It was very thoughtful of you to take the trouble to tell me in person. I don't suppose I'd have found out otherwise.'

'Will you be all right?' asked Wilf.

This small, kind question was enough to undermine Gwen's self-control. She felt her jaw tighten and the unmistakable prickle at the back of her nose as tears began to well. She wasn't going to cry in front of these boys. It would embarrass them.

'Tea,' she said brightly to cover up the signs of emotion. 'I'll go and make some.' She stood up and walked swiftly to the kitchen. Once there she leaned against the sink and allowed the tears to flow. *What a waste, what a shocking waste*, she thought. George didn't deserve to die. He was too exuberant and fun to be snuffed out. She looked at the letter she was still holding in her hand and put it on the kitchen table. She wouldn't read it while his two friends were here. She wanted to be entirely alone when she discovered what he had to say to her. Instead, she reached into the sleeve of her cardigan and drew out her hanky. She looked at the grubby mark that she had cleaned off her face thinking that he was about to stride up the path and through the front door. And he hadn't. He was probably lying in a corner of some foreign field. She snorted as that line of poetry crossed her mind; it was a concept that seemed quite romantic when it wasn't your lover or husband involved, entirely different when it was. She blew her nose and picked up the kettle. Those two boys would be wondering where she had got to. While the kettle hissed on the range she laid a tray with cups, saucers, sugar and milk. She looked in the larder: no biscuits. They would have to make do with bread and marge. She cut a few slices and spread them, then sliced each one in half into a triangle. How banal, she thought. My lover is probably lying dead in the wreckage of his plane and I'm doing this. She blew her nose again and squared her shoulders. Crying wasn't going to bring him back. The kettle boiled and when she'd made the tea she carried the tray back into the drawing room.

Both men were sitting exactly where she'd left them, still perched uncomfortably on the edges of their seats. They looked up as she came in.

'You shouldn't have gone to any trouble, Mrs Clarke,' said Fred.

'Don't be silly; it's the least I can do to repay you for your kindness. And call me Gwen, please. Mrs Clarke makes me sound old enough to be your mother.'

'Hardly,' said Wilf.

Gwen poured and handed round the cups and bread and butter.

'So how did you meet?' asked Fred.

Gwen related the story of George dropping in as the

two men nibbled politely on their dull tea.

'Trust George to land on his feet like that,' said Wilf.

'Hardly. As far as I recall, when I came across him he was on his back, sprawled all over my garden.'

They all laughed and then equally suddenly stopped, embarrassed by their frivolity in the light of recent events. The atmosphere stiffened up once again.

'Well, we'd better get going and leave you in peace and quiet,' said Wilf, putting his cup on the table and brushing a few stray crumbs off his uniform.

'Yes – mustn't outstay our welcome.'

Gwen longed to tell them that peace and quiet was all her evenings were going to consist of for weeks to come. The two men rose to go.

'Thanks awfully for the tea. Jolly kind of you,' they mumbled between them as they headed for the door.

Gwen extended her hand. 'Lovely to meet you and thank you again.' She watched them walk down the drive and then shut the door slowly. When she was on her own, the tears started again, but this time they seemed to be mostly ones of self-pity as it dawned on her just how lonely a lot of her life was going to be from now on.

The Field Hospital

George had spent most of the afternoon dozing. He couldn't imagine how it was possible to sleep so much. Max, in one of George's spells of wakefulness, had suggested it might well have something to do with the anaesthetic that he'd had when they had set his leg. George didn't know, nor did he care much; he revelled in the bliss of knowing that he was out of action for the foreseeable future.

At around six they had been given a meal of some sort of stew and boiled potatoes, which George had had fed to him by a young nurse. It made him feel such a baby, being spoon-fed, but he had no option. He'd rather hoped the delectable Nurse Armitage would do the honours and had felt hard done by when she had decided to help another chap in their tent. Being fed by Nurse Armitage might have made the rather humiliating experience a touch more palatable, but his luck wasn't in.

Max had seen him glowering and, after their plates had been taken away and the young nurse helping George had wiped his mouth, Max leaned across towards his fellow patient.

'You can't always have her to yourself,' he'd said.

'Who?' said George, although he knew perfectly well what Max was implying.

Max didn't rise and carried on, 'We all want a share of her. Besides, I saw her first.'

'I don't know what you mean,' said George.

Max had looked at him knowingly and tapped the side of his nose.

'You've got absolutely the wrong idea,' George blustered.

'Ah, the little woman waiting for you back home?'

George eased himself back on to his pillows as best he could to try and get comfortable. 'Not really.'

'No one special then.'

'I wouldn't say that. Just ...'George would have shrugged, but it would have hurt too much.

'I get it,' said Max. 'You like to play the field – keep your options open.'

It seemed to George that it would be easier to give this impression than to embark on difficult explanations, besides which it had been the truth till he had met Gwen. He made a gesture that was a cross between a nod and a shake of his head.

'So there's no one you need to write to, to tell them how you are?'

That made George think. 'Well, I suppose I should let

my parents know how I am, even though it'll take forever for a letter to get to them in Pennsylvania and I ought …' he paused.

Max picked up on the pause immediately. 'And?' He raised an eyebrow questioningly.

'Well, there is someone. I mean, we're not serious about each other, but it would only be fair to Gwen to let her know too.'

'Gwen: that's a pretty name.'

'She's a pretty girl.'

'Then she deserves a letter. And if you let the delectable Nurse Armitage know, she'll let you dictate one to her.'

The tent had fallen quiet after their supper had been cleared away. Some men read, a couple smoked and George dozed again. He was awoken as dusk was falling.

'I gather you would like to dictate a couple of letters,' said Nurse Armitage, pulling up a canvas chair and settling herself beside George's bed. He supposed Max must have dropped a hint to her. 'I've time to do it for you now, before I go off duty, if they're not too long.' She smiled at him and George smiled back, wondering if it would be an offence against King's Regulations to kiss her. Then he dismissed the idea. She wouldn't be interested in a crock like him. And Gwen might not be either. That was a bit of a facer. He was used to knowing he could get any popsie he set his cap at and, seeing as how he was an invalid, now the girls might not be so keen on him.

Nurse Armitage crossed her legs and set the pad of paper on her knee, her pen poised ready to take down George's words.

George cleared his throat, acutely aware that Max would be able to hear every word he was about to say. 'My darling, er, Gwen.'

Nurse Armitage's hand whizzed across the white paper, leaving a line of neat writing trailing behind it. She looked up encouragingly, waiting for the next sentence.

George cleared his throat again. Gee, what could you say to a girl when everyone else was going to hear? 'I, er, got shot down yesterday but, um, I thought you would be pleased to know I am all right and have been patched up.' George paused and Nurse Armitage looked up again when she had stopped writing. 'I don't think I'll be doing any flying for a few weeks as a result.' He sighed deeply. It was bad enough writing to a girl at any time, but this was excruciating. Love letters had never been his style; he'd always preferred actions to words. 'I say,' he said. Nurse Armitage was about to write this down too when he stopped her. 'I say. I'm not much good at this dictation business. How about I practise with a letter to my folks to start with?'

'Whatever you would like,' said Nurse Armitage, tearing off the top sheet of her pad and putting it on his bed. Behind her George could see Max grinning to himself. He was obviously getting a lot of enjoyment out of George's discomfiture.

'Dear Mom and Pa,' he began more confidently,

'If you've heard any bad news about me, I am writing to say that reports of my death are an exaggeration. I had a bit of a tussle with a Messerschmitt and came off second best, but I am now in a field hospital and …'

'Hang on,' said the delectable Nurse Armitage. 'I am doing dictation, not shorthand.'

'Sorry, sorry. I was getting carried away.' George waited for Nurse Armitage to finish writing. 'Where was I?'

'"I am now in a field hospital …"'

'… and I am being looked after splendidly.' George made a conscious effort to talk slowly as he dictated a brief outline of his dogfight and injuries. He then went on to cover all the usual subjects of the food, the weather and the company:

'I am not sure when I am likely to be back home.
Nurse Armitage says I should be on a ship back to England in no time, which is good.
In the meantime, please pass on my best wishes to the rest of the family.

Your loving son, George.'

'Right,' said Nurse Armitage when she had finished writing. 'Do you want to add a *p.s.* explaining why your writing has changed all of a sudden?'

'Goodness, yes ... *p.s.* Nurse Armitage ... I say, I can't keep calling you Nurse Armitage. What's your Christian name?'

'June.'

'That's a nice name.'

'And so is Gwen,' June replied firmly.

'Oh yes. Absolutely ... *p.s.* June Armitage is writing this for me, as my shoulder is dislocated and my arm is in a sling. Love again, George.'

'Good. Now then, let's get the envelope addressed and we can finish the letter to your girlfriend,' June said as she folded in half the couple of sheets of paper she'd filled and put them on the bed.

'She's not really my girlfriend,' said George. Behind June's head, George saw Max's eyebrow go up. He ignored it and dictated his parents' address. June retrieved the half-written letter to Gwen and got ready to take some more dictation. George repeated much of what he'd said to his parents; then, 'I am looking forward to getting back to England again. Perhaps we'll be able to see each other on my return. In the meantime I wish you all the best ... *et cetera, et cetera*,' he finished, a little lamely.

'She isn't, is she?' said June wryly as she signed off the letter.

'What?'

'Your girlfriend. I'd be livid if my boyfriend wrote to me like that. Or is it how you Americans do things?'

'Well ...' George stopped. 'Is it *really* that bad?'

'Yes,' said June. She glanced at her watch. 'Look, I've still got a few minutes spare.' Her tone was softer and she smiled. 'I know how difficult you boys find this, but I am sure Gwen cares about you and is worried sick about you. Even if she's not your girlfriend, just a friend, I think she deserves something a little more heartfelt – don't you?'

June was right. George took a deep breath. 'Dearest Gwen, The worst thing about being shot down isn't the injuries but the fact that I can't get up to your cottage to see you.' George saw a flicker of a smile cross June's face as she wrote. He hoped it meant that this attempt was meeting with her approval. He carried on, spurred by the occasional nod of encouragement from June. He told her that he hoped she wouldn't be too lonely on her own but that she was to remember he was thinking about her all the time and that as soon as he was well he'd come and see her and take her for a picnic on the back of his motorbike.

When he'd finished, June folded up the letter and got out an envelope. 'Much better,' she said. 'And it wasn't so difficult, was it?' She saw George's glance flicker to Max. 'And don't worry about what *he* says. He a terrible old cynic on the surface but his letters to his girlfriends ...'

'Girl*friends*?'

'Several,' confirmed June. 'His letters are equally lovely.'

Behind her Max shook his head vehemently, but George could see he was blushing bright red. He dictated the address and June said goodnight and warned them that it would be lights-out in a few minutes.

'*Mrs* Clarke?' asked Max with undisguised interest,

when Nurse Armitage had gone.

'She's a widow,' said George shortly and defiantly. 'Anyway, you can't talk. How many girlfriends?'

'Only three. Time is short, old chap. I haven't time to test-drive them one at a time.'

George smiled and closed his eyes. In the distance he could hear guns firing, overhead he could hear a plane, and here he was, tucked up in a comfortable bed and no worries about risking his life for the foreseeable future.

Twelve

Nightfall, Sunday 25 June 1944

Carpiquet Airfield

The roar of fifteen throbbing Maybach engines filled the air at the airfield. Peiper, sitting in the cupola of the lead tank, gave the order for them to move forward. The throbbing deepened and intensified and made the guts of Hoffman and his men vibrate in sympathy, although Hoffmann's guts were also churning with fear. The fact that he'd been ordered to 'hold the airfield to the last man' had been profoundly disconcerting. Clouds of dark exhaust spewed from the Panzers as they slowly ground their way out of the gate and on to the road that led west towards the enemy. Ahead of them the sky flashed with bursting flares and exploding shells, but they heard nothing of the accompanying racket over the deafening roar of their own engines. The tanks thundered and squealed along the road to the next village, a tiny settlement of just a handful of houses, and then Peiper gave the order to turn off and proceed cross-country. Leading his men at the head of a V formation Peiper's tank churned over the fields of pasture, the tracks throwing up great clods of wet turf, crashed through hedges and flattened crops as he took his men by the most direct of routes to his chosen objective. At one point they cut between two even tinier hamlets and had to negotiate a small stream, but nothing seemed to get in the way of the relentless progress of the massive Panzers.

Ahead Peiper could see, even in the darkness, that the

ground was rising gently to a tree-crested knoll. This was his objective. With cover from the trees and undergrowth his tanks could command the low ground between the hill and the village of Le Mesnil-Patry and stop the enemy gaining any more ground. Once he had established a strong base, the division would be able to start the business of repelling the invaders back into the sea. This time there would be no 'Dunkirk miracle'. This time they would be eradicated.

Peiper's tank reached the crest and he signalled his unit to stop. He jumped off the hull of his Panzer and told his driver and radio man to accompany him. They moved forward slowly, squinting in the deep gloom of the almost moonless night. As he walked, his binoculars bouncing heavily against his chest, he was aware of the rattle and crump of an engagement some miles away. His two escorts padded a couple of paces behind him over the soft ground. Initially he smelt the wet, musty smell of leaf mould and the sharper, more pungent tang of wild garlic, but after a couple of minutes he picked up another smell which grew more powerful and more acrid as he moved carefully forward. Suddenly he could see a jagged shape in front of him and a hole in the canopy above. He paused at the edge of the clearing and willed his eyes and brain to work out what the dark misshapen lump was. Then he spotted a faint scimitar-shaped gleam of light running almost vertically: an aircraft propeller. Now he knew what he was looking at he could make out that the plane was on its back. And he could discern that the wings had been ripped off – no doubt as it crashed through the trees. Around him he could see that the undergrowth was blackened and burned. There was no point in seeing if the pilot had survived. If he hadn't bailed out, he was nothing more than a cinder now.

Peiper skirted round the wreck and felt the ground start to slope downwards again. If his map was accurate, he would soon come to the western edge of the wood. Ahead the darkness seemed less dense. Peiper moved more slowly: he didn't want to run into an enemy patrol. Divisional intelligence had told him that they were about two kilometres away, but Peiper had scant regard for the pencil-pushers on the Staff. It wasn't *their* arses on the line. What did they care if their information was out of date or just plain wrong? He reached the edge of the trees and raised his binoculars to his eyes to scan the countryside that sloped gently away to a flat expanse of farmland, criss-crossed with hedges interspersed with a few small copses. About seven or eight hundred metres away the land rose up again equally gently and at the top of the little rise he could make out some dark rectangular shapes of the village of Le Mesnil-Patry. There was no sign of the enemy, but that didn't mean anything. If they had any sense at all – and he had no reason to doubt that – they would be dug in and keeping their heads down.

Peiper examined the ground closer to hand. A hundred metres away and below him – he was level with the chimney – was a farmhouse. In front of it and on the other side of a yard was a large barn. Peiper considered this. The barn might provide cover. He looked through his binoculars again. The outbuildings had possibilities too. He stepped out of the wood and on to the pastureland that bordered it. He walked a dozen or so paces into the field and looked back at the trees. His idea to conceal his tanks in the trees had been reasonable, but the farm might be better still. There were plenty of possibilities to hide his tanks, hull down, amongst the muddle of stone byres, stables and cowsheds. He could even conceal a couple in the barn itself. Besides which, the thought of sleeping in a comfortable bed in somewhere weatherproof had more than a certain appeal. And there would be fresh food on hand. He looked back at the woods and made his mind up. No, the farm would be his choice.

He signalled to his two escorts and made his way back through the trees to his men. Then over the radio he gave the order for the other tanks to follow his into the farm complex near the bottom of the hill.

Thirteen

An Hour Before Dawn, Monday 26 June 1944

La Ferme de la Source

It was the noise that woke Martine, then the strange throbbing vibration jolted her from half-sleeping to completely alert in one thudding heartbeat.

'*Qu'est-ce qui se passe?*' she muttered in sleepy irritation as she thrust her feet into her clogs and grabbed a thick sweater. She opened the window and then threw wide the shutters. The noise was now getting deafening. This hadn't happened before; this was a new aspect of the war. What the hell was going on? Her heart was banging away as the terrifying din got louder and louder, the rumbling roar and squealing, as if a dozen pigs were being slaughtered by whatever infernal machine was approaching.

What in God's name is happening? she wondered frantically. It wasn't planes, it wasn't any vehicle she'd ever heard; then, suddenly, behind the far wall to the farmyard she saw the unmistakable outline of a tank cupola with the sinister pointing finger of its big gun travel past.

'Oh dear God,' she whispered. She felt her knees weaken and her limbs start to shake. The moment she had been dreading had arrived. The war had come to them. She and her father were now in the eye of the storm. Another tank appeared, and then she saw a movement out of the corner of her eye. She turned her head and looked in the other direction. *Mon Dieu,* tanks were on the other side of the farm too. They were surrounded. Instinctively she crouched down so just her eyes and her forehead showed above the sill. She strained her eyes and tried to work out whose side the tanks were on, but if there were markings on their hulls they were below the level of the wall. The noise abated slightly. It seemed from Martine's vantage point that all the tanks had stopped moving forward and they were now idling. She wondered why. Perhaps it was the British or Americans and they were about to be liberated without a fight. A sudden swoosh of joy thrilled through her. Oh, how wonderful that would be. She almost clapped her hands at the thought. Oh yes, that would be so wonderful. Then she saw one man in a helmet silhouetted against the lighter grey of a stone wall. *Germans.* Her heart crashed into the pit of her stomach again and fear replaced the joy.

Martine backed away from the window and crawled across her bedroom floor. She was terrified of being spotted, though she had no idea why. Panic was trying to get the upper hand, but this was not the moment to let it take over. She had to think what was best to do. She shut her eyes and pulled herself on to her bed, then sat down on the edge. Her hands grabbed the edge of her coverlet and she tried to make herself breathe slowly and evenly. The obvious course of action was for her and her father to hide in the cellar. But supposing the Germans found them there. She'd heard terrible stories about things they had done; since the fall of France, years back, the village had been rife with rumours about families disappearing or groups of people being shot because of the Maquis. They had got worse since the Allied invasion; now rumours of entire communities getting lined up and gunned down and whole trainloads of people vanishing had been circulating. From the start Martine had been inclined not to believe them and certainly not the latest scaremongering tales; the old women always exaggerated every story they passed on whether it was the size of someone's baby or the number of lovers the village slut had reputedly had. But it was difficult to be rational when the danger – however real or imagined – was at her gate. And with Otto in the root store her conscience was far from easy. Sitting on her bed wasn't going to help anyone. Her father needed to know what was happening. She had to tell him.

Martine ran to the door to her room and then shot across the corridor to bang on his door.

'Papa!" she yelled. No chance of being heard by the Germans over the throb of their tanks. She hammered with both fists and yelled at the top of her voice. She opened the door. *Merde*, the old soak was dead to the world. There he was, lying on his back, fully dressed, snoring his head off with spit dribbling down his cheek and into his ear. For a second Martine felt nothing but disgust. Perhaps she should leave him here to take his chances. But he was her father and her mother had loved him. Her mother wouldn't have wanted Martine to abandon him – no matter how much he deserved it. She strode over to the bed and shook him roughly.

'Wake up!' she yelled at him.

Jean-Paul opened a bleary bloodshot eye. '*Quoi?*'

'The Germans are here,' she yelled at him. 'Get up.'

Slowly Jean-Paul began to take stock. 'Wass tha' noise?' he slurred.

'I told you.' Martine was beside herself with fear and impatience. 'It's the Germans. It's their tanks you can hear.'

Jean-Paul rolled on his side and swung his feet off the bed. 'Don't be silly. Can't be.' He groaned and held his head.

Serve the old bugger right, thought Martine. She hoped his head was dreadful. 'Want a bet,' she shouted. 'There's dozens of them, all round the farm.'

Jean-Paul was now sitting upright but swaying. He rubbed his face with both his hands and sniffed loudly. 'They've probably come looking for that deserter of yours.' He staggered to his feet and stumbled to his window. Like Martine he opened the inner window and then cracked open one of the shutters. '*Merde alors, tu as raison.*'

'Of course I'm right,' said Martine sullenly. 'It's not the sort of thing you imagine, is it?' She was just about to ask her father what he thought they should do when a thunderous hammering came from the back door. Martine jumped. 'Oh my God!' she exclaimed.

Jean-Paul looked at her. 'One of us had better let the bastards in. If we don't, they'll just break the door down. The Boche will take what they want regardless.'

Martine looked at her father. She really didn't want to be the one to face them. Jean-Paul stared back at his daughter. After a few seconds, although to Martine it seemed an age, he said, 'I'll go.'

Martine sat on her father's bed as he opened the door and clumped down the wooden stairs. His footsteps were lost under the continuing rumble of the idling tank engines outside. The seconds, then the minutes, ticked past. Martine felt more and more anxious. What was happening? What were the Germans doing? Was her father all right? Supposing they had just taken him away – or worse …she wondered about creeping to the head of the stairs and seeing if she could get a glimpse of what was happening, but despite her worry and desperate need to find out what was happening to her father, she was so terrified she couldn't force herself to move off the bed. Her heart was pounding and her legs felt like mush. Memories of all the dire rumours that the old women had passed on flooded into her brain and Martine could only imagine what was going on below. She heard heavy footsteps approaching the top of the stairs. Dear God, they were coming for her now.

The door opened. It was her father. Martine sagged with relief.

'What's happening?' she managed to croak out of a completely dry mouth.

"They're requisitioning this farm,' her father responded tersely.

Martine shook her head in disbelief. 'They can't. What about us?'

Her father shrugged and sniffed loudly. 'They can do what they like. We can't stop them.'

'But the animals …?'

'They said we can shelter in the cellar if we want, but they won't be responsible for what happens. They are expecting fighting round here.'

Martine stared at her father. 'What option have we got? We have nowhere to go, and we can't abandon the cows.'

Her father looked at her sadly and shook his head. 'We can always buy more cows.'

Martine knew he had a point. She was a farm girl and had no great feelings of sentimentality towards the stock on the farm. They were there to provide food; but she had always been taught that the beasts should have decent lives until the time came for their slaughter. They had never allowed any of their animals to suffer and the thought that they might now was a hideous prospect. But if it was a choice between the cows and themselves, she knew the herd would come second. She felt sick. The poor dumb creatures didn't deserve this, but what could she do?

'Do you think we'll be safe in the cellar?'

Her father shrugged again. 'Who knows? I suppose we could stay in the village.'

'If there is going to be fighting, we'll be no better off there.'

'The church?'

But their cottage had stone walls almost as thick as the

church's. And they would have to walk there. Martine shook her head. 'I think we should stay here.' Besides, if they were *in situ* on the farm, they might be able to protect some of it. Martine knew it was a vain hope. If a battle was fought here, everything would probably get pulverised. People in the village had told her what Tilly looked like after the recent battle there. Not a house had been unscathed and most had been reduced to rubble. But the cellar might provide some sort of sanctuary.

Jean-Paul nodded. 'I agree. At least we will know what they are doing.' He briefly rested a hand on Martine's shoulder. 'We'd better get some things together to take with us. God alone knows how long we'll be stuck here.'

Martine nodded and went to her room. She grabbed some clothes, her Bible and a lamp. The clothes and the Bible she made into a bundle, but she carried the lamp carefully so as not to spill any of the precious paraffin. She met her father outside his room and together they went slowly down the stairs. At the bottom Martine gazed dumbfounded at the scene. All their furniture, with the exception of the big table, had been pushed back and the room was now filled with people and equipment. The Boche had only just arrived and already they had taken over completely. *The arrogance of these people*, thought Martine. Her mother's kitchen now resembled a barracks more than a home. Guns were stacked against the sink: there were piles of kitbags and canvas pouches in a corner and around the table were gathered half a dozen German officers, poring over a map. They barely glanced up at Martine and her father.

Martine thrust her bundle at her father and then handed him the lamp more carefully.

'Take these,' she said. He looked at her quizzically. 'We'll need food and water. I don't get the impression we will be able to come and go in the kitchen as we please.' Jean-Paul nodded. Martine, putting on an act of bravado that she certainly didn't feel, left her father to take their few bits and pieces to the cellar while she shouldered her way past the soldiers and went to the larder. Aware that a number of the men were watching her covertly she made herself ignore the glances and took the end of the previous day's loaf, a jug of milk and some vegetables. There had been a hunk of cheese on the shelf too, but that had already gone missing. She tried to remember what provisions there were in the cellar. She supposed there might be a few jars and pots of preserves remaining but she didn't think there was much. In fact, she seemed to remember that the last time she'd been to the cellar the shelves had been pretty well empty. When her mother had been alive and even after the start of the war the racks of shelves in the cool depths beneath the house had been loaded with potted meats, jams, preserved fruit, home-smoked hams and all manner of riches. As the war had ground on and the Germans had taken more and more of their fresh produce, they had been forced to rely increasingly on the stores in the cellar until they had virtually all gone. As each autumn arrived, Martine knew she ought to try to take advantage of nature's largesse, but there had never been enough time for her to gather blackberries from the hedgerows and hazelnuts from the coppice on the hill. And even if she had made time to forage for food, she knew she didn't have her mother's cooking skills. Her mother had started to teach her, but Martine had only been just twelve when her mother had contracted a chill, which had suddenly turned to pneumonia. Martine shook her head to clear away the memory of her mother's last days. She didn't have time right now for the luxury of grieving.

Martine tucked the jug of milk between her forearm and her body and balanced the plate of vegetables, with the bread on top. Then she took another large jug, went to the sink and filled it from the pail standing on the draining board.

As she stood with her back to the group of Germans, she heard one say, 'I bet she could make a man happy at night.'

There was a burst of lewd laughter followed by a couple of other similar comments. Martine froze by the sink; then she pulled herself together. It would do her no good at all to reveal she spoke German. Ignoring the men and shutting her ears to further bawdy remarks, she took her meagre supply of provisions to the cellar.

Jean-Paul had lit the lamp she had given him and a soft glow lit the cavernous space. He'd found a few empty sacks stacked in a corner and had laid them on the floor to make somewhere for them to lie on the beaten earth. Martine looked at the arrangements. *Grim*, she concluded, *but better than having to live with the Boche.*

'There's a bucket over there,' he said gruffly.

Martine nodded. She didn't want to dwell on the prospect of using it. She wandered over to the shelves that ran along one wall of the cellar, which had contained the culinary artistry of her mother while she had been alive. Martine found a couple of dusty preserving jars of beetroot and another containing cornichons. *Edible but not particularly nourishing*, she thought. The jams had long gone, along with the preserved fruit. She crouched down and checked the lower shelves in the hope that something more interesting than pickles remained. At the back was a pot with a glass lid and a clamp holding it fast to the rubber seal, Martine pulled it towards her, but even in the soft glow of the lamp she could see that whatever was contained in it was no longer going to be fit to eat: the contents were a vile green. Martine put it back on the shelf, not even contemplating opening it. Whatever was growing in there could stay in the jar.

The noise from outside grew in intensity again. The rumbling and the squealing made the air in the cellar shake. Dust fell from the joists in the ceiling and the spherical glass shade on the lamp vibrated. Martine lowered the wick, reducing the light still more so that the cellar was in virtual darkness, and climbed on an old packing case that was under one of the small lights that could be opened to let air circulate. She pulled away sacking blackout, fumbled for the catch and pulled the tiny window open, oblivious of the spiders' webs that hung around it. She pressed her face forward so as to get the best field of view possible, but with the window being at ground level she had a very limited one. However, she could see across the farmyard and was able to make out that several tanks had rumbled through the gate and were manoeuvring to take up positions. A couple of Germans strode across the yard as Martine watched and wrestled with the big crossbar that kept the huge double doors to the barn shut. Between them they managed to haul the big plank out of its wooden sockets. They dumped it on the ground to one side and then, taking a door each, they swung them both wide. Martine stood on the packing case aghast and unable to do anything. She instinctively knew what she was going to see next.

'What's going on?' asked her father. Martine swung round. Even in the almost non-existent light her father could see her pallor. 'Tell me,' he said.

Martine gulped. She glanced out of the little window once more to check. 'They're going to put tanks in the barn.'

Jean-Paul swore loudly and fluently. 'You'd best hope they don't find your deserter,' he said angrily. 'God knows what they'll do to us all if they find him.'

'What about what they'll do to Otto?' Martine was beside herself with worry.

Jean-Paul spat. What did he care? He flopped down on to the sacks and sat with his back against the cellar wall staring into space.

Through her spyhole Martine could see the German

soldiers exploring the farmyard, throwing open stable doors and poking around in the various outhouses. At one point she saw one soldier walk past with two pullets, both with their necks wrung. Martine wondered about telling her father, but what good would it do? The old man would only fly into a rage and might end up doing something rash – and just for the sake of a few hens. Martine imagined the pig might have met the same fate as the chickens.

Her attention was whisked away from the matter of the pig by a burst of activity in the barn. A young soldier came running out of the big double doors at full pelt and from behind him Martine could hear shouts and yells, then a shot. Her heart stopped. *No. No. Please, God, no*!

The Field Hospital

George lay awake, listening to the noises of the night. His shoulder ached abominably and the wounds in his legs throbbed. If he hadn't slept for so much of the day he would probably be able to sleep now. He knew he could ask for a painkiller or something to help him to sleep, but the night nurse who had taken over from the delectable Nurse Armitage had made him feel a bit of a baby. *All a bit unfair*, he thought; she'd asked him how he was and he'd told her. He hadn't expected her to reply rather briskly that, compared to many in the hospital, he was one of the lucky ones and some of the really badly wounded weren't making a fuss. George had felt completely nettled by this response – it hadn't been what he'd been expecting at all. And he hadn't been making a fuss – he'd just told her he felt rough. All he'd wanted was a little tea and sympathy. And now, despite the ache in his shoulder, the last person he felt like summoning to his bedside was her. *Mean old bag*, he thought.

Outside the tent the sounds of war and battle drifted

through the night air. In the distance he could hear the sporadic crump of heavy artillery. It was the glass upturned on the open neck of the decanter of water by his bed that made him realise that some big push was taking place on the front line. Some other noise, some steady drone setting up an unheard and unfelt vibration in the air, set the glass rattling against the water container. George turned his head a fraction to watch the St Vitus's dance of the tumbler. He wondered what was causing it; not the traffic, that was obvious. For some reason George thought that the atmosphere had suddenly become oppressive with menace.

He became aware of the noise so slowly it almost seemed surreal. The chinking of his glass was slowly subsumed by an almost imperceptible hum. The hum grew to a drone, then a throb and finally a roar as tens upon tens of aircraft swept over the field hospital. Next to him, Max woke up.

'What on earth ...?' he said.

At least that was what George assumed he said as his words were completely drowned out by the din. George shook his head. 'Big raid!' he yelled back.

Max raised his eyebrows. 'No kidding.'

Nurse Battleaxe bustled into the tent and began checking on her charges. By now all the patients were awake. She took pulses and temperatures, straightened their bedclothes, offered water to the thirsty and pills to the feverish and still the planes roared overhead. She was just getting to George when the racket finally began to abate.

'And how are we?' she asked, her face so close to George's ear he could see the small sprouting of whiskers on her chin.

'I'm all right,' he replied. 'But I don't know about you.'

Nurse Battleaxe sniffed and dropped his wrist. Obviously she wasn't in possession of a great sense of humour.

'You made an enemy there,' said Max as they watched her affronted back view sail out of the tent.

'No loss,' said George. 'Besides we'll be out of here in a day or two.'

'You'd better hope so.'

George realised he might have been somewhat foolish to upset the old biddy, especially considering his vulnerable position. *Oh well*, he mused, if Nurse Battleaxe hurt him, he could always ask Nurse Delectable to kiss it better. Comforted by that thought, he settled down to try to sleep again.

'What do you think the target is?' asked Max.

Max, thought George, had been snoring his head off for half the night and obviously felt rested. *Well, bully for him.* All George wanted was to lie quietly and fall asleep, not while away the rest of the night chatting and speculating.

'Dunno,' he mumbled back, not opening his eyes.

'They're going to get a pasting.'

'Hmmm.'

'Caen?'

'Maybe.'

'I thought you fly-boys would have an idea of what we need to take next.'

'Not me. I go where I'm sent.'

Max lapsed into silence. In the distance, whatever the planes had been heading for seemed to be getting the pasting Max had predicted. A sustained, throaty crashing and rumbling made the decanter and tumbler chink again. George sighed. *Fat chance of any sleep now.*

La Ferme de la Source

Martine bit on the knuckle of her index finger to stop herself from crying out, but she couldn't stop two large tears trickling down her face as she saw a group of soldiers emerge from the barn and drag a limp body across the yard. Jean-Paul saw the wet tracks down his daughter's face and frowned.

'What's happening?' he asked. 'What are they doing to the farm?'

Martine shook her head. She didn't dare speak. If she did she knew she would break down completely.

'What is it? Is it the pig?' Jean-Paul was fond of the creature too. Again Martine shook her head, but two more tears rolled down her face. Jean-Paul stood up from where he'd been sitting and pushed Martine away from the window. 'Here, let me look.' Martine stepped off the packing case to make way for her father, but as he was that much taller than she he was able to see out of the window just by standing on his toes. He pushed his face against the tiny space and Martine could tell from the way his shoulders slumped that he'd seen what was going on. But he wasn't concerned about what was happening to Otto; he was worried about the repercussions that might befall them. He swore softly and crudely.

'You stupid cow,' he said, shaking his head. 'You stupid, stupid cow.' He moved back to the sacks and slumped down again.

Martine sat on the corner of the packing case. 'I'm sorry,' she said. She wasn't sure if she was saying sorry for what she had done to them or what she had done to Otto.

'Sorry? Well that's a big help. "Sorry" is going to make all the difference. "Sorry" is bound to stop us from being shipped off to a labour camp. Or worse,' he added ominously.

'I didn't mean …'

Her father looked up with an expression verging on hatred on his face. 'Didn't mean? *Didn't mean?* What were you thinking about? I knew I should have shot him rather than let you hide the bloody man in the store.'

Martine lowered her head and studied her hands. *What have I done?* she thought. Otto was dead and it was her fault. If only she hadn't suggested that he should desert. He probably would never have thought of it, left to himself. Or if he had, he wouldn't have suggested coming to their farm and so putting them in danger too. She had killed Otto, just as if she had shot him. It was all her fault. And now she'd put her father in danger too. She didn't care about what was going to happen to herself. With Otto dead she didn't care now whether she survived the war or not. In fact, she didn't want to.

They sat in silence for several minutes, each wrapped up in their own thoughts. The sound of jackboots on the stairs, which Martine was expecting, failed to materialise. Perhaps Otto had managed to say something before they shot him that had led the Germans to believe that she and her father weren't implicated. A tiny ember of hope began to glimmer somewhere inside Martine. She brushed her tears off her cheeks and wiped her nose on the back of her hand.

'Perhaps they won't shoot us,' she said.

Her father raised his eyebrows and shook his head in disbelief. 'Haven't you listened to anything when you've been down at the shop? Haven't you paid any attention to what has been going on since the bloody Boche invaded?'

'But …' Martine began.

'There's no buts. Just because that sodding Kraut has brainwashed you doesn't mean the rest of us are blind, deaf and stupid. They've wiped out whole villages, the bastards; men, women and nippers, all lined up against walls and mown down.' Jean-Paul saw Martine start to open her mouth. 'And don't tell me it's just propaganda because it isn't, young lady. So, if they've got a mind to shoot us, they will. You'd best hope that the Allies get here in the next couple of hours; otherwise I think we've had it.'

Her guilt about Otto's fate plus the awfulness of their situation, coupled with shattering tiredness and the fact that Martine was blaming herself entirely for the current state of events, was too much for the girl and she was overwhelmed with misery. Wave after wave of sobs racked her as she sat, perched on the case, until even her father had to put aside his feelings of betrayal and anger and was moved to stand up and give her a hug. Rather than comforting her, though, this just caused an even more desperate flood of tears and wails and Jean-Paul found his eyes pricking with tears of sympathy too. She was heartbroken and scared and no father would have been able to stand by unmoved by such a burden on his only daughter. Despite Jean-Paul's loathing of Martine's relationship with Otto, to see his daughter suffering so was tearing him apart too.

Another sound began to permeate through the walls of the cellar –a deep, rumbling drone. Slowly it also began to penetrate the consciousness of the two occupants. *Aircraft.* Martine looked up. She was used to the sound since the invasion. Every day, sometimes several times a day, a large formation of aircraft would fly over the area on its way to bomb some target or other. But even in her misery and fear Martine realised that this didn't sound like anything she'd heard before. Either there was an awful lot of planes, or they were very low, or possibly both.

The thundering roar of the Allied aircraft grew louder and louder until Martine thought that she would be driven mad by the noise. It invaded every particle of her being and it was such that she couldn't even form thoughts in her head as the cacophony seemed to even deafen what she was trying to say to herself.

She almost fell off her perch when the door to the cellar burst open and a couple of German soldiers entered. They stood either side of the doorway; then two more soldiers appeared, dragging Otto's body between them. Nothing was said, and even if it had been, no one would have heard a word over the racket going on. Martine stood up to run towards her lover, but instantly one of the soldiers threatened her with his gun and Martine froze. Otto was thrown to the floor and then the four soldiers left. As soon as they had gone Martine ran over to Otto, tears streaming down her face once again at the sight of him in his blood-stained tunic. She turned him over so she could kiss his poor dead face and then she lay down beside him and rested her head on his chest, heedless of the blood.

At first she thought she'd imagined it. Under her right ear Otto's chest was moving. Martine lay perfectly still and waited to see if she had imagined or mistaken this movement. How could it be so when he was dead? There – there it was again. Otto's chest was moving. He was breathing. Martine leapt up and knelt beside him, grabbing his wrist.

'He's alive. Papa, he's alive!' she yelled, hoping to be heard over the roar of the planes overhead. She felt for Otto's pulse. She fumbled about trying to locate the right spot and finally she was rewarded with a tiny little beat under her fingertips.

Jean-Paul looked on, bewildered. But his daughter's face was suddenly aglow. She'd gone from utter misery to joy in a matter of seconds. For a moment or two he couldn't work out what was going on. Then he realised.

Martine was unbuttoning Otto's tunic to see the extent of his injuries. Obviously he'd been shot and had lost blood, but she couldn't see how bad his wound was. Gently she peeled back his jacket, sticky with drying blood, and revealed the puncture wound the bullet had made. Superficially it didn't look too bad, but Martine wondered what damage the bullet had done internally. She untucked her shirt from her trousers and ripped a hunk of material off; then she packed it over the wound and put Otto's jacket back over to hold the wad in place. The bleeding seemed to have mostly stopped and Martine's actions were more out of a sense that she should be doing something to tend him rather than a real purpose or knowledge. Having done that, she sat on the beaten-earth floor next to him and patted his hand, willing him to hang on until the Allies could get to the farm. She felt rather than heard the first wave of bombing. The ground she was sitting on seemed to shudder and tremble and for a second she almost felt as if the earth under her was rippling like water and she was bobbing on the surface like a small boat. The sensation was so peculiar she couldn't work out what on earth was going on. After several seconds the feeling stopped, but then it came again and this time with more violence. Martine held Otto's hand even tighter and looked to her father for some sort of reassurance. He left where he was sitting and moved next to her, then gathered her to him as he had when she was small and needed comfort. He stroked her hair with his free hand as the thumps from the falling bombs made the pair of them feel as though some giant force was kicking the structure of the house. Martine was too scared to scream or cry. She was certain that this was how they were all going to die and part of her was praying to God to take her and get it over with. She was terrified of pain but found the idea of death itself strangely acceptable. It had only been a couple of days ago that she had longed for her mother's presence again. Perhaps she was about to get her wish. The thought of her mother comforted Martine somewhat and despite the continuing raid she calmed slightly and loosened her grip on Otto's hand. As she did so, she realised that the hellish pounding was beginning to fade. The thumps and bangs were becoming less continuous and they weren't as close, and the sound of the aircraft was slowly diminishing. Was it over? Had she survived? Perhaps they were all going to make it.

Fourteen

First Light, Monday 26 June 1944

South-east of Brouay

David could see the aerial bombardment a mile or so ahead of his position. 'Armageddon' was the only word he could think of that might even come close to describing the hell that he was witnessing. The noise was indescribable –from the roar overhead of the dozens and dozens of planes to the ear-shattering crump and blast as the bombs dropped on to the enemy positions below. The horizon was lit by shell bursts and fires and black smoke wreathed amongst the flames like demonic spirits. Underneath him the ground shook and trembled. On either flank the artillery were adding their two penn'orth to the mayhem and so all around David huge orange flashes were blossoming like some sort of demented flower display. He glanced at his watch. Only a matter of minutes now before the barrage was due to stop and he and his men would get the signal to go forward. He prayed inwardly that when they advanced it wasn't going to be a rerun of a Great War battle – brave men obeying orders and marching unwaveringly into a hailstorm of machine-gun bullets. He didn't think he could bear to have such slaughter on his conscience.

David couldn't tell if his jelly-like insides were due to the shock waves from the detonations blasting over him or blind fear. He knew he would do his duty. He would lead his men; he would hold his head up and walk forward; he would not cower and quail; but he had no illusions about what might await him. And he knew he feared not dying, but dying badly.

The waves of aircraft began to diminish; the barrage petered out. David looked at his watch again. *Any minute now.* He shut his eyes and prayed silently to God that if it was preordained that he was to die then, please, might hedie quickly and cleanly. Was that so much to ask? he wondered. Overhead a red flare burst. This was it.

He was not supposed to go forward with his men. His three companies were adequately commanded by their own officers and David's role was to be in overall command and control from the rear, but his sense of loyalty to his men had led him to the private decision that, whatever they were going to face, so was he. He would be in amongst his men. It was only fair.

The artillery barrage continued as his men hauled themselves out of the hedges and ditches where they had been sheltering and began to creep forward. The guns blasted and crashed to their left and right and the sound of heavy machine-guns punctuated any momentary gaps in the racket with their staccato bursts of drumming. Ahead and to his right David saw the bright-red stitching of tracer heading lazily in the direction of his men. He knew that the laziness of the stream was an illusion and that dozens of rounds were spaced between each spark of light, each bullet capable of killing or maiming. On his immediate right hand there was a mortar section. He threw himself to the ground and crawled towards them.

'Sir,' said the corporal in charge, looking a touch stunned as David suddenly appeared next to him.

'Over there!' yelled David over the racket of the assault. He pointed at the source of the tracer.

Needing no further instructions the mortar section took a bearing and the loader dropped a bomb down the tube. There was a second's pause, then a tinny clonk and a whoosh. The mortar sailed into the air towards the

Germans. David watched the machine-gun post intently, willing the mortar to land on it. The explosion happened nowhere near. *Damn – short.* The mortar section adjusted the trajectory a fraction and dropped another bomb down the tube. *Failed again.* This time it was to the left. A second adjustment and a third mortar launched. *Yes!* The plume of soil subsided and the smoke drifted away. David looked again. Maybe not a direct hit, but it was pretty bloody close.

The Colonel picked himself up off the ground and ran forward at a crouching run, covering the ground between himself and the German machine-gun in under a minute. He noticed as he ran that a squad of soldiers taking cover at the edge of a field of wheat also joined him. David dropped to the ground about twenty yards short of the position and signalled the men to do the same.

'Allow me, sir,' said a voice at his shoulder. David heard the ping of a grenade pin being pulled and then saw a tennisball-sized object being lobbed with supreme accuracy at the trench. David instantly pressed his face into the soft, wet earth of the field and held his tin hat on firmly. A couple of seconds later the blast wave crashed over him and clods of earth splattered his helmet and back. Tentatively he looked up and saw the muzzle of the MG34 pointing skywards and a smudge of dirty-looking smoke drifting out of the dugout. David leapt up again and ran to the edge of the position. One glance told him the poor buggers weren't going to cause him or his troops any more trouble. He looked away again and swallowed. God, war was grim.

David looked around at the advance of his battalion across the French countryside. He watched his men progress along the margins of the fields, jinking from one area of cover to the next as they slowly but steadily made their way forward. Sometimes they would be pinned down for a while by a German position lurking somewhere in the surrounding countryside, but their advance was relentless. David's fears about his men being decimated like the troops at Ypres and the Somme receded. He began to move forward himself, keeping low, trying not to provide an easy target to be picked off by a sniper waiting for a laggard such as himself. He followed the example of his soldiers and kept to the shelter of the hedges and the undergrowth in the field margins and worked his way forward towards the shallow valley bottom.

To his right he could see a vast array of tanks of the infantry brigade attacking their objective and in amongst them bustled infantry men of another battalion. Thousands of men were involved in this attack and David drew comfort from the numbers he could see. Surely nothing could withstand such an onslaught. Surely the attack would prevail.

David looked at the farm, assessing how he would deploy his troops around it once they had taken it. The briefing from Brigade Headquarters had implied that the place was going to be relatively easy to take and certainly the way the battle had gone so far it seemed as though it was going to be the case. David raised his binoculars to get a better look at the arrangement of the main farm building and its outhouses. He had just got the focus adjusted to his satisfaction when he thought he saw a glint of watery sunlight reflecting off something metallic behind the barn. David looked again. Perhaps he had been mistaken.

The metallic gleam began to change shape. Slowly a large, dark, curved silhouette began to loom forwards from behind the wall of the farmyard. It looked like a tank, but how on earth had the armoured brigade got so far ahead? David couldn't work it out. And what was more, there was something not quite right about the tank. David's fingers tightened on his binoculars until his knuckles were shining white against the black metal. It was a tank all right, but not one of theirs. Good God, it was a Panzer! But Brigade had told him there weren't any in this region. He'd drawn up orders for this attack and sent his men forward, working on the theory that the worst they could come up against was infantry like themselves. But armour was a whole different issue. David scanned the rest of the farm complex and spotted several others. He moved his attention to the woods behind the farm, but the summer foliage was too dense for him to be able to discern anything hidden in it. How many more were there? he wondered. Ten? Twenty? Or were the ones he could see the sum total of the German armour? However, it didn't matter to David whether there were four or twenty-four. A feeling of sick helplessness gripped him. His men, lightly armed, were heading directly towards some of the most deadly weaponry in the German arsenal.

As he watched, he saw a puff of black smoke belch from the muzzle of one of the tanks and then a section of pasture some half a mile in front of it disappear in a shattering explosion. The soldiers who had been advancing across that bit of field had simply disappeared.

David dropped his binos on to his chest and ran back to the mortar section. He needn't have bothered: the section were way ahead of him and had already moved the weapon to target the farm. David put his binos to his eyes again to check the fall of the mortars. He focused on the farm again and saw a fountain of earth erupt from just in front of the barn. Then the whole barn appeared to move. David was perplexed: the mortar hadn't been close enough to bring a structure of that size down. As he watched, the whole wooden back wall of the barn crashed forward and a further two tanks emerged from the shadow. Then the roof of the barn collapsed sideways in a great cloud of dust and debris. As the dust cleared, David was able to see that there were at least a dozen tanks hidden round the farm buildings, maybe more. *Good God*! he thought, his soldiers were facing slaughter.

The aerial bombardment might have ceased, but the crashes and thumps still persisted.

'Artillery,' her father said. Martine recognised the sound too. God only knew, they'd heard enough of it in the distance over the last couple of weeks to get used to the eerie whistles of the shells passing overhead, followed by the crump of the shell landing. This time, though, the shells were landing round about the farm and the blast and noise were quite hellish.

Martine pulled Otto's head on to her lap so she could stroke his forehead and hold him close. She felt completely helpless and useless. There was nothing she could do to help him: she had no nursing skills, no medicines; she didn't have even the most basic of first-aid equipment, but she hoped that he was aware of her presence and that that might help him to survive. She willed her strength to become his strength, her health to transfer to him. All she could do was watch and pray and wait. His breathing seemed steady and the bleeding appeared to have stopped. If they could all just survive the battle and the next few hours, there was hope.

Rhythmically, automatically, Martine stroked Otto's forehead with one hand while the other clasped his fingers. It was the merest fluttering of fingertips that Martine detected at first – hardly more than a pulse. She glanced down at her lover, but he was still deathly white and motionless. Then she felt his hand move again. This time there was definite pressure on her fingers. She lifted his hand to her lips and kissed it.

'Darling Otto,' she whispered, 'stay strong. Don't leave me.'

Otto opened his eyes and looked at her.

'Oh, *Liebling*,'' she said. 'You'll be all right soon. As soon as the British get here, you'll be safe.'

Otto tried to smile, but instead he winced and groaned. 'The bastards came looking for food in the store. They found me instead.'

'Don't try to talk,' Martine said. She kissed his hand again and stroked his forehead.

'What's he on about?' asked her father.

Martine said, 'Nothing, really. He said that the soldiers were looking for food and discovered him.'

'Bah,' said her father, still unable to feel anything for the man his daughter so obviously adored.

Outside, the battle continued and the trio sat or lay in silence, each wondering about what the immediate future might hold for them and trying to keep their fear under control.

The door crashed open yet again without warning. Martine jumped in shock and every nerve in her body tensed in involuntary fear. A tall man dressed in black SS coveralls strode in. Behind him followed a more junior officer, similarly dressed but distinctly lacking the presence of his superior.

'So,' the senior officer said, 'I am Obersturmbannführer Peiper.' He turned to look at Otto. 'And this must be the deserter.' He drew his leg back to aim a kick at Otto's leg.

'Don't,' shouted Martine in German. She lifted Otto's head off her lap and leapt to her feet to stand between him and his aggressor.

Peiper stopped the kick in mid-swing and stared at her, his eyes narrowed. 'My, my, Kowal,' he said, turning to his adjutant, 'I didn't think Norman peasants could speak a civilised language. Why can you?'

Martine refused to answer.

Peiper stepped forward and slapped her hard across her face. 'When I ask you a question, you answer.'

Pain rammed through her ear and jaw. She swayed under the force of the stinging blow but managed to remain standing. Martine heard her father bellow with rage and saw Kowal step forward to restrain him. *Please God,* she thought, *please don't let Father do anything rash and get us shot.* She swallowed and, despite her cheek burning with pain and the taste of blood in her mouth, she said steadily, 'My mother came from Alsace.'

'And then she decided to slum it in France.'

Martine stared at him defiantly, her hands on her hips, but didn't rise to the bait.

'So, this might explain why this scum was hiding out in the barn. You decided you wanted a decent German dick between your legs, isn't that so? – and you managed to seduce this cretin?'

Jean-Paul might not have understood a word that Peiper said, but he perfectly caught the gist of what was being implied. 'She had nothing to do with it,' he interrupted, also struggling to his feet. 'It was all my idea.'

Kowal quickly translated Jean-Paul's outburst into German.

Peiper swung round to the old man. 'Shut up,' he snarled. He picked up the pitcher of water Martine had brought from the kitchen earlier. He threw the contents over Otto's face, then he gave Kowal a signal and the pair of them heaved Otto to his feet then sat him on the packing case under the tiny window.

Otto's dripping face was contorted with pain and Martine noticed that the wad of fabric she'd pressed against his wound earlier was now bright with blood. She moved to his side to support him, hoping that he might be able to draw some strength from her.

'What a touching scene,' said Peiper, thrusting his face into Otto's. 'So, whose idea was it? Yours or the whore's?'

'Leave the girl and the old man out of it,' said Otto in a barely audible voice. 'They had nothing to do with it. They didn't even know I was in the barn.'

Peiper let out a mirthless laugh and slapped his thigh. 'Oh, really. My, my, the Wehrmacht *is* resourceful these days. So resourceful, in fact, that you were able to conceal the entrance to the store room from under the trapdoor. How did you manage that, eh?' He laughed his sinister laugh again and Kowal joined in. 'So you are not only a yellow, cowardly deserter, you are a liar too. My God, I know the Wehrmacht is desperate to take any old rubbish, but even they don't need the dregs that you represent. You are an insult to your country and your uniform, but most of all you are an insult to the Führer.' And with that Peiper drew his pistol from his holster and shot Otto through the centre of his forehead. The bang of the shot in such a confined space was deafening. It was so quick, so sudden, Martine could scarcely believe it. It was unreal.

The bullet entered Otto's head right between his eyes, leaving a neat black hole about the diameter of a pencil; but, as it travelled, the cartilage and tissue that it smashed through caused it to tumble, so by the time it reached the back of his head it took half of the skull with it as it exited. Blood and brains sprayed over the cellar wall and Martine's face. She was so transfixed with horror and fear she didn't even wipe the mess off herself. Then she realised that she could hear someone screaming. When the second vicious blow arrived, she knew it was her. The stunning force of the punch sent her reeling and shocked back to silence. Pain crashed in her head, her teeth jarred and blood burst into her mouth. She slumped down on to the packing case so that she was almost lying across Otto's body. 'No, no,' she said as she fell across him, not wanting to believe what was happening.

'You bastards,' yelled Jean-Paul, devastated by what he had just witnessed. Peiper swung round, levelled his gun at shoulder height once more and fired again. Jean-Paul was dead before he hit the ground.

This time Martine was too shocked to even whimper.

She stared dumbfounded, first at the body of Otto and then at the body of her father. She waited, head bowed, for the crashing finality of a bullet through her skull, but none came. Slowly she raised her head. Peiper was looking at her.

'You see,' he said, 'I am not entirely without compassion. I have decided not to shoot you. Besides, with your language skills I might be able to find a use for you.'

The door to the cellar opened and a young soldier entered. He whipped up a salute. 'Obersturmbannführer Peiper, the enemy is advancing. You're needed upstairs.' Then the young soldier's eyes began to travel round the cellar as he saw the bloody remains of Otto and Jean-Paul.

'Shot while trying to escape,' said Peiper, casually. 'Isn't that so, Kowal?'

'Absolutely, sir,' replied his adjutant loyally.

'Yes, sir,' said the soldier as he exited.

'And it is what will happen to you if you move from this place. Language skills or not. Understand?'

Martine nodded, hardly daring to breathe, and watched them go. The door closed and she was alone with the bodies.

Outside it was growing light and the battle seemed to be getting fiercer and fiercer. The tanks had now opened fire and huge reverberating explosions echoed off the walls of the farmyard. Martine picked up her Bible from the floor and curled up in a comer of the cellar. She didn't care if she lived or died; she was numb with shock, horror and grief to the extent that she was beyond tears. Death or rescue – she was indifferent.

Fifteen

Early Morning, Monday 26 June 1944

44 Selkirk Street, Havant

Nan Viney stood in front of the mirror in her cramped hall and adjusted her hat. Carefully she tucked in a few stray strands of hair under the shapeless brown-felt creation; then she picked up her handbag and gas mask and left the house, slamming the panelled door with its stained glass firmly shut behind her. Tibbs watched his mistress go along the crazy-paving path to the front gate from his vantage point in the parlour window.

Nan walked purposefully down the road towards the bus stop. Her age and girth dictated the speed at which she could progress and since her days for running for buses had long since passed, she always made sure she had plenty of time in hand to catch the seven thirty. Tucked safely in her handbag was her latest letter to Bill and she had every intention of posting it at the box near the corner shop. Puffing very slightly, Mrs Viney neared her destination; but as she did so, she was taken by a board outside the shop.

"*Normandy Latest!*" screamed large black letters.

'Oh my,' said Mrs Viney under her breath. 'Normandy latest,' she said to herself. She wondered what was happening over there – and she *needed* to know, now she knew her Bill was there. As a rule, Nan wasn't a great one for the papers and gleaned most of her knowledge of world events from the newsreels during her weekly trip to the picture house. She sometimes glanced at Mrs Clarke's copy of *Picture Post*, but papers were another thing: all that small print and so few pictures. Reading had never been her strong point.

Taking her purse out of her bag, she walked determinedly into the shop and picked up a copy of the *Daily Sketch*. She paid and walked out again, already reading the caption under a graphic picture of some British troops relaxing by a burnt-out German tank. It didn't say which unit they belonged to or exactly where they were fighting, but it made Nan feel better to think that these chaps looked cheerful and well-fed, all smiling and laughing for the cameras, fags hanging out of the corners of their mouths, as if they were on a day trip to the country. Grubby, she noticed, but smiling – that was the important thing. Why they almost looked as if they were having a really good time. Perhaps that was how the war was for her Bill. Nan made her way to the bus stop still engrossed in the story on the front page of what the 'brave British squaddies' had been up to in Northern France, occasionally glancing up to make sure she wasn't bumping into another pedestrian and completely forgetting about the letter tucked safely in her bag – until she'd climbed on to the bus and was halfway to her destination.

'Oh dash it,' she muttered angrily, folding the paper up and laying it on her lap. And there wasn't a post box anywhere near where Mrs Clarke lived. She'd have to wait to post it on her way home now. That's if she didn't forget it a second time. She shook her head, annoyed with herself. Still, no use crying over spilt milk.

When she arrived at her stop, Nan tucked her paper under her arm – she'd have another read of it with her mid-morning cuppa – and walked up the hill to Orchard Cottage. Twice on the journey Nan had to pause and get her breath and both times she wished Mrs Clarke lived somewhere without quite so much of a view.

By the time she arrived at the cottage she was ready for a sit down. Letting herself into the kitchen, she tottered on to one of the wooden chairs and plumped down heavily. After a couple of minutes she felt recovered enough to get the kettle on. She took off her coat and hat, hung them along with her bag and gas mask on the hook behind the door and slipped her pinny on over her head. Then she took the letter out of her bag and laid it on top of her paper on the draining board so as to remind her to post it on the way home; she didn't want to forget it a second time. Five minutes later she had the previous night's supper dishes stacked in the sink, a pot of tea brewing and had made a start on scrubbing the kitchen table. Engrossed in her work, she didn't hear Gwen come down the stairs.

'Morning, Mrs Viney,' said Mrs Clarke cheerfully. 'Oh, is that tea in the pot fresh?'

Mrs Viney started and slopped water from the pail she was dipping her scrubbing brush into on to the floor. 'Ooh, you gave me a turn there. Miles away, I was.'

'Sorry.'

Mrs Viney busied herself pouring tea for them both, but as she did she glanced up at her employer. *Shameless hussy*, she thought. *Fancy a well-brought-up lady like her having a fancy man.* The thought made her cross and without thinking she banged the cup and saucer down rather hard in front of where Gwen was sitting, lighting up her first cigarette of the day. Gwen looked up and met Mrs Viney's eye.

'Thank you,' she said coolly.

Gwen took another drag on her ciggie. She knew full well what had got into Mrs Viney, but she wasn't going to give the old bat the satisfaction of letting her see how worried she was that Mrs Viney had found out about her and George. Never apologise, never explain – that was the ticket.

'Heard from Sergeant Viney recently?' Gwen asked.

'Not since that last letter, saying he was off to France.' Gwen didn't miss the brusque tone. Mrs Viney was cross and no mistake.

Mrs Viney finished the table and turned her attention to the dishes in the sink. Before she made a start on them she picked up her paper and the letter lying on the top and put them on the dresser.

'Oh is that today's paper?' And before Mrs Viney could say anything Gwen had walked across to it and picked it up. The letter to Sergeant Viney fell on to the kitchen floor. Gwen bent down and picked it up. 'I'll post this for you on my way into Portsmouth if you like.'

'No, it's all right. I'll do it on my way home.'

'Don't be silly. You'll miss the last post if you do that. It'll be no trouble. Anyway, it'll probably get there quicker if it goes from the main post office.' Mrs Viney's back view spoke volumes and Gwen knew she was in even more of a huff. It was obvious she didn't want Gwen to post the letter, but there was no excuse she could make against Gwen's impeccable reasoning. *And why don't you want me to get my paws on your letter?* thought Gwen, though she was certain she knew. She put thoughts of what Mrs Viney's letter might contain out of her mind as she scanned the front page, drank her tea and finished her cigarette. Taking a last drag, she stubbed it out in a saucer and went upstairs to get dressed, taking the letter with her. She wasn't going to take the chance of leaving it downstairs for Mrs Viney to put back into her handbag. Once it was back in there, that would be it.

She sat at the dressing table and stared at the envelope as she tapped it thoughtfully on the knuckles of her other hand. Mrs Viney had told her often enough that she wasn't much of a correspondent and only wrote to her Bill once a week. And if Gwen's memory served her right, that was a task that she saved for Tuesday afternoon, on her day off. So it didn't take much effort to work out why she had taken it upon herself to write again. *Damn*. The last thing Gwen wanted was Mrs Viney spilling the beans to her husband. Once Sergeant Viney knew, there was no telling who else he would pass a juicy bit of gossip about the CO's wife on to – or how fast.

Quickly she got dressed, dabbed on a little powder, applied some lipstick and ran downstairs again. Picking up her handbag and gas mask from the hall table she darted into the kitchen to grab her customary slice of bread and marge to eat as she cycled down the bill.

'See,' she said waving the letter. 'It's safe in my bag and I promise I won't forget to pop it in the first letter box I pass in Pompey.' Or maybe I won't, she added to herself.

Gwen suppressed a smile as she saw the look of annoyance pass across her daily's face. 'Must dash or I'llbe late.'

She crammed her uniform hat on her head and waved as she almost skipped out of the back door to get her bike from the garden where it lived.

'I'll spike her guns,' she muttered as she began pedalling.

Halfway down the hill Gwen braked in a farm gateway and dismounted. She leaned her bike against the gatepost and pulled the letter from her bag. Oh boy, Mrs Viney hadn't sealed it. If all was innocent, nothing incriminating, Gwencould drop it in a letter box as she had promised. Of course, if it wasn't …

Gwen scanned the letter quickly; Mrs Viney's round hand was as easy to read as print.

"The Colonel's lady is having an affair," she read.

"I don't know who with but I know for definite she's <u>seeing</u> someone. Don't ask me <u>how</u> I know, but I do. I know it is none of my business,"

Too damn right it isn't, thought Gwen.

"but I know how much you respect the Colonel
and I want some advice. Also I am not sure I want
to go on working for her when I know what she is
getting up to now the Colonel is out the way.
Do you think I should hand in my notice?
Or maybe you think I should say nothing."

Gwen let the letter fall to the ground, then she hurriedly picked it up. *Damn, damn, damn.* Now what should she do? Well one thing was for sure: Sergeant Viney wasn't going to get to hear about the goings-on in her bedroom. Angrily Gwen screwed the letter into a ball and shoved it back into her bag. She'd bury it in the pig-swill bucket when she got into work.

La Ferme de la Source

Outside the farmhouse, guns crashed, shells exploded and a battle was being fiercely fought while Martine lay huddled in the corner of the cellar clutching her Bible and waiting for death to finally take her. What did life hold for her? Her parents were dead, the only man she'd ever cared about was dead, her farm was being destroyed and all the animals were probably dead or injured. The future held no hope; the past consisted only of misery and drudgery. Death would be welcome. As each shell whistled towards the house Martine willed it to crash through the roof and obliterate her house and her life. *With luck*, she thought, *it will take that bastard who shot her father and Otto with it too.* Obersturmbannführer Peiper would rot in hell – that was certain; but it gave her no comfort. Hell was too good for him. She tried to imagine somewhere worse than hell but could only see a place that resembled where she was right now: a place of death, suffering, fear and despair.

Obersturmbannführer Peiper: a name that she would curse every time she thought about it for as long as she lived. She would pray for his damnation every hour of every day that she drew breath, she thought. If there was any justice, if there was a God, he would make sure Peiper died very shortly. *But what if he didn't*? thought Martine. What if Peiper survived the war? Who would make sure that he was tried and convicted of murder? Martine wondered if anyone would take the word of a French farm girl against that of a colonel? *Pah*, she thought, *probably not*.

She sat up, her legs outstretched on the cold earth floor, her back against the cellar wall, the Bible on her lap. With her hands clasped on the Bible she shut her eyes and made a promise. If she was spared this war she would make it her life's work to make sure that, if Peiper happened to survive it too, he would get what he deserved. One way or another she would make sure that Otto's and her father's deaths were avenged.

Near La Ferme de la Source

David neared the rear positions of his troops. The cacophony around him was overwhelming, with shattering blasts of high explosives, yells, shouts, the sharp crackle of rifle fire, the rattling and drumming of machine-guns. The smell of war hung heavy over the area; smoke mixed with cordite, wet earth, crushed grass, fear and chemicals. The first time David had come across it on a live firing exercise in South Wales he had been instantly transported back to bonfire nights as a child. But this was no pleasurable entertainment; this was a deadly business – kill or be killed – and the shouts and cries were not the oohs and aahs of a delighted audience but cries of pain and fear and desperation.

He could see to his left that one of his companies was making a flanking manoeuvre to get round to the north of the farmhouse and that some of his forward troops were almost within range to attack the tanks with PIATs. The trouble was that a heavy machine-gun had been set up in one of the upstairs windows of the farm building and the fire that it was laying down was proving an almost insurmountable barrier for his men to overcome. Until the machine-gun had been neutralised, getting any closer than they were was going to be nigh on impossible, as it hosed out streams of bullets like some sort of lethal fire tender, across the fields around the farm. Luckily the long grass in the pastures, the waist-high wheat and the thick hedges were providing reasonable cover, but they provided no protection against speeding chunks of metal and high explosives. With bullets flying indiscriminately and with the tanks firing randomly in the general direction of David's men they were bound to inflict some casualties even if they weren't aiming at specific targets. Gouts of soil were thrown up every few seconds, accompanied by gut-churning bangs and crumps, and behind this was a constant rattle of the heavy and light machine-guns firing. Now and again, David could hear shouts and cries from his men, but he couldn't determine which were sounds of anguish from the injured and which were orders and instructions being yelled from one group of men to another.

Without warning a shell landed just a few feet from David. It blew him off balance so that he suddenly found himself sprawled on the ground in an undignified heap. The smell of wet soil and hot gas drifted past him as he lay trembling with the shock of the near miss. Gingerly he lifted his head to see just how close the shell crater was to him. He could almost touch the edge of the saucer shape. *Jesus, that was close.* He got to his hands and knees and scrabbled over the few feet to the hole and rolled in. He was probably no better off than before, but the fact that he was now invisible to the enemy gave him a certain comfort. He crawled through the churned earth to the leading edge of the crater and carefully lifted his head so that he could see over the rim. He needed to get further forward and join his troops. He was doing no good to anyone here. He assessed the lie of the land and worked out a good position he could sprint to next. About fifty yards away there was an old water trough towards the edge of the field. If he could reach that it would afford him some shelter before making another dash to the corner of the hedging by the gate into the lane. Once there, David thought, it might be relatively easy to make his way to the back of the outbuildings that formed the western side of the farmyard. The trouble was, it would just be so much easier to stay where he was.

David took his pipe out of his top pocket and clamped it between his teeth. Just sucking on the empty bowl made him feel a bit more resolute and, with a sudden surge of determination, he picked himself up and ran, jinking left and right to make himself less of a target, to the water trough. Someone obviously had a bead on him, as little splashes of earth, like hailstones hitting a pond, kicked up around his feet as he ran. He reached it and threw himself flat on the ground, jarring his pipe stem against molars. He heard bullets ping on the aluminium above him as he lay panting with fear and exertion. After about a minute, once his heart rate had regained something like a normal rhythm, he leopard-crawled to the end of the trough and squinted round the edge. The corner of the field, his next objective, didn't look as close as he had hoped. *Shit*, he thought, he was really going to have to motor if he was going to reach there unscathed. He withdrew slightly and breathed deeply. Glancing to his immediate left and right he could see he was now level with other members of his battalion. Like him they were huddled behind any available cover: bushes, fence posts, a lump of rusting farm equipment – anything.

David, feeling recovered, his breathing back under

control, jumped up and hurled himself, bent double, at the corner of the field. Again he knew bullets were zipping past him, but again he seemed to be charmed as he reached the cover of the thick hazel hedge unscathed. Panting, he flopped down amongst the tangle of hazel stems, nettles and ivy.

'Hello, sir,' said a voice.

Chest still heaving, David looked towards the speaker. 'Hello, Mr Brown. Fancy seeing you here.'

'I could say the same myself, sir. I thought you were supposed to be keeping out of harm's way.'

'I can't think what gave you that impression.'

They both ducked and paused as a shell landed perilously close again, showering them with clods of earth.

The RSM adjusted his tin hat and brushed earth off the front of his battledress. 'SOPs and orders from Brigade HQ.'

'You must have been mistaken.'

Mr Brown smiled wryly. 'As I had a hand in writing the standard operating procedures for the battalion, I don't think so.'

Another shell whistled overhead. 'Tell you what, RSM, you can report me to Brigade when we get back to Blighty.'

'It's a deal, sir.' The RSM grinned broadly as he said it. 'Not sure what the charge'll be though, sir.'

'Conduct to the prejudice of good order and military discipline? That usually covers most eventualities.'

'I'll make a note.' The RSM glanced over his shoulder. 'If we could get to that corner over there,' – he indicated an angle between two outbuildings – 'and if we had a mortar, we could probably take out that MG42.' He nodded at the heavy machine-gun poking out of the upstairs window of the farm.

'That's a couple of big "ifs", Mr Brown.'

Brown nodded. Then he got on to his hands and knees

as if he was about to start a race and, having checked around for enemy activity, shot off up the line of the hedge, keeping so close that the twigs and branches whipped and tweaked his battledress jacket and snatched at his webbing. Five minutes later he was back.

'The mortar section is on its way. They'll be with us in a little while.'

'Well done, RSM. So now all we have to do is get to that position unscathed.'

'That's about the size of it, sir. But there's a couple of lads with a PIAT round the corner. I saw them on my way back. They're closing in on those two tanks there.' The RSM indicated the ones to the side of the ruins of the barn. 'When they start engaging the Panzers it'll probably take the heat off us.'

Just as the RSM said this there was a whoosh followed by a weird, almost tinny, bang as a shell from a PIAT burst inside the confines of one of the Panzers. A plume of black oily smoke rose out of the turret.

'Go!' yelled the RSM.

Taking his eyes off the grisly spectacle of the tank, David raced for their chosen objective. Machine-guns clattered about them, but David didn't know if they were his men's or the enemy's. All he concentrated on was getting to the safety of the cover of a stone wall. He threw himself at it as he neared it and slid into it. The impact knocked the wind out of him momentarily. Half a minute later he was joined by the RSM.

David sat up, his back against the rough grey stone, massaging his shoulder where he had bruised it against the wall and looking back the way his battalion had come since crossing the start line at first light. Dotted up the far side of the shallow valley he could see huddled khaki shapes, perhaps thirty or more – the dead, the dying and the wounded. He wondered how many other casualties there were hidden in the hedges and ditches. The lush pastures and fields of crops had, in places, been reduced to a pockmarked moonscape of mud and craters. A couple of trees had had their crowns blown off so that the trunks were denuded of their leafy branches and now stood shattered and stark, like misshapen obelisks.

'*Dulce et decorum est*,' he muttered angrily. 'My arse.'

'What was that, sir?' asked the RSM.

'Nothing,' said David. Now was not the moment to get distracted by the utter bloody futility of war.

La Ferme de la Source

The sounds of battle were now overwhelming and from time to time Martine could feel the fabric of the entire house shaking. Surely the Allies must be almost upon the place if the fighting was all so fierce. Still clutching the Bible, Martine levered herself up and crept over to the little window. Despite her shock and grief she was driven by some strange imperative to find out what was happening to her farm. She'd lost everything else; was this being completely ruined too? Otto still lay sprawled backwards on the packing case, his head at a weird angle, his arms thrown out sideways, just as he had fallen. She couldn't get to the window without moving him. Carefully she placed her Bible on the floor and put both arms under Otto's armpits. Gently she lifted him and then, pulling him sideways so that his weight transferred off the case and on to her, she was able to manoeuvre him sufficiently to be able to lay him on the ground. She put his feet together and arranged his arms by his side. Lying like that he looked almost at peace. She drew her fingers down over his eyelids to shut them and then kissed him gently on his lips.

Blinking back tears she turned her attention to her father. He might have been an old soak, he might have let her down in recent months, but he hadn't deserved this fate. She arranged his body too and shut his eyes. She stood between the two bodies and bowed her head. She wanted to pray for them, but she couldn't think of anything to say. Besides which, what had God been doing that he had turned his back on her and her loved ones? What had she done that had been so bad that she deserved this? Maybe she hadn't gone to mass for a few months. Maybe she had been sinful, but if she'd been so bad, why wasn't she dead too? Her tears of grief became tears of anger. One day, if she survived, justice would be done. Peiper would pay, and until God gave her that satisfaction she wasn't going to go to mass again.

She climbed back on to the packing case, carefully trying not to look at the dark smear on the wall where Otto's head had rested, hauled herself into a kneeling position so that she could peer over the sill of the tiny window. The yard was full of smoke, which billowed and eddied in the wind. But despite that there was something else that was wrong. She couldn't work out what it was for a second; then it occurred to her. The light level was all wrong. She glanced at her watch and saw that it was still quite early in the morning, but the yard was bright. Then she saw why: as the smoke drifted away, giving her a clear view for several hundred metres – the barn was no longer there. Martine's hand flew to her mouth and she gave a gasp of shock. Where the barn had once stood there was now a pile of rubble and planks around two tanks, which were loosing off shells at the fields across the valley.

The barn! How would she manage the farm with no barn? Martine sagged back on her heels and her head sank on to her chest. Everything was hopeless. If she didn't die in the next few hours, she would starve over the next few months. Even when the battle passed she wouldn't be able to get any of the crops in from the fields on her own, and if she did she would have nowhere to store them. The cows were probably dead; she knew the chickens had gone and more than likely the pig too. She would have no way of making a living and who would employ her? She was only a girl and people wanted girls for cooking and household tasks; what did she know of such things? Martine began to sob. *Why hadn't Peiper killed her with the others*? At least she would have been spared the miseries the future promised.

The Field Hospital

'Morning, George, and how are we today?' George opened his eyes and saw June Armitage smiling down at him. 'Sleep well?' she continued.

'Terribly. Those bloody planes had me awake half the night.'

'You seemed to be fast asleep just now.' June picked up George's wrist and checked his pulse.

'I was examining the insides of my eyelids.'

June raised an eyebrow but didn't say anything for a couple of seconds as she counted off the seconds against her watch. 'Hmm. Open wide.' She dropped his hand and slipped a thermometer under his tongue. While George was silent, June turned to Max and took his pulse, and then silenced him with a thermometer too. She turned back to George and removed his. She twisted it so she could see the reading clearly, then shook it hard a couple of times and put it in the glass by his bed. 'Hmm,' she said again. She moved to the end of the bed and picked up George's chart.

'Come on, Nurse, what does "hmm" mean?'

'It means what it means.'

George let out a snort of annoyance. 'Which is ...?'

'That your temperature and pulse are up a bit – that's all.'

'Much?'

'Enough.'

'But I feel fine.'

'But I have to decide whether you are well enough to move.'

'Where to? Move where?'

'My, what a lot of questions you're asking today.' Nurse Armitage straightened George's coverlet, pulled the top sheet taut and tucked it in. Immediately George moved his chest a bit so as to stop feeling quite so constrained.

'There's a hospital ship due to leave today.'

'Oh.' George realised he rather wanted to stay put.

A hospital ship would mean repatriation to England and then, after convalescence, he'd be back on ops.

'But I'm not sure you're well enough.'

Well, that was a relief. But darned bad form to show it. He summoned up a lie. 'Oh but I feel well enough. If my leg wasn't crook I'd show you how fit I feel.'

'Trust me: if I thought you were fit enough, you'd be on it. We're going to need the beds.'

Max sat up and took an interest. 'So that big stonk we heard going on last night was in support of an op.'

'I have no idea,' said Nurse Armitage. 'And if it was, it's of no concern to you boys now.' She filled in the details on Max's chart too and then went to her next patient.

'I bet it was Caen,' said Max. 'Stands to reason. We've got to take it to move on.'

But George was thinking about the hospital ship and wondering how long he was likely to be delayed in France; wondering if there was anything he could do to prolong matters. 'Why can't they move me if I'm running a temperature?' he asked.

'Search me. Do I look like a medic?'

'Is that the only reason why they don't move people? Don't they move people worse than me?'

'I don't know.'

'But haven't you watched the newsreels?' George wanted to get any information he could glean as to what he could have wrong with him that would delay his departure.

'Well, maybe they think you're really dodgy. You know – plague-ridden or something. The last place they're going to put you is on board a ship where there might be rats. Look what happened last time someone did that.'

George had sufficient sense of humour to see the funny side of what Max said. He laughed drily. 'Maybe.'

Max had obviously misunderstood George's anxiety. 'Look, I want to get home too. I can't remember Nurse Armitage saying I was due to be moved.'

George felt a heel for being such a coward, but he buried it with a joke. 'But, on the bright side, the longer we stay here the better our chances with her.'

Max nodded slowly. 'I like your logic. Yes, you're right: there are advantages to every situation. One just has to know where to find them.'

Portsmouth Docks

Gwen climbed off the bus outside the dockyard gates and got her pass out of her handbag to show to the sentry. As she did so, the crumpled envelope addressed to Sergeant Viney tumbled out on to the pavement. A passing matelot picked it up and smoothed it out before he handed it back to her.

'Don't want to go losing letters to your sweetheart, miss,' he said. 'Looks like this one's been through the wars before it even gets to him.' He winked at her and strode on.

'Huh,' said Gwen stuffing it into her bag. 'That's the one thing it isn't going to do – get to him.' She showed her pass and made her way over the old cobbled roads of the dockyard, past derricks and wharves, past HMS Victory and the old Wren chapel, till she got to the mobile canteen.

'How I never turn my ankles on those blooming cobbles I'll never know,' she muttered as she let herself into the van. It was cold in the van, as it had been empty overnight and it smelt faintly of sour milk. Gwen looked about to see if there was an obvious source, but it was clean enough. Perhaps someone had spilt some and it had seeped under the cupboards. Well, she wasn't going to start pulling things out to find it. The niff would go once she got the shutter at the front open.

Gwen switched on the electric boiler, which was powered by a cable that was run in from a nearby building, and topped up the water using a big saucepan that she filled from the sink. The water came from the same building, this time via a hose attached to an outside tap. Years back they had been promised something more sophisticated, but as the months passed, everyone had got used to the Heath Robinson arrangements, so there didn't seem much point in altering them now. The boiler made funny hisses and bumps as it heated up and Gwen kept her mac on while it got going. When she had a hot cup of tea in her hand she might think about taking it off, but right now she felt decidedly chilly. June, and she was cold; it wasn't right. Gwen looked in the fridge to make sure the girls who had manned the van on Sunday had left her with enough provisions to get going this morning. There were several loaves, a couple of pints of milk and some marge. In the cupboards were tins of corned beef and spam so she could make sandwiches, but no biscuits. When Marjorie arrived, one of them could go to the WVS store and get a couple more boxes of digestives or whatever was available. *And tea*, thought Gwen, looking in the canister. In fact, she needed to make a list of all the stuff that was getting low. She cast about for a piece of paper. Surely there should be something to write on here. Nothing, not a scrap. She fished in her handbag for an old receipt or the back of a previous shopping list, but the only paper she came across was Sergeant Viney's letter. As it wasn't going anywhere, Gwen felt no compunction about taking the writing paper from the envelope and shoving it back into her bag until she could get rid of it once and for all. Then she ripped the envelope down its edges and opened it out. Perfect. Getting busy with a pencil she leaned on the counter, while behind her the boiler made ever more frantic noises.

She was about halfway through her list when Marjorie bustled in.

'Brrr. Brass monkeys again. I thought we were supposed to be enjoying summer now.'

'No chance. Vile, isn't it?'

Marjorie took off her coat and peered over Gwen's shoulder. 'If this is a list of things we need, I think we ought to see if there are any pickled onions available, and we could do with some more mustard.' She put her hand against the side of the boiler. 'I think this has nearly boiled. Tea?'

'Oh please. I'm gasping.'

Marjorie busied herself with warming the teapot and measuring tea into it. 'Have you heard from that man of yours yet?'

For a second Gwen thought she meant George and felt a renewed lurch of guilt surge through her system. Taking a slow breath, she answered, trying to sound as casual as possible. 'No, not yet. But I don't think the post had come before I left the cottage.'

'Oh well, I expect you'll get a letter soon. And I know itis banal and trite but I always think that no news really is good news.'

'Maybe.' Gwen opened and closed another couple of the cupboards.

'Looking for something?'

'Just wondering if we could do with more piccalilli.'

'Put it down. It isn't as if it'll go off if we have more than we need. And we do need more scourers.'

Gwen wrote these things on her list. 'And maybe we

could ask for some bleach or something like that. There's a funny smell in here.'

'I thought so too. But I can't think where it is coming from.'

Marjorie poured some boiling water into the teapot and put it on the side to let it brew. Then she began moving plates and canisters about on the counter to see if she could locate whatever it was that was off. As she did so, she sent Gwen's handbag flying.

'Dash,' she said as it tumbled on to the floor and the contents cascaded out. In the narrow confines of the van Gwen couldn't squeeze past Marjorie to rescue her belongings, and in any case Marjorie said cheerfully, 'Silly me. Never mind: I'll pick it all up for you.' She began to gather up Gwen's ID card and ration book, her purse and her door key and other bits and pieces; and then she picked up the letter. Gwen watched her closely. It was obvious Marjorie had cast her eye over it, but had she seen anything that actually mattered? Nan had wittered about inconsequential stuff other than her worries about her employer's morals. Without a word Marjorie put the things she had gathered off the floor into Gwen's bag and handed it back to her.

'Thank you,' said Gwen.

Marjorie continued to stare at her. Then she said, 'I'm sorry, I don't think I should have seen what was in that letter. Is it about you?'

Gwen felt her face burn. She couldn't bring herself to speak so she just nodded.

'So how have you got … sorry, it's absolutely none of my business. You must forgive me. I'm a nosy old woman who shouldn't pry.' She turned away to make the tea.

But Gwen suddenly felt the need to confide in someone. The burden of guilt and remorse was gnawing at her; she'd been a fool and she'd been found out. Perhaps Marjorie could help her find a way forward.

'Actually,' said Gwen quietly. 'I think I would like to talk about it.'

So while they buttered bread for the sandwiches and sliced spam, Gwen recounted her short affair with George, her reasons for her actions, how much she realised she loved David and how ashamed she was of what she'd done, and Marjorie listened patiently.

'You don't look shocked,' said Gwen when she'd finished.

'My dear, I'm a doctor's wife. You'd be surprised how much it takes to shock me.' She smiled at Gwen kindly.

'I know, but I've made such a mess of things. And if David finds out …'

'But he hasn't. And I doubt if Mrs Viney will mention it again to her husband. I can't say it was right of you to take her letter, but under the circumstances I fully understand why you did it. By the time this wretched war is over and everyone is home again this will be just so much water under the bridge. The important thing is that you love David and that you realise what a silly goose you've been and it won't happen again. I suppose you've told George it's over?'

Gwen told Marjorie about the visit from his friends in the mess.

'Ah,' said Marjorie. 'Well, if he does turn up, you must tidy up that loose end, but I don't suppose he'll be heartbroken. I think chaps like him live life rather fast and loose until they're ready to settle down and they regard failed love affairs as honourable battle scars.'

'But supposing Mrs Viney says something when David gets back?'

'I very much doubt she will. Would you snitch like that?'

Gwen shook her head.

'Well then …the main thing is you've learned a hard lesson. You won't do it again, will you?'

'No, never.'

'And you've also realised just how much you love David.'

'Oh yes. George was fun, but when I thought I might have made such a mess of things, that David would go ...'Her stricken face said everything.

'Then that's the main thing.' Marjorie smiled at Gwen again. 'Right, well I think we should open for business now, don't you?'

Gwen looked at her watch. 'Goodness, we're terribly late.'

'Never mind. It's all been in a good cause. Just one more thing.'

Gwen looked at Marjorie questioningly.

'Can I have that letter?'

Gwen fished it out of her handbag and handed it over.

Marjorie tore it into dozens of tiny pieces and put it in the bin. 'There, all over.'

Gwen felt such a bubble of relief well up inside her, and as it came to the surface and popped she felt an overwhelming lightness come over her.

Sixteen

Mid-morning, Monday 26 June 1944

La Ferme de la Source

'Over here, lads!' yelled the RSM, using his considerable lung-power to get his voice to carry to the mortar section over the noise of the battle.

Ducking and weaving, the men carrying the mortar, dismantled into various sections to make it portable, joined David and Mr Brown. After being told their objective they reassembled the weapon and not long after that they began lobbing mortars at the upstairs of the farm. The first two mortars pitched over the ridge of the roof and landed out of sight; however, judging by the slates which fountained into view, they did considerable harm to the room with the heavy machine-gun. But then the soldiers got their eye in and the third hit the roof square on above the dormer and a great gout of smoke erupted out of the window followed by two stunned and bewildered German soldiers, who seemed to be desperate for fresh air. Mr Brown picked them off with his rifle. The machine-gun was silenced.

Not that it was the only defence of the farm. There was the matter of a number of tanks each armed with its own machine-gun, to say nothing of their main armament of a 7.5-centimetre gun. However, with the heavy machine-gun silenced, the men armed with PIATs were now able to mount a more concerted attack. And it appeared that some of the tank crews had had enough. Over the row of the raging battle David discerned the sound of engines starting up and saw half a dozen of the remaining tanks start to pull back.

'Don't let them get away, men!' he yelled, although it was doubtful if anyone heard his order. Fired with an urgency to finish the job, he dashed from behind the wall and instantly took several bullets in his chest and arm. David felt as though he had been punched and the force of the impacts threw him backwards. His tin hat connected with the cobbles of the farmyard with a sickening, brain-numbing force and he lay on the ground, fighting for breath, the wind knocked out of him. He felt curiously detached as the action raged on; he could hear the noises and see some of the events, but it all seemed as though it was happening elsewhere, as though he wasn't really a part of it any more. And he felt so tired. Quite exhausted. He shut his eyes.

'Sir, sir. Look at me, sir.'

David tried to summon the strength to open his eyes.

'Over here. Stretcher-bearer!'

David wondered who needed one. Then he felt himself being lifted.

'Careful now. You don't want to go dropping the CO.'

The CO? That was him, wasn't it? What was going on? He was aware of the light on the other side of his eyelids suddenly becoming much less bright and the noise was suddenly less raucous, more muffled. He wondered if he was now indoors, but still he couldn't open his eyes to find out. It was all too much effort. What he really wanted to do was let go, fall asleep.

'You'll be all right now, sir. The doc's going to take care of you.'

David wanted to express his thanks and ask what was going on, but it was almost as if he was trapped inside some sort of airtight vessel and everything else was happening outside it. Hands seemed to be undoing his webbing and taking off his battledress; then there was a prick in his arm and he slid into welcome blackness.

Martine was still slumped on the packing case when the door to the cellar opened again. So what could they do to her now to make life worse? Death would only be welcome and anything else ... well, so what? Life was a living hell. Her father had hinted about other things that could happen and there had certainly been talk in the village of horrors that had been meted out elsewhere, but Martine was past caring. Death, rape, torture? Nothing could be worse than the pain of what she was going through right now.

But nothing happened; no hands grabbed at her, no orders were shouted, she didn't hear the sound of a weapon being cocked. Nothing. Curiosity got the better of her and she looked up. For a second or two she couldn't work out what was going on. Why had the Germans changed their clothes? This wasn't what they had been wearing a few hours earlier. Then slowly realization dawned on her. The Germans had gone. She'd been liberated. She had survived. For a second she almost felt happy.

But Otto and her father hadn't made it. This was all too late for them. Her heart, which had lifted momentarily, plummeted again. She'd survived – for what? What was the point of continuing to live if all that the future held for her was loneliness and drudgery? She could have faced rebuilding the farm with Otto beside her. Life would have been bearable with his love, but now ... it was all so pointless, so bleak.

The man said something to her.

Martine shrugged. Then he beckoned. Perhaps he wanted her to follow him. Wearily she climbed off the packing case and made her way over to him. She noticed him staring, fascinated, at the bodies on the ground.

'Peiper did it,' she told him.

The man said something and looked blank. Martine thought about trying to act out what had happened, but what was the point? With all this death and destruction, who the hell would care about a couple of mindless, brutal executions of a French farmer and a lowly German soldier?

She followed the soldier up the stairs and into the kitchen.

Mon Dieu! The destruction. Her house was virtually wrecked. The ceiling had come down, there was lath and plaster all over the floor. Half the furniture was broken or smashed. Her mother's best china was in pieces and the windows and doors had been blown off. If Martine had thought what had happened to the barn had been bad, it was as nothing to what had happened to her home. She stared around her, trying to take in the damage. She felt tears welling up as she saw the remains of items that had been part of her life, little things like the vase her mother had put the bunches of wild flowers in that Marine had gathered, the wooden carver chair that her father had always sat in, the sewing machine that had been her mother's pride and joy – all wrecked, all in pieces.

Miraculously the kitchen table had survived, but now it seemed to have been pressed into duty as a makeshift operating table. A man a bit younger than her father was lying on it while another British soldier was prodding around in his chest trying to remove a bullet. Or that was what Martine supposed he was up to. On the surface of the table were wads of blood-soaked cloth. The injured man looked in a bad way.

The man looked at Martine. He asked her a question.

She shrugged; English was beyond her.

'*Nom?*' he said.

'Martine,' she replied.

'Martine?'

She'd said so, hadn't she? Anyway, what did he need to

know for?

'*Draps*,' he said

'*Draps?*' she repeated. What the blazes did he want with cloth?

He held out a bandage.

The penny dropped. 'Oh, *draps de lit.*'

He nodded. Martine went to the old oak chest that stood by the wall and lifted the lid. Inside were the sheets her mother had told her were for her bottom drawer. As if she was going to need them now. What chance did she have of finding someone to marry her now? What could she offer? Once she might have been considered a bit of a catch, with the prospective inheritance of a farm. But who would want her for this wreck? And the only man she had ever felt love for, and who had loved her, was lying cold and dead in the cellar. *Marriage? Pah.* The sheets might as well be used for something useful. Without hesitating, Martine took out the fine white linen and shook it out with a crack of starched fabric. Then, grasping a hem between both hands, she gave a sharp pull and the cloth ripped. She repeated the exercise a few more times until she had a couple of strips about ten centimetres wide and a couple of metres long. The doctor looked grateful as she handed them over.

'*Savon?*' he asked.

Martine just snorted. The doctor nodded and turned away. He obviously understood just how ridiculous his request was. Perhaps they had similar shortages in England.

'Do you want hot water?' she asked him, but he looked blank. 'Should I light the range?' More blank looks.

The doctor seemed to be collecting his thoughts. '*Les morts*,' he said. He pointed at the floor beneath his feet. Martine reckoned he meant the bodies in the cellar. '*Qui?*'

'My father and a German soldier.' He seemed to understand that, despite his execrable French.

'Why the German?'

Martine wasn't going to admit her relationship with Otto to anyone. She wasn't going to suffer as a collaborator on top of everything else, so she just shrugged. But even as she denied their affair by her omission, she expected to hear a cock crow. 'Peiper did it. He killed them.'

The doctor shook his head. Martine sighed. Didn't this man understand any French? He turned away and began jabbering to the soldiers around him. Martine wandered off across the kitchen to be out of the way.

'All right,' said Mike Barton, the Regimental Medical Officer, 'we'll just have to manage as best we can. She says there isn't any soap. At least we've got some bandages now. Can someone organise the stretcher-bearers to get the bodies out of the house? Apart from the two upstairs there are a couple in the cellar. Get them laid out in the yard. The RSM will organise burial parties later. I gather the older one is her father, so be respectful.'

'Right you are, sir,' said the soldier who had brought Martine up from the cellar. 'And what do you want me to do with the bint?'

'Young lady,' corrected Captain Barton. 'She can stay here. She may be able to help me. If nothing else, she can get the range going so we can boil up some water. I have no idea how this load of scrap metal works.' He nodded at the antique stove that dominated one side of the kitchen but which was standing cold and useless. He turned to Martine again. '*Feu?*' he said hopefully, wishing he'd paid more attention in French lessons all those years ago when he'd been doing his school cert.

The girl gabbled something back at him and looked exasperated. What was getting her goat? Mike wondered. He just wanted her to light the range.

'*Feu,*' said Mike again hopefully and with a smile.

Perhaps a bit of charm would win her over.

Martine shook her head at him and sighed, then picked her way over the debris on the floor to the door and came back a couple of minutes later with an armful of kindling.

Mike was pleased and relieved that the language barrier appeared to have been overcome. He got on with tending his patient while behind him Martine opened the door of the range and began to lay a fire.

Then she disappeared again and returned, this time with an armful of sticks. She inserted them into the grate expertly and put the rest beside the range for later use.

'*Briquet, allumette,*'' she said to him sitting back on her heels.

'Sorry, I don't understand.' Mike watched her mime striking a match. 'God, I'm sorry. How stupid.' He ferreted around in a pocket and handed her a box of matches.

Martine struck one and put it to the kindling. In no time, the fire was raging away. Martine slammed the door and pulled a big pan on to the hot plate.

'*Eau? Chaud ou bouillant?*'

'*Oui, merci.*'

'*Chaud ou bouillant?*' she repeated slowly.

Mike knew what *chaud* meant; he guessed *bouillant* meant boiling.

'*Bouillant, s'il vous plaît.*' He smiled again; his French was coming on in leaps and bounds. Well, not really; it was rubbish, but he was getting by.

The girl tipped water into the pot from a bucket by the sink; then she went and picked up a three-legged stool from where it was lying on its side at the back of the big room and sat on it, out of the way.

Martine observed the activity in the room. Soldiers came and went, some carrying stretchers, others moving bits of military equipment. Others came in and spoke to the doctor and yet more appeared with a reel of wire and seemed to want to set up some sort of telephone. Martine watched the comings and goings dispassionately. Now she had got the fire in the range going, the English seemed to have worked out how to feed it more wood. Martine was ignored and she dozed a little, leaning against the stone wall of the fireplace at the far end of the living room, as the morning wore on. She'd had no sleep the night before and the exhaustion of the months of drudgery finally caught up with her, despite the grief that lay like a cold stone deep inside her.

Some bangs and thumps roused her. She opened her eyes to see a couple of men struggling to bring up a stretcher with her father's body on it from the cellar. Wearily she hauled herself off the stool. 'Where are you taking him?' she asked the doctor as he dressed a soldier's mangled hand.

'What?' he answered. He sounded irritable. Perhaps he was tired too; he certainly looked it.

Martine repeated her question.

'Outside,' was the answer.

Martine went into the yard, following the stretcher. The men carefully laid the body at the end of a line of British soldiers who had also lost their lives. Otto was on the other side of the yard with the German dead. Martine didn't want him there. The other soldiers weren't his comrades: the SS had been his enemy as much as they'd been hers; but she didn't dare say anything. And again she knew she was betraying him to save herself. God would make a cock crow any minute. But goodness only knew what the English would do to her if they found she'd had an affair with a German. She'd survived, she was alive and her future was horribly grim; but what was the point of making it needlessly worse? She might have wanted to die along with her father and Otto, but she hadn't. God obviously had a reason for her survival, so she just had to get on with it. She took a last look at her father and Otto, and then returned into the house.

As she entered, she noticed a pile of army kit stacked by the remains of the dresser. There were a couple of kitbags, a tunic or two and a belt with a revolver in the holster. Martine eyed the revolver. A gun she already possessed, but it was her father's shotgun and an unwieldy weapon. But a revolver she could hide in a pocket or a bag. A revolver might be extremely useful. Martine was no fool. Times had been tough under German occupation, but now the invasion had happened life was destined to get a whole lot more difficult. She knew she wasn't the only person to have lost everything and now be in desperate straits. Desperate people did desperate things. Hunger and fear would drive the most ordinary people to extremes of behaviour they would never have considered under normal circumstances. While the foreign troops were here, people would pay lip-service to the law; but what would happen once they had gone? She had very little, that was true, but even the little that she had might be more than other people, and she wasn't prepared to lose out just because she couldn't protect herself.

Casually Martine went over to the oak chest and removed another sheet. Then she returned to her stool and began tearing it up into strips. When she had made half a dozen, she picked up the sheet, together with her rough bandages and walked over to the doctor. As she passed the pile of kit she dropped the sheet on to it and then proffered the home-made dressings to the MO. He took them with a smile. Martine walked back, picking up the sheet again – and the gun that lay underneath it. She dropped it all in the chest and shut the lid.

Seventeen

Early Afternoon, Monday 26 June 1944

Carpiquet

Since dawn Major Hoffmann had watched the battle raging just a few kilometres away with mounting horror. First the aerial bombardment, which had made the ground shake even where he was standing, and then the armour had come rumbling over the countryside, flattening or shelling anything that lay in its path. From his position in the control tower on the airfield he could see for miles and now what he saw was terrifying him. He had known since 6 June that he was going to have to fight sooner or later, but the prospect still filled him with dread. Hoffmann wasn't a natural soldier and had only joined up when it became compulsory. His father had used his money and influence to get him into officer school and Hoffmann wondered if his father hadn't used the same levers to get him posted in the opposite direction from the main fighting as soon as he had passed out. However, four years of living in relative comfort in occupied France had now come to an abrupt end and Hoffmann was in a state of panic. He knew that his complement of just over one hundred men was not going to be enough to prevent the enemy from taking the airfield, but he knew he was going to have to put up a fight. There were enough bastards like Peiper in the area to have him court-martialled or shot if he didn't put up a proper show of resistance, so he had no choice. But what was the point? The enemy was going to get the airfield regardless. No one but a fool would think that the small number of German troops stationed in Normandy was going to be capable of holding back this massive tide of men and materials. It was like a mouse trying to stop a steamroller.

Trying to look confident, he had issued orders and the men were now manning various pillboxes and dugouts around the perimeter on the northern and western sides of the airfield. Hoffmann himself reckoned they could probably hold out for about half a day if they were lucky. Privately he hoped that his men would surrender rather than do anything brave and foolhardy such as try to fight to the death. He knew Peiper's lot were in the area – *somewhere in the valley to the west*, he thought – but other than that he didn't think there was much else in the way of German troops between him and the British. As far as he was aware, most of the German forces were concentrated round the high ground to the south at Bourguébus ridge and in the city of Caen itself. Perhaps there had been other troop deployments that he wasn't privy to, perhaps there had been reinforcements; but right now he and his men seemed to be a dot of field grey amongst a sea of khaki.

Hoffmann was seriously beginning to think about what his best route out of the battle zone was going to be when he saw half a dozen Panzers come powering over the fields towards the airfield. The tank commanders gave no thought to hedges or gates as they crashed through any obstacles that threatened to impede their progress.

'Thank God,' he mumbled to himself as he saw the reinforcements appearing. With the presence of Panzers as well, his men might be able to hold out long enough for other reinforcements to arrive. Maybe if he held the airfield he'd be a hero. For a second Hoffmann revelled in the delusion that he might be able to alter the course of the war, that decorations might be his, that he might be fêted in Berlin …

The first of the tanks reached the outer barbed-wire perimeter fence. Without stopping, it crashed straight through it and then treated the inner, higher fence in the same way. For a second Hoffmann was furious, but then he told himself that there was a war on and anyway, a few strands of wire weren't going to make any difference in a battle for this piece of ground.

With a renewed sense of self-worth given to him by the thought of having tanks to command, he strode down the stairs from the control tower to meet the tank drivers. However, when he reached ground level all he could see of the tanks was the blue haze of their exhausts as they thundered over to where their column of soft support vehicles were still parked up from the night before.

Hoffmann hurried over, formulating his orders for the deployment of the armour around his airfield as he went. He was puffing heavily when he reached his objective and paused, out of sight around the corner of a building, while he caught his breath.

'Hey! You,' he yelled to a black-clad back view. The individual turned round slowly. '*Scheisse*,' Hoffmann said under his breath. It was Peiper.

'Yes?'

'Herr Obersturmbannführer,' said Hoffmann, letting a tone of obsequiousness trickle into his voice. 'Thank you for returning to help me hold this important position.'

Peiper looked genuinely bewildered. 'I don't understand you, Hoffmann. Hold what, exactly?'

'The airfield.' It was Hoffmann's turn to be bewildered.

Peiper sniffed. 'The airfield is your problem. I have to regroup and fall back to Caen. You're on your own, Hoffmann.'

'But what good will my lot be against all that?' Hoffmann gestured wildly at the western horizon. 'We can't possibly hope to hold them.'

'Well, I expect you to try very hard, Hoffmann. And if

you can't, I expect you to die in the attempt.' Leaving
Hoffmann lost for words Peiper strode off to issue orders
to his own men.

Half an hour later Hoffmann felt utterly beleaguered as
he watched the column of tanks, accompanied by their
support vehicles, drive out of the airfield and rumble down
the road towards Caen. All visions of honour and glory
disappeared like the exhaust fumes of the tanks in the
breeze that stirred across the countryside.

Eighteen

Late Afternoon, 26 June 1944

The Field Hospital

Earlier in the day Max and George had enjoyed a couple of hours of being the sole inhabitants of the tent that constituted their ward and had therefore revelled in having the delectable Nurse Armitage to themselves. In the event she'd been rather too busy, stripping beds and making them up again, to spare them too much of her time, but she'd found a few minutes to chat with them when she served them their lunch. Then, as the day wore on, the stretchers began to arrive until all the beds were full again.

Max and George assessed the occupants as they arrived and compared clandestine notes on how much competition they might pose for the attentions of Nurse Armitage and how ill they were. Their conclusions were that, happily for their own selfish ends, most of the others were pretty poorly and, that being the case, they were in no state to muscle in on June Armitage's affections. The officer next to George even had the screen pulled round his bed. Max caught George's attention and pulled his hand slowly across his throat to indicate what he thought were the chances of that particular casualty. George shrugged. He disagreed – after all, if the chap had survived this long, his chances had to be getting better now rather than worse; but then he was no expert. Max had been here rather longer and presumably had seen more comings – and goings – than most.

A doctor arrived a few minutes later and disappeared behind the screen. Nurse Armitage came and went, ferrying kidney bowls and bandages and taking away bloody dressings and used equipment. Max shook his head again and George, this time, decided he was probably right. After about ten minutes the doctor pulled the screen back and told Nurse Armitage to call for the stretcher-bearers again.

The poor bugger hasn't made it, thought George, feeling uncharacteristically emotional. But it was probably because he'd never been really near to someone who had bought it. The people he knew who had got shot down and the enemy pilots he'd dispatched himself had all died well out of his sight, so he'd never actually seen a dead body. Out of sheer ghoulish curiosity, George turned his head to see what one looked like before the stretcher-bearers took him away.

His heart missed a beat. Good God, it surely couldn't be? Unless Gwen's husband had a twin, this was David Clarke. And now the poor sod was dead.

'Take him to the operating tent,' said the MO.

The two male orderlies lifted the Colonel on to the stretcher and carried him off.

George didn't understand. The man was dead, wasn't he?

Nurse Armitage came back and began to straighten the covers of die now vacant bed.

'I thought that chap was dead,' he said as casually as he could.

'No. But he's in a bad way. The doc thinks he's got some internal damage that needs sorting out. We'll have to hope for the best.'

'Is he likely to make it?'

June Armitage shrugged and paused in her bedmaking. 'We'll know one way or the other soon enough.'

'What's his name?' George had to know for definite.

Nurse Armitage moved to the end of the bed and picked up the board hanging there. 'Colonel David Clarke.'

George willed his face to remain expressionless. 'Let's hope he pulls through,' he said.

'Yes, let's.' The nurse went off to perform other duties.

'Seems you were wrong, old chap,' said George. 'He's not dead yet.'

'"Yet" seems to be the operative word, though, doesn't it?'

'You can be a callous bastard, can't you?'

'"Pragmatic" is a nicer word, though, don't you think? One has to be a realist, after all.'

But George didn't want to be a realist. He remembered a few days before when he'd caught Gwen looking at a picture of David and he'd seen the expression on her face. She'd be heartbroken if David died. He couldn't bear the thought of her being so upset. He prayed that David would make it. *Please God,* he asked, *Gwen doesn't deserve the misery. Don't punish her for what I encouraged her to do.*

George had no idea if his prayer would be answered or not, but he lay back feeling better for having asked.

It was two hours later that David was returned to the ward. For some reason that George could not fathom, he felt a strange sense of relief and gratitude that he had pulled through. Lying as he had been in his hospital bed, he'd had time to reflect on his affair with Gwen, and although it had been huge fun, he realised that it wasn't something he was terribly proud of. Being spurred into writing a love letter to her had really brought home to him the fact that he was deceiving himself and her. And to cap it all he was now lying next to her husband, who looked a thoroughly nice, decent sort of chap – the sort of chap who absolutely didn't deserve to have his pretty young wife carrying on behind his back with a heel like him. Well, no more of that. He lay back on his pillows and felt that, if nothing else, he could look the Colonel in the eye now. He might have done wrong in the past but he wasn't going to go any further down that path.

David stirred and opened his eyes. Dazed he looked round his immediate surroundings.

'Welcome,' said George.

The Colonel blinked slowly.

Was he acknowledging the greeting? George couldn't tell. 'How do you feel?'

The Colonel shut his eyes for a second or two as if he was trying to work out the answer to that knotty question himself.

'Not great?' George thought he detected the minutest of movements of David's head. 'Do you want anything?' That movement was there again. 'I'll leave you to get some sleep then.' The Colonel's eyes shut again and this time stayed that way.

Nineteen

Early Evening, Monday 26 June 1944

La Ferme de la Source

Martine could still hear the guns but the shells were falling well away from her farm. Most of the soldiers seemed to have moved on. The front had passed now like some hurricane from hell and, like a hurricane, behind it was nothing but destruction and ruin. Martine sat on the mounting block in the yard and surveyed the mess. The barn was gone, most of the roof to the house was gone and an entire corner of the building had been blown off; not a window was unbroken, the hen house was a ruin and the sty was empty. The dairy was still standing, but what use was that without any cows to use it? Not that she was certain her cows were dead. She hadn't plucked up the courage to go to the meadow to see. She thought she could cope if they had all been blown to bits or killed outright, but supposing one was terribly injured – or they all were? Would she be able to bring herself to destroy the poor creatures to put them out of their misery? Her father had always done the slaughtering as he hadn't considered it a job for a woman. Well, she could forget such considerations now. Whatever the job; however distasteful, if she didn't get on and do it, then who would?

She sighed miserably as yet again she had a sharp reminder that her father was dead. It seemed at the moment that it didn't matter where her train of thoughts began, they always ended up by reminding her that she was alone in the world. And not just that: she had almost no money, no home, no farm, livestock … destitute and orphaned. What on earth was her future going to be like? She blew her nose on a piece of rag she found in her pocket. *And what good is crying going to do me?* she wondered. Time enough for that – the rest of her life, perhaps.

She looked into the field behind where the barn had stood. There were a couple of dozen fresh mounds of earth in a line. Under one of them was her father. The graves were marked with very simple crosses, each bearing the name of the body buried below. Martine got up and walked slowly across the yard and through the gate into the field. She paused at each cross to examine the names. 'M. Bracque' said the cross at the far end. Underneath the name were the date and some words in English. Some yards away was a larger mound of earth. Martine went over to examine the cross on that. She didn't understand the English written on it, but she saw the number '48' written and the date again. She assumed that was the number of Germans killed at her farm. And one of them was Otto. *He shouldn't be in with them*, she thought. He didn't deserve to be treated like those SS monsters who had shot him. Martine looked at the mass grave and wondered if she could rescue him from an eternity of being entombed with the very soldiers he had loathed. It simply wasn't possible, though – not on her own. If she told anyone of what she wanted to do, she'd be branded as a collaborator. The thought of being tarred and feathered, or worse, was too terrible. So now she had betrayed him a third time – and still no cock crow. She wondered if worse retribution was awaiting her than a nasty audible reminder of her treachery.

Martine wandered back to the farm. She had no energy to do anything. There seemed no point in trying to clear up anything in the farmyard or weatherproof her house. And how on earth could she manage such a big job on her own? She supposed she might be able to ask for help in the village, but that was supposing there was anyone there left to ask. It was quite possible the locals had fled, and those that hadn't would have their own properties to try to sort out. She felt herself sag under the sheer weight of the feeling of hopelessness. Besides which, the Germans might counter-attack and what a waste of time it would have all been. Better to wait until it was certain that France was liberated from the Boche for good. She picked her way over the splintered wood that had once been her front door and looked about her kitchen. It was still full of soldiers. A big radio set had now been installed; her table had stopped being used as a first-aid post and was now some sort of administrative centre with a meeting taking place around it. Someone looked up as she came in and shouted at her.

Martine was completely bemused. What had she done wrong? 'This is my house,' she explained. 'My house,' she repeated.

A soldier pulled at her arm as if he was about to eject her. Martine wrenched it away from him.

'Get your filthy hands off me,' she hissed at him. She didn't know if he understood her words or not but he certainly got her meaning. He let go instantly.

A man with red bits on his collar and some gold stars and crowns on his shoulders came up to her. 'I apologise for this but we need your house.'

At last someone who spoke French. 'I won't get in your way,' said Martine.

'It wouldn't be safe for you to stay here.'

'Why not? I was here, down in the cellar, when you were fighting the Germans over this place. I survived that.'

The man looked taken aback. Martine didn't know who he was, but he looked important. Perhaps he wasn't used to people arguing with him. Well, that wasn't her problem.

This was her house and she had a right to be here and she didn't give a damn what he said. He turned away and said something in English to one of his men. The soldier came forward and took her arm, but this time quite gingerly. He led her away from the table and over to a chair on the other side of the room.

She cast a look at the oak chest and hoped that none of the soldiers would take it upon themselves to see if it contained anything worth looting. She didn't want any of them finding that gun. She wasn't worried that there would be any repercussions if they did; she would deny all knowledge. But she did want that gun for her own protection for the coming months. Well, *tant pis*. There was nothing she could do about retrieving it yet. Patience.

The meeting broke up. Chairs scraped back on the stone flags and the men made preparations to leave, gathering up briefcases and caps and tucking notebooks into the pockets of their battledress jackets. Finally the French-speaker was alone, apart from a couple of subordinates who were clearing away papers and pencils off the table.

'Sir,' she said. The English officer glanced up in surprise as if he'd forgotten her presence. 'I need to see if any of my animals, my cows, need attention. Is it safe for me to go down the lane?'

'To where, exactly?' Martine began to describe where the pasture was in relation to the house, but the officer put his hand up. 'Show me.' Martine began to make her way towards the door when the officer called her back. 'No, on the map.'

Martine came back into the room. She peered at the map. She saw the name of the village, and there was the airfield. 'So is this the road to the village.' She pointed to an orange-and-white dotted line.

'Yes, and here's the railway.' The man pointed that out. 'So whereabouts do you keep your cows?'

Martine thought. It was about halfway along the lane, before you got to the village and across the stream. She made a guess and stabbed her finger at a place between La Ferme de la Source and the village.

The man scratched his chin. 'Hmm. I think you'll be safe going there, but I'll send an escort with you. We don't want you getting shot by accident.' He didn't say which side might be trigger-happy nor did Martine ask. He barked out something in English and several men appeared. He spoke briefly to them and then turned back to Martine.

'These boys will go with you and bring you back here when you have done what you have to do. They don't speak French but I'm sure you'll cope.'

Martine led the way out of the kitchen and into the yard. The men escorted her like sheepdogs around a flock. They kept close to her as she strode through the gateway, the gate now hanging on one hinge at a drunken angle and she'd been on at her father about the hinges on the gate to the Long Meadow –God! That was the least of her worries now – and into the lane. The soldiers kept their guns cocked and ready as they walked along between the flower-filled verges. Their caution transferred itself to Martine and she began to feel apprehensive too; jumping at a sudden rustling in the hedge, looking for sinister shapes in the shadows cast by the undergrowth; but their journey to the meadow was uneventful.

Martine approached the gate to the field with some trepidation. Until she actually reached the entrance to the meadow she could not see what was behind the thick hedges that surrounded and sheltered it. She had to force herself to walk the final few paces, dreading what she might see. Her heart thumped and her palms sweated as she peered round the edge of the thick hazel and hawthorn enclosure.

Four of her six cows were lying on their sides, already

bloated with the gas of their decomposition and buzzing with flies. However, the warm breeze that wafted past them didn't carry the stench of death – not yet anyway. The cows could only have been dead for half a day and it would be a bit longer before they really began to stink. Martine looked around the field to see what had happened to her other two cows. She saw part of a leg in the earth thrown up by one of the bombs. She guessed that poor brute had taken a direct hit. But where was the last one? She lifted the latch on the gate and pushed it open wide. The soldiers darted into the field ahead of her and checked the hedges on either side of the entrance. Martine almost felt touched at this concern for her welfare, but then she realised that they were just as concerned for their own safety. If there were snipers in the field, they were just as capable of taking out the Tommies as her. Having ascertained that the field was clear of any lurking enemy, they beckoned her forward. There appeared to be no sign of the missing animal. Martine scanned the hedge, but there was nothing, so she moved forward. As she did so, she heard a mournful lowing. She walked in the direction of the noise. The poor brute had fallen into one of the craters. Martine stood on the edge and looked at her one remaining cow. Not only was the poor creature in desperate need of being milked but she appeared to have hurt her leg, Martine slid down the soft, muddy side of the depression.

'You poor old thing,' she said to it as she reached it. Again the cow mooed, her flanks shivering with pain, her eyes dull, her head hanging low. Martine patted the beast reassuringly as she moved to its rear to examine the injured leg. It was broken. No doubt at all. There was no way the leg could be mended; she wasn't going to be able to climb up the steep sides of the bomb crater; it was hopeless. She had to destroy the creature. Martine shut her eyes and let out a long sigh. The prospect was dreadful.

'Here,' she called to the nearest Tommy. Oh God, how was she going to get across to these men what she needed to do? She gave the stricken cow another reassuring pat before scrambling back up the side of the crater.

'Watch,' she said, pointing to herself and then her eyes and then at them. She pointed to the cow and then one of the soldier's guns. Then she mimed holding a gun to her head and pulling the trigger. The soldiers looked at each other and then one spoke some words to her. He repeated what he had said and, although Martine had not the first idea what he was saying, the way he spoke and the way he nodded seemed to indicate to her that he had understood. She held her hand out for the rifle. He shook his head but took her hand and led her back down into the crater. He stroked the cow's nose, then he put Martine's hand on the animal's head and indicated for her to continue. He looked at her and nodded. Martine breathed a sigh of relief. He had understood and he knew what to do. Martine whispered words of comfort to the poor animal as the soldier stood by the animal's shoulder and cocked his weapon. Then he put the barrel of his rifle to the animal's head just behind its right eye and pulled the trigger. The report made Martine jump out of her skin, and the creature slowly sagged to the ground and flopped onto its side. Then, what with the horror of what had just happened over the past hours, her gratitude for the kindness and sensitivity of the soldier who had helped her and the overall exhaustion that was engulfing her, she began to sob her heart out. The soldier put his arm round her as he led her away from the poor dead cow and Martine clung to him, grateful for the support, as she no longer felt capable of anything.

David opened his eyes when he felt a hand on his wrist.

'Ah you are awake? Good.' The nurse concentrated on taking his pulse. 'Open wide,' she said, offering him a thermometer. 'You gave us a scare, but you're all patched up now. How are you feeling?'

'Rough,' David managed to say before the nurse slipped the cold glass stick under his tongue.

'Would you like something to eat? I can find some tea and biscuits for you.'

David nodded. He wasn't very struck by the idea of biscuits, but he was devilish thirsty.

'I'll run and get you a cup just as soon as I've finished doing this.'

David waited patiently until the nurse deemed that the thermometer had been in his mouth the right amount of time and smiled gratefully when she removed it, noted the reading, shook it and disappeared with a promise that she'd only be two ticks.

'So what happened to you?' asked the young lad in the next bed.

'I think I took several bullets when we were attacking a German position.'

'Bad luck. I'm George, by the way – and, before you ask, I was named after Washington, not one of your kings – and this is Max.' The young lad gestured with his thumb to where Max lay propped up against his pillows.

'David – David Clarke.' He smiled at the two chaps in the next two beds. 'Been here long?'

'Got here the day before yesterday and Max was here before that. We're assured we'll be on a hospital ship home to Blighty soon, but the last one sailed without us.'

'Yes,' said Max. 'They were shipping people out of here left, right and centre to make room for some push there seemed to be going on.' He paused for a second. 'I say, were you part of it?'

'I suppose I was.'

'And what was the objective? That is, if it's all right to tell me. It's a bit frustrating being laid up here and not knowing how it's all going.'

'I shouldn't think what I was involved in is much of a secret now. We were hoping to take Caen.'

'So that would explain the stonk that went on last night,' said George.

'It's a big operation,' said David.

'Did you pull it off?' asked Max.

David shook his head. 'I'm not the man to ask. My battalion ran up against some tanks that we weren't expecting. Pinned us down for a while and it was while trying to take them out that I picked up this load of lead. 'Fraid I don't have the first clue about how my lot are getting on. I can only hope they're doing all right.'

Nurse Armitage came back carrying a cup of tea. She put it down on the chair by David's bed. Instinctively she straightened his covers and smoothed the counterpane. 'Now I don't want these two tiring you out. You've lost a lot of blood and you need rest.' She turned to the other two. 'So don't you go pestering the Colonel with questions, you hear me? The invasion is going just fine and will carry on like that without you plaguing anyone for information.'

She turned her attention back to David and supported him while he sipped his tea. 'Can I get you anything else?' she asked.

'I was just wondering about a soldier of mine who was injured a couple of days ago. I was wondering if he had come here.'

'I can ask around and let you know.'

'He's called Sergeant Viney. He was quite badly wounded. It would be nice to know if he made it all right.'

'I'll do my best and get back to you. No promises,

mind. There's a lot of comings and goings here and things can be a little bit chaotic.'

'Thanks. His wife works for my wife, Gwen. I feel more than usually responsible for him. Mrs Viney would never forgive me if something really bad happened to her Bill.'

'I'll see what I can find out. And what a coincidence: young George's girl is called Gwen. It's a name I haven't come across for years and then I hear it twice in a couple of days. How odd. Still it gives you two boys something in common, doesn't it?'

She smoothed George's bed covers, bestowed a smile all round and left to continue her duties.

'So your young lady is called Gwen too, is she?' said the Colonel.

'Yes.'

'I bet she's a lovely girl.'

'Yes, she is. She's a real peach.

'Any plans for the future?'

George shook his head. 'My Gwen is a wonderful woman. She's everything anyone could want. The only trouble is, I think she's in love with someone else.'

The Colonel looked discomfited. 'Oh I say … I mean, I didn't wish to …'

'That's OK, Colonel. The guy she loves is a swell chap. I know when I'm beat. I'll find someone else, I expect.'

'I hope you do. You are being very gentlemanly about things. You deserve to.'

'I'm not sure I'm a gentleman, sir. But thank you.'

Orchard Cottage

Gwen let herself into the cottage and patted poor Jasper, who greeted her as if he hadn't had a scrap of human company for a month, not just the couple of hours since Mrs Viney had left. With Jasper pressed so close he was in danger of tripping her up, Gwen made her way into the kitchen. A short note from Mrs Viney informed her that her supper was in the larder and Gwen didn't fail to notice that the note was addressed to 'Mrs Clarke', not her more usual and chatty 'Mrs C'. Gwen sighed.

'I'm in the doghouse with Mrs V and no mistake,' said Gwen to Jasper. Jasper looked up at her and licked his lips. 'But you want your supper, not moans from me,' she said, scratching him behind his ears. She went into the larder and brought out a bowl of cooked lights. Jasper was, by now, almost drooling with anticipation, though Gwen found the smell of the ox lungs quite repellent.

She slopped some into Jasper's dish, added some biscuits and put it on the floor. Jasper fell on it, gulping it down in a way that wouldn't have put a stray to shame. Now Jasper was happy, Gwen made herself a pot of tea and took herself into the drawing room. She had letters to write, her conversation with Marjorie had convinced her of that, and there was no time like the present. All day she had been thinking how silly she had been to have taken up with George and how she needed to put a stop to the foolishness before she really did some damage. The trouble was that it was going to be difficult to write to George to tell him how the land lay. She could risk sending a letter to the mess and asking them to keep it till he returned, but would they? Or would she be better off sending one to the mess and asking them to forward it? But if he'd died, might someone else open it? She didn't want to risk that. It was so difficult to know what to do for the best.

But the one thing she could do was write a proper letter to David – not the gossipy rubbish she usually wrote but one telling him that she really did love him and miss him, that she understood and admired him for being selfless and giving up his chance of a weekend pass, that she'd been a silly goose for getting angry with him about it, and that she regretted everything except the fact that she'd fallen in love with him and married him. And now that he was serving in France she was so proud and worried that she didn't know if she was coming or going, but she just longed for him to come home safe to her once more.

Gwen pulled a pad of writing paper out of the bureau drawer and began the letter that she had been planning in her mind for half the day. She wrote without a break until she had covered several sheets and then put her pen down and read it back to herself. She smiled as she finished it. David would be in no doubt that she really loved him – which was how it should be.

She folded the paper and tucked it into an envelope. She'd post it in the morning. Now she was hungry and it was time for her supper.

Twenty

Nightfall, Monday 26 June 1944

La Ferme de la Source

The soldiers were still in the farmhouse and now there were all manner of trucks and vehicles parked up round and about. They had also erected tents in a field opposite but some distance away from the graves, and there were bits of equipment scattered around the place which, like the trucks and vehicles, were hidden under netting with strips of canvas and other fabric woven through it. Martine imagined it was supposed to hide the stuff from the air, but as it didn't look anything like the trees and bushes that grew near the farm, she couldn't imagine that it would work.

Martine wandered around the farmyard at a completely loose end. For the first time in years she had nothing to do. There were no cows to milk, no hens to shut up, no pens to muck out –nothing. She was at a loss to know what to do with herself She didn't even have to cook, as the soldiers had made a meal for themselves on her range and had allowed her to share it. It hadn't been wonderful, but it had been warm and filling – some sort of stew and a fruit sponge out of a tin to finish off. They had given her tea to drink too, but that had been disgusting, as they had added milk that had also come out of a tin.

That was the point at which she'd made a fool of herself by bursting into tears as she thought about her lovely Normande ladies all lying dead in their field, and that she'd never get to taste their warm, creamy milk again. The soldiers had all stood around looking desperately embarrassed as she'd tried to pull herself together, but the combination of all the events of the last twenty-four hours overwhelmed her. Someone had passed her a hanky and she'd busied herself mopping her face and blowing her nose, and when she'd sorted herself out she found all the men had gone outside to smoke cigarettes. It had cheered her up to notice that none of them looked at her in case she was still crying. She'd heard about the English not liking displays of emotion but had thought it was just a joke. Apparently not.

She approached the man who spoke French. He didn't look at her until she stood directly in front of him and said, 'Excuse me.'

'Yes?' he answered, not unkindly.

'I want to go to bed,' she said. 'Am I allowed to sleep in my own home?'

'Ah.' He paused. Perhaps he hadn't thought about practical arrangements like this. 'I don't know. I mean, do you want to?'

'Where else can I sleep?'

He nodded. 'There's no one you can go to?'

'Who? I shouldn't think there is a house with a roof for miles.'

'No relations?'

Martine lifted her chin and looked him in the eye. 'Only my father.' She nodded towards the graves.

The man looked uncomfortable. 'Quite. Well, most of us will be in the tents over there. There'll be some chaps manning the radio in the house throughout the night. If you want to find somewhere to sleep, you're welcome to.'

'Thank you.'

Martine went back into the house. She looked up the stairs, at the debris that littered them, the plaster from the walls and ceiling and slates off the roof. Gingerly she made her way up them, testing each tread and hanging on to the banister. The stairs felt reasonably safe underfoot, but Martine was wary: no house could take the sort of battering hers had taken and be completely safe.

The sight that greeted her, when she reached the landing, was dreadful but hardly a shock. If she was honest, it was no worse than she had expected, being much the same sort of damage as she had found downstairs. There was plaster dust everywhere and a couple of holes that went through the attic and roof so that she could see the steely-grey of the twilit sky. She wondered what state the bedrooms were in.

She looked through the door to her father's room. It seemed a lifetime since she had raced in there to tell him the Boche had arrived, but the reality was that it was less than twenty-four hours. So much had changed, however; her whole life had turned upside down. The room was a wreck. The window had been blown out completely and in the hole where it had been there was a big machine-gun with its barrel pointing up at the sky. The floorboards were splintered and stained – Martine didn't want to contemplate with what – and the walls were pockmarked with shrapnel.

She turned her back on it, took a step across the corridor and looked into her room. Amazingly, it wasn't too bad. It was habitable at any rate, although the glass in the window was shattered. So what? – she could pull the shutters across, which would keep out the worst of the weather for the time being. Dust was everywhere. She patted the covers on her bed and a great cloud rose up. Martine threw open the empty window frames and grabbed her bedding. She shook her sheets and blankets vigorously then remade her bed. Then she slipped her boots off and climbed into bed without undressing. Despite the traumas of the day, she was so exhausted that she slipped into a deep sleep almost immediately.

Twenty-One

Morning, Tuesday 27 June 1944

The Field Hospital

George watched June dish out the tea, waking the patients as she went around the half-dozen beds in the makeshift ward.

'And how are you this morning?' she asked George as she placed the tea on the table by his bed.

'All right, thank you. In fact, if my leg wasn't crook I'd feel like getting out of bed.'

'Well I expect we might be able to find a wheelchair and get you into the fresh air, if you'd like that.'

'Very much. I say, could you?'

'No promises, but I'll see what I can do.' Nurse Armitage gave tea to David and then walked around the foot of George's bed to deliver Max's before disappearing. 'You jammy thing,' said Max.

'Why don't you ask to get out of here for a few minutes too?'

'Because, old chap, I'm probably going to face a lifetime in a wheelchair and I don't really relish the prospect.'

George felt a heel for not realising that Max was never going to make a complete recovery. He didn't know what to say, so covered his embarrassment by slurping his tea. In the next bed David stirred and groaned. 'How are you, sir?' asked George. The Colonel passed a hand over his face as if to wipe the effects of sleep away. 'Sore.' He looked at his tea, which was on the table beside him. However, sitting up and reaching for it wasn't an option. 'And thirsty.'

'I'll get Nurse Armitage back,' said George. He levered himself up on his good arm and hollered, 'Nurse!'

She came running through the entrance of the tent, looking about her anxiously.

'Over here,' said George.

She walked briskly to his bed. 'What is it? What's wrong?'

'The Colonel can't reach his tea.'

Relief, quickly followed by anger, clouded her face. 'I thought … I …' Then she laughed. 'Never mind.'

'I really didn't mean this young man to cause trouble. He called out for you before I could do anything to stop him.'

'It's all right, Colonel. No harm done. Here' – she slipped an arm under the Colonel's shoulder and raised him gently, edging him up with pillows. Then she picked up the cup and held it to his lips.

David sipped it gratefully. 'Thanks,' he said when he had drained the mug. 'If you're not too angry with me, could I ask you another huge favour?'

'I'm not angry at all. Not with you, at any rate. This troublemaker, on the other hand …'But the smile she gave George gave the lie to her words. She turned back. 'What is it you want?'

'I'd really like my wife to know I'm all right, but I can't write.' He nodded at his dodgy shoulder.

'That's no problem at all. I'll come back later on today, if you'd like, and you can dictate a letter to her.'

'You're an angel.'

Nurse Armitage smiled and shook her head. 'All part of the service,' she said as she walked away.

George flopped against his pillows, a feeling of dread seeping through his body. He had no doubt that, when

June Armitage honoured her promise, she would put two and two together. How many Gwen Clarkes were there living in homes called Orchard Cottage? Would she say anything? George groaned at the awfulness of the situation. All the time he'd been having an affair with Gwen he'd thought they were fireproof. Living where she did, miles from anywhere, he'd been certain they would never get caught out; but now there was the very real prospect he'd have to face the irate husband. *Damn, damn, damn.* And, what was worse, he'd never meant to wreck Gwen's marriage. Neither of them had. All they'd wanted was a bit of fun and companionship. No strings, no complications, an affair that meant nothing to either of them. Except that it was now becoming apparent to George that it was more complicated than that. There was every possibility that Gwen was going to wind up in the divorce courts, and that was the last thing he wanted to happen to her. He had become fond of her, more fond than he had meant to, and he absolutely didn't want to see her hurt. Oh, God! What a dreadful mess.

'I say, are you all right?' asked Max, noticing George's sudden change in demeanour.

'Yes, fine,' said George.

'You're worried about the competition for the delectable Nurse A, aren't you?' said Max with a knowing wink.

'Hardly – he's a married man.' *And who is he to make moral judgements?* George thought.

When Nurse Armitage returned a few minutes later, George pestered her about being taken out in a wheelchair.

'I haven't time now. I've dressings to change apart from anything else.'

'But when?'

'When I've got time,' she snapped.

George knew he had gone too far. Nurse Armitage seemed to have an inexhaustible supply of patience and he had just drained it. 'Sorry,' he apologised.

'No, I'm sorry too. It must be horrid for you young men to be all cooped up like this. I'll see if I can get an orderly to get you into the fresh air.'

'No.' It came out all wrong; he sounded angry. 'No, I mean, I can wait until you've got time. Really I can. It's just that … well … I want to ask you something.'

Nurse Armitage's eyebrows went up and George was well aware that Max and David were more than likely eavesdropping.

'I see,' said Nurse Armitage slowly. 'How intriguing. Well, in which case I'll see what I can organise in my lunch break.'

'Thanks,' said George. He lay back on his pillows, staring straight ahead. He really didn't want any smutty comments from Max at this point. He had a lot of thinking to do and he didn't want any distractions.

La Ferme de la Source

Martine awoke and stretched. Then, as she opened her eyes, she realised that the light shining through the chinks in her shutters was much brighter than it should have been.

'*Mon Dieu*, the milking.' But even as she thought about the start to her day's labours, the images of the previous day's events cannoned into her consciousness. Slowly, wearily she climbed out of her bed. She went over to the shutters and pushed them open. Outside, the sun shone, the air was warm and puffy clouds were scattered across a speedwell-blue sky, but Martine was oblivious to the glories of the summer morning. All she could see was the pale faces of her father and Otto, each with a neat round black hole in the middle of his forehead. She returned to her bed and pulled on her boots before making her way back down the damaged stairs to the kitchen. She paused at the bottom and took in the activity going on in her house. An easel had been erected where the dresser had once stood – the remains of that shattered piece of furniture had gone: she wondered if the soldiers had used it for firewood, which was all it was good for – and a group of men were gathered in front as the French-speaker was reading stuff from a notebook to them.

A soldier sitting at the back of the group noticed her at the bottom of the stairs and said something. Silence fell and half a dozen pairs of eyes turned her way. Martine felt appallingly self-conscious.

The French-speaker said something and then turned to her. 'Good morning. Would you like some breakfast?'

Martine nodded nervously. She didn't like being the centre of attention like this.

'Good. If you go into the yard, a canteen has been set up. The soldiers there will look after you.' He said something to a young chap sitting by the door, who stood and beckoned to Martine.

'Jacobs will look after you,' said the French-speaker 'Go with him.'

Martine walked through the room, past the staring eyes to the front door and escaped into the air. The lad touched her arm and led her over to the dairy. In the shelter of the one undamaged building on the farm a couple of soldiers were overseeing some pots on a big portable stove. One of them smiled kindly at Martine and dolloped some beige goo on to a plate. She looked at it. What was this? Jacobs took a spoon and sprinkled some sugar over the top, poured some milk on and gestured for her to eat it.

Martine wasn't sure. What she wanted was *tartine* and butter, but as that wasn't being offered, she took a taste anyway. The sugar was nice, but the other stuff, the goo, tasted of nothing. But it was warm and she wasn't sure where her next meal was likely to come from. She ate some more.

'*Bon*?' said the soldier.

'Not really,' she replied. The lad looked blank. She took her bowl and went and sat on the mounting block, where she carried on eating until the bowl was empty. At least she felt pleasantly full, even if her breakfast had tasted of nothing. The lad was approaching her again, this time carrying a steaming mug.

'Tea,' he said in English as he handed it to her.

'*Merci*,' she replied.

He nodded happily. Martine reckoned he understood that word. She took a sip. Ugh, it had the same horrible tinned milk in as yesterday.

'*Bon?*' the lad asked, nodding in anticipation that she would think it delicious.

Martine looked at him. He barely looked old enough to be away from home, let alone fighting in a foreign country. He was trying so hard to be kind; she didn't have it in her heart to tell him it was dreadful.

She smiled. '*Oui*.'

From across the yard a voice called out her name. 'Martine. Martine!'

She looked up. Mme Boiselle was coming into the yard, her black skirt grey with dust and her hair uncombed. Martine put her mug down on the mounting block and stood up.

'Oh, Martine, you are all right.'

Martine nodded. 'And you, madame?'

'The shop took a direct hit. The village is in ruins. We are all destitute and homeless. We are in such straits.'

Martine nodded. She understood the feeling well.

Mme Boiselle looked at the mess that was Martine's yard. 'You had a bad time too.'

'There was fighting here, yes.' Martine saw that Mme Boiselle was eying her mug of tea. 'Would you like a drink?'

Mme Boiselle nodded hungrily. Martine mimed to Jacobs what she wanted, who understood readily enough and went off to the canteen in the dairy to get another mug.

'It's terrible stuff, but it's hot.'

Mme Boiselle shrugged and looked about her some more. Martine thought that the old biddy had been so wrapped up in her own misfortunes that she wasn't really able to absorb that it was the same for everyone. 'What are you and your father going to do about the barn?' asked Mme Boiselle while they waited for the tea to arrive,

'My father isn't going to do anything,' said Martine. As if Mme Boiselle cared what happened to Martine and her father. She had a feeling that the old bag had only come to the farm to see if there were any foodstuffs she could scrounge and not to check up on their well-being.

'Pah,' said Mme Boiselle. 'You really ought to make your father see that he can't leave the running of the farm to you. You must take a stand and stop him drinking. We all know he does. It's no secret in the village.'

'My father is dead,' said Martine.

Jacobs arrived with the tea and Mme Boiselle nearly dropped the proffered cup as she flapped about trying to make an apology. Martine stared at her so as to make her feel even more uncomfortable. Who did Mme Boiselle think she was, criticising her father like that? Martine knew the drink had been a problem but her father had been a good man in his way.

Martine turned her back on her unwelcome visitor and picked up her own mug.

'I'm sorry, Martine. I really am.'

Martine shrugged. She didn't believe her. 'What have you come here for?' she asked. She wanted rid of her.

'Oh, well …' The old woman shuffled her feet. 'I was wondering if you had any spare food up here. With the village the way it is, we have nothing there. We thought.'

So she'd been right. The old cow was here on the scrounge. She might have guessed she wasn't the least bit interested in Martine's welfare. 'If you can find anything, take it,' said Martine. 'But I doubt if you will. The Boche were here before the Allies. What they didn't take they wrecked.'

Mme Boiselle looked at Martine over the rim of her cup as she took another gulp of her hot tea, her beady little eyes looking cold and calculating. 'But the Allies have food.'

'So?'

'So you'll be all right as long as they stay here. You could probably persuade them to give you something – extra rations, I'm sure there is something you could exchange for food.'

Martine didn't like the implications this woman was making, but she wasn't going to rise to the bait. 'But they might go in a couple of hours,' she said calmly. 'They're not here for my benefit or protection. And any food they have is for the soldiers.'

'But can't you get them to leave you some of their rations? I'd give you money for the food.'

'I don't want money.'

'Come on, we all need money.'

'I don't.' Martine had lost so much, money wasn't going to make a sou of difference to her circumstances.

'Hah. If you don't need my money, I can only guess it's because you're already earning plenty. You're earning money from the soldiers already?' said Mme Boiselle nastily. 'I always guessed that was your game. I've seen the way you look at men. And the way they look at you.'

Martine was speechless. She was trembling with anger. Just because Mme Boiselle's husband was a randy old goat who fancied any woman who had more life to her than his dried-up harridan of a wife. How dare the old hag suggest she was selling herself. How dare she! 'Get off my land,' she yelled. 'Get off.'

Mme Boiselle drank the rest of her tea and handed the mug to the bemused Jacobs, who wished he understood what was going on.

'There's a name for girls like you,' she shrieked in turn: 'whore.'

'And there's a name for people like you,' countered Martine: 'bitch.'

Mme Boiselle turned and flounced out of the yard. Martine took a deep sigh and returned to the mounting block.

Jacobs wondered why someone had called Martine a whore. He only knew a couple of words of French from his basic schooling, but on the ship coming over, the older men had been at great pains to teach him what they considered to be the essentials: *vin, pain and putain* were now firmly in his vocabulary. And Martine didn't look like a whore to him. Mind you, he wasn't sure he would recognise a whore anyway. As far as he knew, he'd never encountered one. But perhaps he was wrong; perhaps Martine was one.

Twenty-Two

Afternoon, Tuesday 27 June 1944

The Field Hospital

With help from an orderly, Nurse Armitage got George in a wheelchair and covered in a blanket. The weather was pleasant but still not hot enough to be out of bed in just pyjamas and a dressing gown. His bad leg stuck out in front like some sort of signal advertising his dodgy state of health and like a warning for people to keep away from him. *Still*, he thought, *at least I've a leg to stick out. Not like poor old Max.*

Nurse Armitage wheeled him carefully past the beds in the ward and out into the sunshine. The breeze had dropped and the sun was strong, and instantly George felt the warmth of a glorious early summer's day. He breathed in the fresh air greedily, thankful to get away from the musty smell of damp canvas and the other, even less pleasant odours emanating from half a dozen bedridden men. He supposed it was all right for the chaps that were used to living and fighting in trenches, but he went home to the mess every night – or he had done till he was shot down – and he didn't like this communal living lark one bit.

He looked about him, appreciating the view over the Channel and the Mulberry harbour. The makeshift port was teeming with activity, as were the beaches below him. As far as the eye could see, armadas of ships were coming and going. He'd seen the sight often enough from the air till he'd got shot down; the first time he'd seen the quantity of ships involved he had been completely dumbstruck, but he'd assumed that after the initial push of D-Day the shipping activity would tail off. Now, though, three weeks on, as far as he could determine it hadn't decreased a jot. It was a remarkable sight.

Nurse Armitage saw him staring at the fleets of naval and merchant ships. 'And one of those is probably the hospital ship to take you home.'

'Really?'

She nodded. 'You and Max should be going tomorrow. It's not definite, so don't get your hopes up too much.'

'What about the Colonel?'

'Maybe. We'll see.'

June wheeled George over to the edge of the field-hospital compound to where they had an uninterrupted view of the sea. She parked George's chair by the bench that had been placed where the view was best and so that George could see the coastline.

'So what is it that's so urgent I have to give up part of my lunch break?'

'It's about the Colonel.'

'Oh.' She sounded disappointed. 'And there was me thinking you were going to talk to me about something else entirely,' she said as she casually examined her empty ring finger.

'Oh Lord,' said George, flustered.

'I'm joking,' said June gleefully. 'I was just teasing you.'

'Oh.' He almost added, 'Good,' but decided that might sound churlish and ungentlemanly. The last thing he wanted to do right now was annoy June. He needed her on his side more than anything.

'So what is it about the Colonel? Have you discovered he's some terrible double agent or something?'

'Hell, no.' George paused. This was darned difficult. Of course he had no one else but himself to blame for the whole situation, but it didn't make things any easier. 'Look, this is as difficult as hell and I have to ask you to keep whatever I say to yourself.'

June looked at him with her eyebrows slightly raised. 'Now I really am intrigued. And yes – whatever you tell me won't go any further.'

George looked at her and took her hands. 'Promise?'

'Promise.' She nodded as if to emphasise her trustworthiness.

George took a deep breath. 'You know you noticed that my girlfriend and the Colonel's wife are both called Gwen.' June nodded.

'Do you remember what surname you wrote on the letter to my Gwen?'

The penny dropped and June nodded again, her eyes just slightly wider than before. 'Clarke,' she whispered.

It was George's turn to nod.

'Oh my goodness,' said June.

'I had to talk to you before you wrote the Colonel's letter for him. You mustn't react.'

'For heaven's sake.'

'No, you mustn't. You promised that whatever I said you'd keep to yourself.'

'That was before I knew.'

'But it's over between Gwen and me. I shall make sure we never see each other again.'

'It didn't sound like it when you wrote to her.'

'No … but …'

'But nothing. That was before I met her husband and found out what a decent, nice bloke he is. I can't bear the thought of what we got up to spoiling their lives forever. What Gwen and I did was just a fling. It meant nothing.'

'I wouldn't be too sure it'll mean nothing to the Colonel. You had an affair with his *wife.*'

'Which is why it's all over between Gwen and me. I mean, I knew she was married, but it was just a bit of fun when it started.'

'Some fun,' interrupted June, her voice oozing with sarcasm.

'As soon as I get back I shall telephone her and end things. If I'd have known what David was really like, I would never have got involved.'

'So if he'd been a complete rotter it would have been all right to make love to another man's wife – to have an affair with a married woman.' June was really angry and she had raised her voice.

George looked about them, afraid someone might overhear their conversation.

'No, of course not.'

'Well that's what you seem to be saying.'

'Look, I don't care what you think of me' – which was a lie: George did care terribly. He hated the idea that June now thought him lower than the low, but he had to put up with it out of loyalty to Gwen. He'd been less than honourable and he had to give it his best shot to stop things going from bad to worse. 'But I do care enough to do anything in my power now to stop Gwen's marriage from falling apart. David obviously adores her, and I think Gwen loves him. I'm in the way. And I should never have done what I did. It was wrong, I know that now. I shall make sure I extricate myself from the whole business and leave them to it.'

June gave a little snort. 'A bit late for that now. Talk about shutting the stable door …'

'I know.'

'Suppose Gwen doesn't want David.'

'That's up to her. But I think she does. If I'm wrong, then so be it. But I want to make sure I'm not getting in the way or the cause of anything getting between them.'

June gave a derisory snort. 'You just want to make sure you don't wind up as co-respondent in a divorce court.'

'No!' He was so vehement in his denial he surprised

even himself. He really hadn't thought about having to make an appearance in a divorce court; he'd just been determined that Gwen wouldn't have to.

June stared at him. 'I don't know whether to believe you or not.'

'What is there not to believe? I just don't want Colonel Clarke to find out about it.' He paused and gripped her hands even tighter. 'So will you do it? Will you pretend you've never heard the name Gwen Clarke before?'

June looked at him, mulling over what he'd asked her. 'And what about Max? You know how nosy he is. What are you going to do about him?'

'I thought I might be able to engage him in a game of cards or something. If he's distracted he won't be able to earwig what's going on a couple of beds away.' George stared at June, willing her to agree. 'Does this mean you'll do it?'

'Maybe.' June didn't look at all happy.

'Please,' wheedled George.

'Understand one thing,' said June sternly: 'if I do go along with this, it's because I think Colonel Clarke is a good and honourable man. I like him and he doesn't deserve to have his life made miserable because of you. I am not doing it to stop you from looking a total cad. I think what you did was despicable.'

George felt a complete heel and knew his face was flushed with shame. 'Yes. It's not something I'm proud of, believe me.'

'Good.' June Armitage stood up and grabbed the two handles of the wheelchair. She pushed him back to the ward without another word.

'You look like she slapped your face,' said Max with a knowing wink.

'She did, sort of,' said George. He slumped down in the wheelchair and shut his eyes, hoping Max would take the hint that he really didn't want to talk.

Twenty-Three

Evening, Tuesday 27 June 1944

Orchard Cottage

Gwen let herself in and was greeted, as normal, by rapturous barks and wriggles from Jasper. On the hall table was a neat pile of letters, which had obviously been delivered after she had left for work in the morning. Gwen picked them up and flicked through them as she walked into the kitchen, accompanied by the dog. She was delighted to see several from David. Taking her hat and coat off and dropping them on a chair, she pulled up another one and eagerly opened the first of them. Quickly she scanned his writing, hoping for news of his well-being and safety; but the letter seemed to be full of trivialities. She read the date at the top: it had been written before he'd gone to France. She discarded it and picked up another envelope. The postmark was smudged, so she ripped that letter open too and checked the date. *Still too early*. She tried the third, but that was no good either. They had all been written long before he'd gone to France and this wasn't the news she wanted at all. She knew he'd been all right when he left England, she thought irritably. She would have been told instantly if something had happened to him while his battalion had been in training. What she wanted to know was that, now he was on active service, he was still safe and well.

She threw the letters on to the kitchen table and got up to put the kettle on the hob. Of course she wanted to read what he had to say to her, but now she knew the letters were old ones, the urgent desire for his news had left her. He couldn't have that much to say from a training camp in the back of beyond. She filled the kettle and pushed it on to the hotplate of the range and then, while she waited for it to boil, she gathered up the pages she had left on the table and began to read them more carefully.

"My dearest, darling Gwen," wrote David in one of them, *"I can't tell you how much I am missing you stuck here in a training camp 'somewhere in England'.*

The work is deadly dull because the lads all know what they are supposed to be doing and we're really just cooling our heels until the Brass decide to make use of us. If it was possible I'd come home like a shot to see you and tell you how much I love and adore you, but all leave has been cancelled so we are all stuck here for the foreseeable future. Of course we're all hoping against hope that we'll be allowed a bit of embarkation leave before the balloon goes up but Mr Brown says that he heard from another RSM that the War Office isn't authorising any at the moment, as they are too afraid of the men going AWOL. I do not know where Mr Brown gets his information from but he is usually right. This is one occasion when I am praying he is mistaken and I'll be able to get home.

Whether or not I am able to see you once more before being sent away will not make any difference in my determination to fight, with all my courage, for you and the country I hold almost as dear. I could not bear the thought of Hitler's forces prevailing and putting you in mortal danger so I will do everything in my power to prevent this – and I will do it gladly, if it means you will be safe."

Gwen put the letter down, her eyes filling with tears at the implication of David's words: that he was willing to lay down his life if that would make any difference to her future safety. *And how have I repaid him?* she thought. She shook her head as the shame of her previous actions washed through her. She brushed her hand over her eyes and put the letter down. If – no, *when* David got back, she would make it up to him. She offered up a little promise to God. If God spared David, she would be the most attentive, faithful wife any husband could wish for. Never again would she grumble if he didn't want to go dancing and wanted to listen to the Home Service instead, or go walking rather than go up to London. She would comply with everything he wanted. If only he was spared. *So, please God, please listen to me and believe me*, she prayed.

The telephone rang. Gwen, immersed in her thoughts and prayers, jumped.

'My goodness, Jasper, who on earth can that be?' Leaving the kettle hissing on the range, Gwen walked briskly into the drawing room.

'Hello,' she said into the receiver. 'Gwen Clarke speaking.'

'Hello, Gwen my dear,' said a faintly crackly voice over the line. Gwen thought it sounded vaguely familiar, but she couldn't place it. 'It's Reggie Day here from Regimental HQ.'

Of course, Reggie Day. Gwen had met him on a number of occasions when David had taken her to RHQ for cocktail parties and the like. David's battalion was just one of half a dozen in the King's Yeomanry, all administered by their Regimental Headquarters in Worthing. Every now and again the officers and their wives were summoned for social functions –Gwen always said it was so that the Brass could give the wives the once-over and make sure they were all still up to snuff – and Gwen had got to know quite a few of the officers who ran the Yeomanry. Reggie Day was a delightful old buffer who had lost a leg in the last war, who was full of charm and bluster and always made Gwen laugh.

'Reggie, dearest. How are you? Keeping well, I trust.'

'I'm top-hole, dear lady, top-hole.'

Gwen laughed. 'Glad to hear it. So tell me why I've got the unexpected pleasure of a telephone call from you?' Gwen was anticipating something nice, like an invitation to a croquet tournament or a curry lunch. There had been a number of pleasant social events that had taken place at RHQ since the war had started. Nothing elaborate – just jolly get-togethers to take everyone's mind off the horrors of the war, rationing and the blackout, and to give the newcomers to the Regiment a chance to get to know some of the old hands.

'Actually, my dear, I've got some rather bad news for you.'

Gwen felt her heart lurch. After the anticipation of something jolly this was like being doused in cold water. No. No! She leaned against the piano to steady herself and willed her voice to stay calm. 'What is it, Reggie?'

'It's David.'

Gwen sagged and felt tears spring to her eyes again. *No, it couldn't be. Please God, no.* Please God it was some ghastly mistake.

'We've just had a signal through from Brigade. David's been injured.'

'Injured?' Gwen breathed again. 'Injured' meant he was still alive. She clutched the phone in relief.

'Yes. I don't have any details, but I thought you would want to know.'

'How bad is he?'

'I'm sorry, Gwen, I'm afraid I don't know. I do know they're expecting him to be put on a hospital ship in the near future. But I've nothing more than that. And I only know that much because we've been asked to recommend who should take over as acting CO of his battalion until he is fit to return to duty. The Regimental Colonel asked me to tell you. He thought you'd like to know as soon as possible rather than get the news through official channels, which could take days.'

'Yes, of course. Terribly kind of you.' Gwen's mind was functioning automatically and making her say the right words to an old friend of her husband's when all she really wanted to do was sob her heart out.

'I'll ring through if I hear anything more, shall I?'

'Please. That would be most kind.'

'Right.' There was a slightly awkward pause. 'Well, all the best, my dear. I'm sure David will be as right as ninepence in no time.'

'Yes. 'Bye.'

Gwen put the receiver back on its rest. She'd longed for news. Now she'd had it.

La Ferme de la Source

Martine watched the last of the vehicles pull away from the farm. The tide had rolled in and now the tide had rolled out again. The silence was overwhelming. She sat on a chair in the kitchen and tried to take stock of her situation. It didn't take her long. Orphaned and destitute. But, she thought, she wasn't homeless. The house was battered, but it was still standing and a couple of the rooms were almost weathertight. She wasn't too sure how it would stand up to the winter gales, but at least she had somewhere to live for the time being. And on a practical note, with the barn wrecked she had plenty of lumber that she might be able to use for repairs. What she didn't need for herself she might be able to sell, too.

Wearily she got up and went into the yard to assess how much of the timber from the barn might be reusable. She glanced at the graves in the field as she crossed the yard. She wondered if it was normal to carry on as she was doing. Perhaps she ought to be prostrate with grief, crying her heart out for her lost father and lover; but, although she had a deep dull ache in her chest and half her waking thoughts were about them, she needed to survive. Grieving wasn't going to put bread in her stomach or mend the roof.

She looked at the pile of planks and beams that had once been their barn. The tanks and the shell fire had reduced much of the wood to little more than splinters, but Martine reckoned there was enough left of reasonable quality to make some basic repairs to the house. She went to the pigsty and was pleased to find that, although the walls were reduced to rubble, the sheets of corrugated iron that had formed the roof were certainly salvageable. She wondered if she was going to be able to haul them up on to the farmhouse roof to cover the holes in the slates left by the shelling. She gazed up at the roof of her house and decided that it was not a job for one person. She'd have to get help from somewhere.

The trouble was, where? Most of the young men had been taken for forced labour and those that remained were the old and the sick. There were a few able-bodied men around, M. Boiselle being one; but Martine would rather have frozen or starved than gone to him for help. She'd just have to manage somehow. At least she had the gun. Then she remembered that she also had a shotgun. At least she might be able to get meat for the pot. There were still plenty of rabbits around. If she could bag a few of them, she'd be able to barter for bread and other basics. What with that and the lumber, she might be able to survive for a while.

Thinking about the gun, she returned to the house and opened the linen chest. Under the torn sheet were the web belt and the service revolver. She looked at it with satisfaction and shut the lid again. She'd get by. She'd survive. And if she did, she'd make damned sure that

Obersturmbannführer Peiper paid for what he'd done to her and her loved ones. If he survived the war and if it took her the rest of her life to find him, she'd get her revenge.

The Field Hospital

George saw June approaching Colonel Clarke's bed. In her hand she had a pad of paper. He turned to Max and picked up a pack of cards he'd managed to scrounge earlier in the day. He'd persuaded June to let him stay in his wheelchair since they had got back from their outing and she had agreed, as long as he didn't go about 'making a nuisance of himself'.

'How about a game, Max?' he offered.

'What of?'

'Five-card stud? We could play for matches.'

'I'd rather play for money.'

'Can't help you there, bud. When I was shot down I didn't have my pocketbook on me.'

Max sighed. 'Matches it is then.'

George turned his chair so that he was pulled up alongside Max's bed and started to deal. They had both just picked up their cards when Colonel Clarke called across to them.

'Nurse Armitage has just given me some good news, boys.'

'The Germans have surrendered?' asked Max hopefully.

'She's breaking open a bottle of Scotch?' suggested George even more hopefully.

'No. Better than that.'

'Doubt it,' said George *sotto voce*.

'We're all due to go home on a hospital ship tomorrow. We're being transferred to Portsmouth first thing.'

'Fantastic,' said Max. 'Hey, George, did you hear that!'

'That's good,' said George, although he was lying through his teeth. *Damn*; he'd been hoping that June had got it wrong. Or that there'd be another reason why he shouldn't get transferred. The last thing he wanted was to be put on some dumb boat and shipped back to England. As long as he was here in France, no one was expecting him to fly another sortie. Once he got back to England, someone would be on his back to hurry up and return to the fray. And that was just what he didn't want to do. He'd had enough of being frightened, enough of being shot at and enough of fighting. It had seemed such a 'lark', as the Limeys would have put it, when he joined up back in thirty-nine, but it wasn't a lark now. He'd done his bit and now he wanted out. The thing that was terrifying him now, though, was that he reckoned the only way he was going to get out now was DD – discharged dead. But he couldn't tell anyone what he really felt, so he fixed a grin to his face and tried to look happy.

George and Max played several hands of cards and George tried to concentrate, even though he was trying to listen with half an ear to what David was dictating to June. He suspected, though, that June had deliberately positioned herself so that she was sitting facing George's bed; thus the Colonel was talking away from him. Try as George might he could only pick up the odd word.

'Hey, George,' said Max indignantly, 'you can't do that. That's not in the rules.'

George looked at the cards he'd laid on the coverlet and scooped them up again.

'What's the matter with you?' asked Max grumpily. 'You're the one who wanted to play and you don't seem to be paying any attention at all. There's no point in going on with this if your mind is elsewhere.'

'Sorry,' mumbled George. He sorted the cards out in his hand and made a real effort for the next couple of minutes; but then he saw movement out of the corner of his eye. He swivelled round. June was standing up to leave. She gave him a long, cool look and pushed some folded paper into an envelope; then she walked towards the entrance to the tent.

'Just a mo,' said George, throwing his cards on to Max's bed. He grabbed the end of the bed and, giving himself a mighty heave, he propelled his chair into the gap between the two rows of beds.

'Nurse,' he called. June turned. 'Please. Just a tick.'

She walked back to him. 'Yes,' she said coolly.

'Is it …? Did you …?'

June bent forward, pretending to tuck in the rug over George's knees more securely. 'I did as you asked,' she said in a low voice. 'And I want you to know that you don't deserve it. I hope your girlfriend realises what a truly wonderful man she is married to.'

George read between the lines of what June had said perfectly. 'I know. And I hope she does too. Thank you.'

June straightened up and walked away.

Twenty-Four

Dawn, Wednesday 28 June 1944

The Field Hospital

'Come on, look sharp, boys,' Nurse Battleaxe boomed from the entrance of the tent.

The exhortation wasn't aimed at the patients for once but at the stretcher-bearers, who were trying to move several patients as gently as possible from their beds on to the stiff canvas litters so as to transport them to the waiting vehicles.

'I can't believe I'm really out of here,' said Max, glee lighting up his face.

'No,' agreed George, who was keeping the lid on his true feelings.

'Just think: by tonight I'll be back in Blighty and as soon as I get my tin legs I'll be back home.'

'That's great,' said George, trying to sound enthusiastic. A couple of hefty medics approached George with a stretcher. He stopped talking as they rolled him on to his uninjured side and positioned the stretcher behind him. Then they carefully rolled him back and finally gave him a shove so that he was in the centre of the canvas.

'Watch the arm,' he remonstrated.

'Sorry, sir,' they said cheerfully, not sounding the least contrite.

Max was made of sterner stuff and he carried on the conversation as he was transferred, ready for moving to the beach-head. 'So where will you go to convalesce?'

'Home isn't an option for me.'

'Exactly.'

'I guess I'll find somewhere.'

And the conversation went no further as Max was lifted up and carried off, waving goodbye to the other ward inmates as he left. George followed him a few minutes later and,after a glimpse of blue sky outside the tent, he was shoved into the back of a waiting truck.

'Chauffeur-driven transport to the beach,' said Max, nothing appearing to shake his good humour.

'Yeah, so I see,' said George. The pair of them were right at the back of the truck, lying side by side, their feet pointing towards the tailgate. A couple of minutes later they felt the truck jolt and rock and then the sound of another stretcher being pushed into it. Neither of the men could see who had been loaded in with them and they lay quietly in the gloom at the rear of the truck until the fourth and final stretcher was loaded.

There was the sound of the tailgate being slammed into position followed by a couple of sharp bangs on the side of the vehicle and a voice calling, 'That's all, take her away.' Then the engine started and they were off.

The truck bounced and ground its way slowly over the uneven grass of the field where the hospital had been set up and then the engine note and the motion changed as they moved on to something smoother and firmer.

'England, home and beauty, here we come,' said Max ecstatically.

'Whoopee,' said George with no enthusiasm.

It didn't take long for them to make it down to sea level from the cliff top where the hospital was perched. They could tell they had made it to the beach as they could see a cluster of roofs of houses and villas through the open back of the truck and knew they had to be at one of the little resorts that had peppered this coast before the war. The truck ground on and then the roofs receded into the distance as it drove across the huge expanse of sand to reach the sea. Finally it came to a halt.

'All aboard the Skylark,' said a wag as he dropped open the tailgate with a crash. One by one, the stretchers were unloaded and placed in a line on the sand. To one side of George he could see the sea and various landing craft, like so many beached whales, ramps lowered, loading and unloading men and materials. To his other side, in the distance George could see a couple of small villages nestled under the low cliffs behind the Mulberry.

'We'll soon have you loaded,' said an unknown voice. 'In the meantime, enjoy the fresh air.'

George had to concede it *was* rather pleasant lying out on the sand in the clean, fresh morning air. Despite not wanting to go back to England, he almost began to enjoy himself. It was about an hour later that all the casualties being transferred with George were finally loaded on to the LCT. There were quite a few cases who were being sent back in ambulances, but the majority of the men were like Max and George, lying on stretchers in the flat tank well. Colonel David was a couple of rows along from the two chums. They'd waved at him when they'd seen him get loaded on and George had been thankful he wasn't any closer. He hoped that, once they got back to Portsmouth, he wouldn't be put in the same hospital, let alone the same ward. He'd felt enough guilt to last him a lifetime. Nurses moved amongst them, handing out cigarettes and extra blankets. They were helped by some of the walking wounded, who distributed life jackets and cheerful banter. With the sun streaming down and knowledge that the war was distant, the atmosphere in the LCT was light and good-spirited.

George wondered if he imagined the feeling of movement as he thought the deck beneath him gave the faintest of shudders, but his suspicions were confirmed when Max said, 'Looks like we're off.'

'But I can't hear the engines.'

'The tide has got to float us a bit first. Give this poor old tub a chance.'

George gave an embarrassed chuckle. 'I guess I know jack-shit about ships. As I said to an old friend a while back: if I'd wanted to get my feet wet I'd have joined the navy. As it was, I chose the air force.'

'But not your own lot,' observed Max.

George explained about his English mother.

'Well, that explains it. I wondered what the attraction was. Apart from our vastly superior aircraft.'

George laughed. 'Yeah.'

The movement under the keel began to get more pronounced.

'I expect we'll kedge off soon. Once we're properly afloat.'

Almost as Max said this, they heard the engines and winches start up.

'Home – here we come.'

The LCT began to use its kedge anchor to drag itself off the beach. The very shallow beaches of Normandy were ideal for the use of the flat-bottomed landing craft and the tides that refloated the vessels, after they had unloaded, swept over the almost level sands with amazing speed. When the tide was low, acres and acres of clean, flat yellow sand were revealed and on days like this one the LCTs were forced to beach hundreds of yards from the high-water mark. In fact, the tide was unusually low on this day and the LCT was even further than normal from the dunes and cliffs of the coastline.

As the craft got under way, the nurses began to help the wounded soldiers and officers to don their life jackets. However, the day was fine, the sea was calm and for most of the men on board there seemed no point in struggling into the cork-filled preservers. George, for one, couldn't be bothered. What with having his right arm in a sling, to say nothing of general aches and pains from his other wounds, it was all too difficult. Max put his on and tied the tapes around his waist.

'Not taking any chances, me. I'm going home, no matter what happens.'

George let his buoyancy aid rest on his chest and watched some clouds drift overhead. *Well, this is it. Next stop, England.*

A few hundred yards ahead of the LCT, lying on the seabed but closer now to the surface than it had ever been before because of the extremely low tide, lay the magnetic mine that had been dropped five days before by Gerhard Werner. It had stayed in roughly the same place since it had landed – in the relatively shallow water of the Channel, moving a few feet now and again as the tides and currents caught it, but really hardly drifting at all. On several occasions its magnetic fuse had detected the hull of a passing ship or craft, but the physical attraction of the steel had never been quite enough to activate it, owing to the depth of the water or the fact that the vessel had not been on a heading that would take it directly over it. However, as the LCT moved off the beach and turned to get under way the fuse began to react. The physical draw of the steel got stronger and began to activate the mechanism. The LCT only had to keep the heading for a few more minutes and the mine would detonate.

For an instant George thought that their LCT must have struck another ship. The front reared up and then a huge ripple passed under the thick steel hull, but George swore he could feel the whole structure and his stretcher rising up as though he had been riding a wave at sea and then dropping back again. As the shock wave moved beneath him, he was flung sideways off his stretcher, causing him to cry out as his shoulder crashed off the canvas and on to the deck.

'What the …?'

'Jesus!' yelled Max, his face white with fear.

Then they both registered the echoing reverberation of the underwater explosion and saw the plume of water like a fountain off the starboard bow, which subsided in what seemed like slow motion, drenching those near the front.

From the bow of the ship they could hear screams and shouts. Then, slowly, the vessel began to tip to one side. George looked to where the mayhem was loudest. Another plume of water was spraying through the side plates of the ship.

'Shit,' said George. 'We must have been holed.' He tried to sit up and began to fumble with his life jacket. Beneath him water was already beginning to seep over the metal decking. Cigarette butts, chewing-gum wrappers, oil rainbows and other detritus floated under him.

'Here,' said Max. 'Let me give you a hand with your life jacket.'

George tried to sit up, but with the angle of the ship he found it difficult. Around him men were thrashing about, grabbing items they thought would help them to float, struggling into life vests or just trying to hobble or limp to the ladders that led out of the tank well. George looked at Max. There was no way he was going to be able to climb to a higher part of the ship to keep out of the water. George wondered how far from the coast they were. Would the LCT sink? Or would it founder in the shallow water? The angle of the deck increased. The filthy water sloshing around on the flat tank deck was deeper and it began to flow to the side, thus increasing the tendency for the ship to list still further.

Suddenly, without warning. Max lost his balance and tumbled down the slanting deck.

'Max!' yelled George, after him. But Max was lost to sight in the press of struggling men and sliding stretchers.

George managed to get his broken leg over the side of his stretcher and braced against a metal rib that formed part of the decking. Thus wedged he looked for a way he could lever himself upright. In front of him, on the downhill slope and not far from where Max had disappeared in a mass of men and kit, was a ladder that led to a companionway that ran around the top of the tank well. If he could only just grab hold of that ...

Jamming the tapes of his life jacket between his teeth, he turned and in one movement flung himself downhill towards the ladder. He just managed to grab it with his good arm, though the shock of all of his body weight plus that of a plaster cast being transferred in a second to his shoulder joint and ribcage as he crashed against it made him grunt with pain and knocked the wind from his lungs. He scrabbled with his good foot until he managed to regain some sort of balance before finally levering himself against the ladder, which by now was at an angle distinctly off the vertical. He turned round to assess the situation of the LCT and saw David struggling across the slope to join him. David wasn't disadvantaged by a plaster cast, but he was still far from well. He reached George and grabbed a rung.

'If we get up here,' he shouted over the noise of the ship's engine and the shouts and screams, 'we can see how far we have to swim.'

George nodded. 'You go first,' he said indistinctly, his teeth still clamped round the tapes. 'If I get stuck, you may be able to help pull me up with your good arm.'

David nodded and began to crawl up the ladder. What would have been difficult, if not impossible, if it had been upright was made much simpler by the fact that he could lean against it between each step to move his good arm up a rung. He moved slowly up and George, who had shoved his life jacket behind him so that it hung down his back, followed him, though his progress was painfully slow as he dragged his broken leg.

By the time he reached the top and joined David the

companionway was only a matter of feet above the smooth surface of the sea. The two men looked at the drop. Already in the water were dozens of men, thrashing around, supported by their life vests and trying to make their way to the shore. The beach didn't look so very far away. Maybe they could make it.

'Where's your life jacket?' asked George, hauling his back to where he could reach it.

'I seem to have lost it. Never mind,' said David. 'Let me give you a hand with tying the tapes. There's no need for both of us to have to get a ducking.'

George looked at David's calm face. 'Can you swim?'

'A bit,' said David, not looking him in the eye.

'Don't you want to be sure of seeing your wife?'

David nodded. 'Of course.'

'I expect she's a wonderful woman. Beautiful too, I shouldn't wonder.'

David nodded again.

'So tell me the truth: how much is "a bit"?'

'Enough,' said David defiantly.

George stared at him. He made a decision. He had to be sure David got back to Gwen. 'Really, bud? Well, I was high-school champion. Which is a darn sight better than "enough". If either of us needs this, it's you.'

George wedged himself against a stanchion and thrust the jacket at David; then with each using his good arm they managed to get the tapes around David's body and tied in a secure knot. David smiled gratefully.

'You were lying about the swimming, weren't you?' said George. 'I don't think you can swim at all.'

'Well …'

'Thought as much. Now jump, damn you,' he said.

David turned to look at the water and braced himself to jump. Then he turned back. 'But what about your leg?' he asked.

'It's fine.' And without giving David the chance

George gave him a shove that propelled him into the water. For a ghastly second George thought he'd done wrong as David disappeared under the surface, but a second later he bobbed up again. Supported by the cork floats he lay on his back and kicked with his feet away from the sinking LCT.

George, who had never swum a stroke in his life, wished he had a last cigarette to enjoy.

Twenty-Five

Evening, Friday 30 June 1944

Portsmouth Hospital

David saw Gwen as soon as she got through the doors of the ward. He felt his heart give a squeeze as he saw her slim figure in a pretty dress appear. He saw her ask a nurse something, and then she followed the direction the nurse pointed in and saw him. David felt such happiness when he saw her smile.

'Gwen, dearest.' He held out his good hand and she clasped it and pressed it to her cheek. Then she bent forward and kissed him.

'Hello, darling,' she said. 'I've been so worried. Then I heard through the WVS that you were being brought here.'

'I'm fine.'

'But they said the hospital ship you were on sank.'

'Yes. It looks as though I've been using up my nine lives a little quickly recently.'

'But you're home now, that's the main thing.' David was touched to see that Gwen's eyes were damp with tears. 'There, there,' he said. 'Look, I made it. I'm safe. There's no need for all this fuss.'

'But I was so horrid to you before you left.'

'That's all forgotten.'

'But I wouldn't have forgiven myself if you hadn't come back.'

'But I did.'

'I am so thankful.'

'And so am I. I wouldn't have made it if it hadn't been for this wonderful American pilot who gave me his life preserver. He was a lovely chap, called George. Made sure I knew he was named after George Washington and not our King. Sadly, I don't think he made it. One day I'll have to tell you about him.

Gwen nodded. She couldn't speak because of the tears.

Epilogue

Like many on the LCT, both Max and Sergeant Viney were drowned. Nan Viney was devastated by the death of her husband and went to stay with her sister in Wimbledon while she got over her grief. She never returned to the south coast.

David spent several weeks in hospital and then convalesced for another month before being sent back to his battalion. He fought with them all the way through Europe and came home in November 1945, having spent several months in Hanover after the war waiting to be demobbed.

Peiper retreated with his Regiment into the Ardennes. After the war he was accused of massacring American POWS in Malmedy during the fighting through the Ardennes. He was tried in Dachau and sentenced to death, but his sentence was later commuted to life. In the end he served eleven years in jail before being released in 1956. He found it difficult to settle after the war, owing to his war record and the fact that people he worked with were keen to denounce him to political extremists. He finally went to live in Traves in the Haute-Saône region of France. He was shot on 13 July 1976 and his house set on fire. By his body was found a British service revolver. The French police never found anyone responsible for his death, although they questioned the local Communists closely. No one thought to query the presence of a small, middle-aged woman from Normandy who was holidaying in the area at the time and who returned home the next day after first attending mass.

Kate Lace

A Question of Loyalty
The Eye of the Storm
A Regimental Affair

For more information about **Kate Lace**

and other **Accent Press** titles

please visit

www.accentpress.co.uk